A DUBIOUS SET O

Who would believe that hea
parson's daughter who had the audacity to elope with the
younger brother of an Earl, would cap all her previous
misadventures by running away the night of her husband's
funeral?

Who would believe that the upstanding Earl of Raeburn, who
had intemperately tried to seduce his brother's bethrothed,
would then threaten to steal her child if she refused to return
to the home she detested?

And who would believe that these two passionately inclined
people—beset by the most perturbing memories yet irrevocably
connected by family ties—could live under the same roof?
Beautiful Jessica thought it the most impossible of arrangements.
But then she hadn't considered the strong will of her infuriatingly
handsome brother-in-law—or her own treacherous heart. . . .

THE
CLERGYMAN'S
DAUGHTER

THE CLERGYMAN'S DAUGHTER

Julia Jeffries

A SIGNET BOOK

NEW AMERICAN LIBRARY

TIMES MIRROR

NAL BOOKS ARE AVAILABLE AT QUANTITY DISCOUNTS WHEN USED
TO PROMOTE PRODUCTS OR SERVICES. FOR INFORMATION PLEASE
WRITE TO PREMIUM MARKETING DIVISION, THE NEW AMERICAN
LIBRARY, INC., 1633 BROADWAY, NEW YORK, NEW YORK 10019.

SIGNET TRADEMARK REG. U.S. PAT. OFF. AND FOREIGN COUNTRIES
REGISTERED TRADEMARK—MARCA REGISTRADA
HECHO EN CHICAGO, U.S.A.

SIGNET, SIGNET CLASSICS, MENTOR, PLUME, MERIDIAN and NAL BOOKS
are published by The New American Library, Inc.,
1633 Broadway, New York, New York 10019

First Printing, January, 1983

1 2 3 4 5 6 7 8 9

PRINTED IN THE UNITED STATES OF AMERICA

For the River City Writers—
Phyllis, Beth, Dolly, Kathryn, Wanda, Georgia,
Nancy, and E. J.—
for all their patience and support

Chapter One

As Jessica Foxe stepped out of the receiving office into the freshening October breeze, she heard the bells begin to ring, announcing the arrival in town of some person of importance. Despite the watery sunshine the afternoon was chill, the salty air damp and heavy with the promise of fog by nightfall, and she wondered idly what notable had chosen to grace Brighthelmstone with his presence so long after the Season had ended. By now the members of the *ton*—who during the summer had flocked like tropical birds to the sleepy little seaside village for a few raucous weeks, turning it into a glittering carnival known familiarly as Brighton—had all migrated once more, this time to their winter habitats, there to garner their waning energies as they awaited the "Little" Season of Christmastide. During the cold months, when the sand on the beaches was damp and clammy and mist lay like a shroud in the streets, the town was home only to fishermen and their families, a few tenacious shopkeepers, pensioners, and cast-off mistresses—people like Jessica, who had nowhere else to go.

A gust of wind whipped around Jessica, fluttering her long black veil. She caught it impatiently and adjusted the folds so that once more it hung smoothly from the deep brim of her somber bonnet that was covered with inky crepe the color of her hair. Shivering, she pulled her pelisse tighter about her slender shoulders, trying to ignore the cold that pierced the thin fabric like a bodkin. Clutching her newspapers and the familiar envelope from Mssrs. Haxton and Welles, Engravers and Publishers of Clerkenwell, London, she quickened her step. When she left the house earlier in the afternoon, she had thought that if her monthly letter had indeed arrived, she would go directly to her bank to deposit the draft it contained. But instead, before she could reach the receiving office, the fickle sun had lost its warmth, and bleak, threatening clouds loomed on the horizon. She could feel a cough growing with burning insistence deep in her chest, and she knew she needed to go home.

She hurried along the plank sidewalk, heedless of the occasional eyes that turned appreciatively to watch her progress. With the Peninsular War apparently doomed to go on forever, with politicians squabbling and Canning and Castlereagh actually fighting a duel over the best way to end it, the sight of women garbed in deepest mourning was increasingly less uncommon, but even the anonymity of her weeds could not disguise the womanly curves of Jessica's slim body or the youthful grace of her step. When the Brighton season had been at its height, Jessica had been careful never to venture out without Willa, her maid and companion, firmly at her side, to discourage the importunings of any bucks, young or otherwise, who might have been disinclined to respect her bereavement. Now that the gentry had gone elsewhere in their never-ending search for amusement, Jessica knew the townspeople would leave her unmolested. Her only wish was that she had had the good sense to borrow Willa's cloak to wear over her rather threadbare pelisse.

Willa had suggested the loan, but just then the feeble sunshine had looked so inviting to Jessica through the shuttered windows of the cottage, and her maid had already been so voluble in her disapproval of Jessica's going outside at all when she had only just recovered from a debilitating cold, that as usual Jessica's hackles had risen alarmingly at the first sign of opposition and she had refused to heed anything Willa said. "I *must* get out of here for a while!" Jessica had snapped irritably, gesturing around the dark interior of the modest parlor. "I've not been abroad for over three weeks, and if I don't get some sunlight soon, I'll probably come down with a green sickness!"

Willa, dandling the baby on the settle next to the fireplace, regarded her mistress with outward calm. At nineteen, two years Jessica's junior, Willa Brown had an extensive and practical knowledge of human nature, and as she studied the other woman's set features, slanting emerald eyes wide and intense in a pale, shadowed face, she knew that further objections would only bring on another outburst. "Aye," she said quietly, "I'm not questioning your wish to walk out a bit. That's understandable enough, but please remember, if you take a fever again, your milk will dry up"—Willa's work-hardened hands delicately stroked the infant's red curls—"and then what will become of this little one?"

As Jessica had gazed down tenderly at her daughter, cradled lovingly in Willa's arms, her hands had risen to cup her rounded breasts in an unconscious gesture of protection, as if guarding the vital fluid that filled them, the palpable link that still connected her to her child, and through her, to her husband. "I'll take no chances, Willa," she had reassured firmly. "I'll be back long before Lottie's next feeding. You know I'd never do anything that might hurt my baby. Besides, I'm certain the weather will remain quite mild. . . ."

Mild, she thought ironically. She pressed the newspapers close against her bosom, relishing the tiny bit of extra protection they afforded her against the sharp breeze that assailed her. She forced her tired feet to move still faster as cold air licked at her ankles. By what right did she, a child of the Midlands, dare to offer opinion on the state of the climate here at the seaside? She had seen sailors raise their craggy faces to the sky and comment sagely on the shape of clouds

3

and the color of the setting sun, predicting with uncanny accuracy a storm that might not arrive for several days. When she looked to the sky, she saw its beauty as depicted by painters she admired, the turbulence of Turner or the serenity of Constable, but its mysteries remained hidden from her. In the year and more since she and Willa had fled from Renard Chase, absconding with the precious secret she had carried undetected beneath her heart, Jessica had learned about despair and anger and self-sufficiency, but nothing of the sea.

Behind her, the sound of hooves fast approaching and the high-pitched rattle of some light rig, utterly different from the low rumble of the heavy carts the draymen drove, caught her attention, and she glanced back curiously, assuming this was the arrival the bells had announced. From the far end of the street a sleek curricle raced toward her, drawn by a matched pair of geldings so lathered and mud-spattered that their ebony flanks looked dingy gray. Behind the shelter of her long veil Jessica sneered with disgust at such wanton mistreatment of a pair of beautiful animals. Since moving to the seaside, she had learned that the London-to-Brighton-and-back circuit was a favorite challenge among young Corinthians, and more than once she had seen a team driven almost to death by a so-called nobleman who considered some paltry wager of greater consequence than the well-being of his horses. In fact, one of Erinys' earliest cartoons had dealt with just such an incident. . . .

Aware that the inclement weather made racing hazardous for the driver as well as his cattle, her green eyes narrowed as she peered beneath the folding calash of the chaise to see if she could identify him. During her abortive introduction to the *ton*, Jessica had learned to recognize many members of that restricted group on sight, although few had deigned to acknowledge her in return—a small loss, she was inclined to think. Her veil obscured her vision somewhat, and as the curricle drew ever nearer at first she had only an impression of size and power, a massive figure cloaked in a many-caped riding coat, large hands gripping the reins tightly, intent features shadowed by a high-crowned beaver hat pulled low over his wide brow.

Then, just as the curricle pulled abreast of Jessica, a gust of wind caught under the edge of her veil and lifted it upward, clearing her vision. The newspapers slipped through her fingers and fell unimpeded to the sidewalk as, rigid with shock, she stared into the harsh, set face of her brother-in-law, Graham Foxe, the fifth Earl of Raeburn.

Perhaps it was the flutter of the loose papers, she thought later, that made him look in her direction as he raced past her, that or the weird, scraping cry of a seagull overhead—or, more likely, the mischievous prank of some bored demon—but just in that fraction of an instant when her face was uncovered, Raeburn lifted his gaze from its intense scrutiny of the road before him, and as Jessica gaped at him from across the expanse of the damp, rutted roadbed, his gray eyes stared directly into her white face.

As quickly as it had happened, the moment was past. The curricle roared on, headed for the beachfront, and Jessica's veil fell in place once more, covering the mittened hand that clamped tightly over her quivering mouth, holding back the strangled cry that threatened to issue from her lips. Clumsily she scooped up the newspapers and the precious envelope that tumbled end over end along the planking, then she stumbled backward into the shelter of a shopfront doorway. After a breathless moment she peeked furtively around the corner to gaze after the receding vehicle. She fully expected to see him likewise peering back at her as he reined in his horses, but relief flooded her slim body as she realized that the chaise had not veered from its breakneck course, nor had it slowed. He must not have recognized her. For yet a while longer, she and her child were safe. . . . Clutching her load over her

5

pounding heart, Jessica slipped around a corner and hurried the rest of the way to her cottage along back streets.

By the time she reached the welcome shelter of her home and at last could escape the wind that whipped ever stronger through the narrow streets, carrying with it the dank odor of the gray water of the Channel, Jessica was chilled and coughing. She stumbled into the overheated atmosphere of her little kitchen, where Willa knelt before the fire to stir a steaming kettle, while with her other hand she tried to rock the squawling baby in her cradle. When Willa saw Jessica, she exclaimed with relief, "You're back! This little lady has been screaming ever since—" She choked back her words as her mistress dumped her bundle onto the scoured tabletop. Jessica yanked off her bonnet and veil and collapsed into a chair, her face pallid under the pleated edge of her black widow's cap.

"Good Lord, what's happened?" Willa gasped, dropping her spoon onto the hearth with a clatter and rushing to Jessica's side. "You look like death. What have you done to yourself?" Jessica shook her head helplessly, trying to find her voice. Willa's rough hand touched Jessica's forehead experimentally, while with her other she chafed her cold fingers. "You're feverish, and your hands are like ice, and after I warned you so particular about—"

Hoarsely Jessica croaked, "Raeburn's here."

The baby's hungry cries almost drowned out her words, and Willa, uncertain she had heard correctly, asked, "What did you say?"

"I said—" Jessica began again, louder, but she broke off when she saw her daughter's tiny fists wave indignantly in the air. "Here, you'd better give Lottie to me," she said as she quickly unbuttoned her bodice over her swollen breast. Willa handed over the swaddled baby, whose famished wails soon changed to slurpy sighs of infant contentment. Distracted by that first moment of communion with her child, Jessica smiled lovingly at her, stroking her small perfect head

6

and shaping a soft coppery curl around the tip of one finger-nail. But when she looked at Willa again, who had returned to the hearth, her green eyes were apprehensive. Coughing slightly, Jessica repeated, "I saw Raeburn."

Willa glanced at her sharply. Beneath the voluminous mob-cap, her plain round face was wary. "Did he see you?"

Jessica shrugged in confusion. "I don't know. He could have." She tried to remain cool, but by the time she had sketched the details of that chance encounter to her friend, she was trembling. "Oh, damnation, why he had to come today of all days, the first time I've been out of the house in weeks—"

"Miss Jess," Willa reproved sternly, consciously trying to soothe the agitation her usually sensible mistress displayed whenever she mentioned the earl, "we've always known there was a possibility he might find you again. It was a risk you accepted when you ran away. . . . If you want my opinion, you've been lucky not to be spotted before this. England's not so big a country, not like, say, America or—"

"That's what I should have done," Jessica said jerkily. "I should have emigrated. Things would have been different in America. Andrew and I used to talk about—"

"Miss Jess!" Willa snapped, banging the spoon on the edge of the kettle. Jessica jumped at the noise, blinking hard. "Miss Jess," Willa repeated, more softly, "compose your-self. You're not thinking right. You're sinking your boats when you don't know for certain that His Lordship even recognized you. If he passed you on the streets as quick as you say, then truly, he probably paid you no heed at all; 'twas but an accident that made him seem to look in your direction."

Jessica coughed again, disturbing the baby, who fussed for a moment and then bit at the nipple with greater force. Grimacing, Jessica said quietly, "I'm sorry, Willa. You're right, of course. It's just that—you know how that man that addles me—"

"More likely, you've not yet recovered from your cold," Willa pointed out, relaxing when she saw that Jessica had regained her composure once more. "The mind can't work when the body's not right. . . . If you'll finish tending to the little one there, as soon as she is tucked safely back in her cradle, I'll fix a hot brick for your feet and a bowl of the restorative broth I made yesterday. When you're warm and settled, you'll be more in a state to think calmly."

Jessica smiled ruefully. "Calmly," she echoed. "Do I ever do anything calmly? Poor Willa, sometimes I think I must be a great trial to you."

Willa shook her head, reaching up to brush back a yellow curl that had escaped her serviceable cap and lay plastered against her sweating brow. "A trial, Miss Jess?" she said, her wide mouth curving indulgently. "How can you be a burden to me when I owe you so much? You were my salvation. . . . But in truth," she added with wry fondness, "you do tend to act first and count the cost later."

"I know," Jessica murmured, dropping her sooty lashes over her wan cheek as she gazed down at her nuzzling daughter. "My father used to order me to pray for God to make me less impetuous. I don't know how many times I had the parable of the wise and foolish virgins read over me." She smiled cynically. "I never thought that particular story fit the situation precisely, but then, my father's sermonizing always did seem just slightly askew. . . ."

She trailed one finger over Lottie's rounded cheek, delicate skin flushed with the effort of nursing, and the baby's lids flew open, revealing eyes that seemed even greener than her mother's against the fiery blush of her small silky curls. Jessica's heart flipped. "Oh, Charlotte Andrea Foxe," she crooned, "what a beauty you're going to be. . . ." As she

8

watched tenderly it seemed to her that her daughter smiled back at her.

After Lottie had been burped and changed, Jessica tucked her back into her cradle, rocking it gently. For a long moment, as she gazed down at her sleeping child Willa's words came back to her: "You act first and count the cost later." True enough, Jessica supposed, sighing, but how did one count the cost of love? She had given her heart without thinking, and that rash action had caused her more pain than it seemed possible for one human being to bear; she had lost her family, her good name, ultimately even the regard of the man she loved. Sometimes she wondered whether, had she known in the beginning exactly what lay ahead for her, she would have hardened her heart against Andrew's blandishments, resisted the soft appeal of his gentle brown eyes. . . .

Thinking of the suffering she might have been spared, there had been occasions during the past year when she almost wished she had never been called to Renard Chase to give drawing lessons to a spoiled young girl, had never laid eyes on the Honourable Andrew Foxe. And yet—and yet, had she not met him, had she not defied the ukase of society and married him, by now she might have been forced to take a position as art mistress in some dismal, third-rate girls' academy or, worse, have been coerced into a loveless union with one of her father's parishioners, just to make room at the vicarage for the latest of her mother's annual babies. At least with Andrew, she had known a few shining moments of tenderness, of passion. And because of Andrew, she now had a daughter whom she could cherish and nurture with all the love she herself had been denied. . . .

Willa, gingerly pulling a brick from the edge of the fire with tongs, asked suddenly, "Begging your pardon, Miss Jess, but did your letter come today?"

Jessica stepped away from the cradle. "Yes, it did, Willa,

but I forgot all about it when . . . What's wrong? Do you need money?''

" 'Twould be a great help,'' Willa agreed as she wrapped a towel tightly around the heated brick. ''While you've been ill we've had to use extra coal, and then there was all the eggs and meat to help you keep your strength. . . . Here now,'' she murmured, setting the brick on the floor before Jessica's chair, ''you come make yourself all warm and cozy, and I'll pour you a dish of broth.''

Jessica sat down again, slipping off her damp shoes and putting her feet on the warmer. For a few seconds she allowed herself the luxury of being coddled, then with a sigh she reached for the forgotten envelope. Like the similar envelopes she had received each of the past ten months, it was addressed to ''J.F., Brighthelmstone,'' the simplicity of its direction more than balanced by the ornate, flowing penmanship that Jessica now recognized as the hand of Mr. Haxton; Mr. Welles's copperplate script was equally attractive, but somewhat more controlled. Breaking the seal on the envelope, Jessica withdrew the bank draft made out to ''Bearer'' and noted with a sinking feeling that it was for about half the amount she usually received. With a grimace she foresaw a month of porridge and meatless soup for her and Willa; then she chided herself, remembering that there had been times during the first months after she ran away from Raeburn's domain when the pair of them would have been grateful for porridge alone. . . . She turned her attention to the letter.

''Dear Sir,'' it began as usual, making Jessica's mouth curl up in a smile of sardonic amusement. She had never met the men who published her drawings, but she envisioned them both as rather short and exceedingly stodgy, and she could just imagine their chagrin were they ever to discover that their unknown satirist was a woman. . . . ''Dear Sir,'' she read again, ''we were most distressed to learn of your recent illness, and we regret that your indisposition has affected the number of drawings you were able to submit to us. While the quality of those you did send was, as usual, excellent, and although the sketches of 'Erinys' are becoming increasingly popular—the first printing of the cartoon 'Cornelia Weeps' sold out in two days—we hope you will understand that we cannot pay your usual—" She skimmed the rest of the page to the final, "Wishing for your renewed health and productivity, we remain," then she wadded the paper into a ball and flung it into the fire, just missing the edge of the soup kettle.

Damn those clutch-fisted old bastards! she thought irritably. Would it really have been asking too much to expect them to pay her the extra few pounds she usually received for her work, especially when, by their own admission, the satirical cartoons of Erinys were proving to be the most popular item produced by their shop? Of course she deserved better compensation. She wasn't a beginner anymore, begging for someone, anyone, to publish her work. Her scathing and expertly drawn indictments of the *ton* were enjoyed by the same people who relished those of Gillray and Rowlandson, and while she hesitated to equate herself with those master satirists, she knew that her work was superior to, say, the crudities of John Mason, her nearest competitor. She was certain that Mssrs. Haxton and Welles knew it too, and she found herself wishing desperately for a chance to go to London and confront them.

But she could not to go London. Her carefully guarded anonymity was as much a trap as a protection. She could not face her publishers without revealing that "Erinys," named after one of the avenging Furies of the Greek myths, was not only a woman, but also the notorious Jessica Foxe, the drawing teacher, upstart daughter of an impecunious country parson, who eloped to Scotland with the younger brother of an earl, and then, when her noble brother-in-law magnanimously recognized the marriage and allowed the errant couple to live at Renard Chase, his palatial country estate, proved

11

herself to be quarrelsome and encroaching and utterly blind to the gracious condescension being shown her. The same Jessica Foxe who capped all her previous misadventures by running away the night of her husband's funeral.

Willa, reading with the accuracy of long acquaintance the grim expressions playing over Jessica's bloodless features, handed her mistress a steaming mug of broth and said, "Here, eat something. There's no problem in the world that doesn't seem more solvable when you're warm and have food in you."

Jessica accepted the cup with thanks, but she only half heard her friend's comforting words. Smooth brow furrowed, she was lost in the memory of a dream-washed spring day eighteen months before, the day she had been made brutally aware that, for a poor clergyman's daughter, at least, even some dreams could be dangerous. . . .

Looking back, she wondered if the day had really been as beautiful as she remembered, or if her memories were tinted by her own emotions. She had been nineteen and in love. Her eyes had challenged the fresh new leaves on the elm trees for greenness, her step had been light despite the heavy wooden sabots she wore, almost a skip, undaunted by the prospect of the eight miles she must walk from the Palladian grandeur of Renard Chase back to her home in the village. She knew that at the vicarage she would have no time to rest before she was expected to oversee the feeding and bathing of her numerous younger siblings, and later she would have to help her worn and ailing mother, who was rake thin except for her expanding belly, try to find enough good bits of fabric left in cast-off garments to piece together a new dress for the forthcoming baby. The twice-weekly drawing lessons Jessica gave—or rather, tried to give—to Lady Claire Foxe, the incredibly spoiled half sister of Lord Raeburn, a gawky fifteen-year-old with red hair and freckles, were regarded by her father as something of a holiday, a frivolous waste of time that he permitted only because the money she received helped eke out his inadequate stipend.

Jessica herself knew how little enjoyment she received from those lessons. Lady Claire was willful and capricious, and when crossed, she was inclined to draw herself up like a disapproving dowager and try to intimidate Jessica with unsubtle reminders of her great wealth and rank. Occasionally Jessica had felt as if she would explode with the effort to contain her temper when Claire made some cutting remark about her shabby clothes or hinted that her unfashionable slenderness was less the result of diet than of genuine hunger. Long used to dealing with unruly children, Jessica had forced herself merely to laugh at the girl's airs, knowing how disastrous it would be ever to permit her to see that some of her cruel jibes had found their mark. But Andrew had known, Andrew, Lady Claire's brother, twenty years old but looking younger, so like his little sister in coloring that they might have been mistaken for twins. . . . From beneath a drooping lock of bright red hair he had gazed at Jessica with brown eyes soft with a sympathy she had never encountered before in a man, and she had fallen in love.

Of course she had known that it was hopeless: poor clergymen's daughters did not aspire to the sons of peers. Her father had already made it quite clear that as soon as her mother had convalesced from this latest lying-in, now that Jessica's younger sisters were of an age to help with the new baby, Jessica herself would be expected to leave home, find herself a husband, preferably a prosperous merchant or at least a farmer who could help supply food for the vicarage table. To dream of someone like the Honourable Andrew Foxe was vanity, so utterly impossible that it showed wanton disregard for the well-being of her family. Jessica had known all that, and yet, the mere fact of being in love had been so novel, so strangely pleasant, that she succumbed without a fight, expecting no more from Andrew than an understanding

13

glance now and then, a murmured word, perhaps—perhaps the furtive brush of fingers as they passed in the portrait gallery at Renard Chase after one of Claire's lessons. . . .

She never dared hope that Andrew might also have dreams.

In her stuffy kitchen Jessica remembered how blithely she had walked back toward the village that bright spring day, strolling along the edge of the dusty roadway, her portfolio in one hand, her shabby straw bonnet dangling by its strings from the other. Ahead of her, in the shade of a spreading oak tree, she had noticed a clump of butter-colored daffodils with white trumpets, and she debated whether she ought to pick some to take to her mother, who was weathering her eleventh pregnancy with less fortitude than she had the previous ones, especially after suffering two miscarriages in six months. Finally Jessica reluctantly decided against the flowers, knowing that if she arrived at the vicarage with anything so frivolous as a fragrant armload of daffodils, her father would accuse her of dawdling; if he was in the right mood, he would proceed to issue a sermon on indolence and the perils of admiring earthly beauty. . . . Wistfully Jessica had resumed her walk. Although she was sorry to have left Andrew's home, she reminded herself philosophically that each passing moment brought her that much closer to the time when she would return to him again. And, she admitted, a little confused by the contrariness of her emotions, in some ways it was much easier to be in love with him when they were apart, when she could weave her fantasies without practical considerations, without having to worry about the watchful eyes of servants or the chaperon, or his spying brat of a sister. . . .

Suddenly her thoughts had been interrupted by an unusual sound just behind her, the growing thunder of galloping hooves. Jessica knew that on the highways mail coaches traveled as much as ten miles an hour, and once she had overheard two men discussing the work of some Scottish engineer, McAdam or something like that, who had devised a new type of road surface that would allow even greater velocities, but here in the country, ungainly vehicles and poor maintenance of the rutted and uneven roadways meant that horses and people traveled at only two speeds, slow and slower. She turned curiously to see what fool could be risking his neck by riding at such a pace.

She was greatly surprised when she recognized the man galloping *ventre à terre* on the huge smoke-colored stallion as the Earl of Raeburn, Andrew's much older half brother, who, she was certain Andrew had said, was in London on business.

Quickly she jumped aside onto the grassy verge to let horse and rider pass, but to her amazement, just as they pulled abreast of her, Raeburn yanked back on the ribbons, and the stallion whinnied and reared, forelegs slashing the air. Alarmed, Jessica shrank back still further, inadvertently stepping into a puddle that slopped muddily over the toes of her wooden shoes. "Oh, Lud," she groaned in dismay. The sabots belonged to her next younger sister, who had grudgingly loaned them to Jessica so that she could save wear on her one pair of "good" shoes during the long hikes to Renard Chase. Momentarily forgetting her fright, she dropped her bonnet and sketchbook onto the grass and, pulling the damp hem of her skirt above her ankles, leaned over to survey the damage.

"Very pretty," a deep voice drawled, and she glanced up to find Lord Raeburn staring down at her appreciatively with hooded eyes the same smoky gray as his horse. Even afoot, the earl was a big man, broad and heavily muscled, but still mounted, he towered above her like some monumental colossus, and suddenly Jessica felt cold with dread. The skirt slipped from her chilled fingers, and she stood upright again, bewildered and threatened by his slow, insinuating appraisal. His gaze roved the length of her body, passing over her green eyes and long raven hair twisted into a thick knot at the nape of her slender neck, to linger on her swelling bosom that strained the bodice of the outgrown dress. Watching him

15

apprehensively, Jessica blushed and crossed her hands over her breast in a futile effort to shield herself from him. The earl smiled lazily at her discomfiture. His eyes moved lower, tracing her narrow waist and the long, sleek curve of her thighs with such accuracy that Jessica's color deepened; too late she realized that in the bright sunshine her body must be clearly outlined beneath the worn fabric of her gown. . . .

Just when she thought she could bear no more of his scrutiny, the earl touched the brim of his hat with affected courtesy and murmured, "Tell me, pretty miss, have you seen—" He broke off abruptly as his gray eyes flicked away from her to the portfolio lying on the ground. His mouth hardened. "*You're* the drawing teacher?" he exclaimed.

"Y-yes, my lord," Jessica stammered, bobbing a curtsy, confused as much by his initial gallantry as by his inexplicable change of mood. "I'm Jessica Marsh."

Raeburn's fair brows lifted. "You're not what I expected," he muttered under his breath. "There must be more to Andrew than I . . ." With a sudden lithe movement, unexpectedly graceful for so large a man, he swung down from the saddle. He patted the great stallion firmly on its gleaming flank, and it moved away a few paces and began to crop the grass, docile as a sheep. Stalking across the space the horse had vacated, Raeburn loomed over Jessica, tall and blond and oddly threatening. She wanted to retreat, but she was brought up short by the puddle, and she had no choice but to let him approach her.

He stood so close that she could smell the hot, masculine scent of his powerful body, and the intimacy of that odor disturbed her. She had never seen him before except at a distance, usually in the autumn when he and a collection of elegant houseguests rode through the village on their way back from a hunt, and now she caught her breath, not daring to meet his flinty gaze. Instead she kept her eyes carefully trained on the white tops of his spurred boots. He was so *big*, she thought; almost too big for gentility—utterly different from his younger brother, a slender, fine-boned patrician of the mode that she had always assumed was the pattern for members of the aristocracy. Raeburn was far above average in height, and while the tight buckskin riding breeches and fashionable Newmarket coat revealed a body that carried not an ounce of surplus flesh, he was so heavily muscled that he gave the impression of being stocky. Remembering the lavish parties that Lady Claire claimed her older brother often attended in London, Jessica drooped her silky lashes low over her eyes, just for a second diverted by the spectacle of this—this human mountain tripping his way through the intricate figures of a country dance. . . .

Her faint smile disappeared when large, blunt fingertips hooked in the soft skin under her chin and jerked her head up roughly. Jessica's green eyes widened with pain. "Lord Raeburn!" she choked indignantly.

His hand dropped away as he scowled at her use of his title. "So you do know who I am," he muttered.

Jessica nodded, rubbing her jaw. "Of—of course. You are the earl. Everyone knows that."

Studying her wan face grimly, he demanded, "Does everyone also know that you are my brother's whore?"

The accusation was so unexpected, so completely unfounded, that for a moment Jessica could only gape at him, rigid with shock, uncertain that she had heard him correctly. Her mouth worked mutely, but she could make no words come. Raeburn, watching her efforts unsympathetically, snapped, "Oh, don't bother to deny it. I have it from numerous sources. Andrew himself—"

At this betrayal, Jessica found her voice. "No!" she cried hoarsely, her mind whirling. "You're lying! He's never—he would never—"

"He wrote to me in London and told me he wants to marry you," Raeburn rasped. "Just now, when I reached the Chase, he told me the same thing again. With a moon-minded adolescent like Andrew, that can only mean that you've fallen for his baby and he has some idiot notion of making—"

Utterly shaken, Jessica did not listen to the rest of the man's ranting. Marriage? she echoed silently, stunned. The Honourable Andrew Foxe, the peer's son, who had never kissed her, had never declared his love in anything but speaking glances, had actually applied to his autocratic brother for permission to *marry* her? She shook her head fiercely. No. It was impossible. Somehow the earl had misunderstood. Huskily Jessica said, "There's been some mistake."

"I know," Raeburn answered drily, his eyes raking over her with scathing intent, "and you made it. You set your sights too high, my girl. I don't know how you've managed to convince my sister's chaperon that you're fit to teach her drawing, but don't think that the fact that you've been permitted inside the Chase makes you better than you are. I will never permit my brother to be trapped into marriage with a scheming little doxy who has probably tumbled in the hay with every—"

"But I am not—not with child!" Jessica persisted, wanting to scream hysterically. Her eyes glistened with tears of embarrassment and temper. "I have never—no one has ever—"

He snorted, "Don't play the innocent with me, miss! I know what life is like on the farm. The country girl hasn't been born yet who could keep her maidenhead to the age of fifteen."

"But you're wrong about me!" Jessica shrieked, so shrilly that she shocked herself. With great effort she brought her voice back under control. "If I were . . . what you think, it would be unlikely that I would know how . . . the drawing lessons . . . my—my father is a clergyman," she finished lamely.

Raeburn regarded her with patent disbelief. He said, "I always thought clergymen's families were expected to main-

18

tain an air of respectability, however shabby. That dress you're wearing . . ." His voice trailed off suggestively.

Jessica colored again, recalling the times she had pleaded with her father to be able to replace the outgrown dress. His response had been to charge her to consider the lilies of the field. . . . "I have seven younger brothers and sisters," she said stiltedly, hating this man who was forcing her to make excuses. "My father's parish is a small one, and of necessity we must . . . practice economy."

"Indeed," Raeburn drawled, beginning his outrageous appraisal of her body once more. "It sounds to me as if it would be more to the point were your father to practice a little abstinence."

Jessica slapped him.

The action came so quickly, so unexpectedly, that she had no time to debate its wisdom, in that moment of fury knowing only that no matter who he was or what he might say about her, she would not allow him to insult her family. But even as the sound of the blow still echoed across the empty, sunlit fields on either side of the road, and her small hand stung as if she had struck it flat against a boulder, the rashness of what she had done seeped into her, and Jessica stared up at him fearfully.

He did not flinch, but even in the shadow cast by the brim of his tall hat, the star-shaped imprint of her hand glared ruddily on his tanned cheek, and as she watched, in the pupils of his eyes tiny flames began to blaze like bonfires set in the gray London snow. Jessica retreated, heedless of the puddle behind her, but before she could take even one step, large hands lashed out and captured her thin arms in living manacles, hauling her toward him and crushing her against the granite wall of his chest.

"Listen to me, clergyman's daughter," he growled, as she gasped for air, "do you know who I am? Do you know what behavior like yours invites? I could take you here, now, in

19

the mud, with no one to hear your screams, and even if they did, they would not dare to interfere. . . ."

His long fingers wound painfully into her thick hair, jerking her head back so that the curve of her slender neck clear down to the swell of her burgeoning breasts was exposed to his contemptuous gaze. His head moved closer, and she could feel his breath hot on her sensitive skin. "A-Andrew would s-stop you," she stammered, her heart fluttering against the inside of her chest like a wild bird caught in a cage.

Raeburn snorted cynically. "My little brother would be the last person to come between me and my pleasures. He's never defied me in his life. Once he discovers I want you for myself, he won't look at you again—"

"But you don't want me!" Jessica squealed in protest. "This is just some scheme to punish me for daring to—"

"Of course I don't. . . ." he began scornfully, but his deep voice trailed off, and the expression in his eyes altered subtly. Since confronting the recalcitrant Andrew, Raeburn had been drinking himself into a blind fury, and when he first touched the girl, he had been intent only on subduing her, bending her to his will as easily as he arched her body over his arm. Now he seemed to become truly aware of her provocative posture. His nostrils flared as he muttered, "By God, I think I do want you," and he lowered his head toward hers.

Like one mesmerized, Jessica watched the descent of his mouth, her green eyes wide and staring as he moved closer, closer. . . . But when she felt his quickening breath tickle her lips, she could almost taste the brandy scenting it, and the realization that he was more than a little in his cups revolted her. With rekindled frenzy she tried to twist away from him, yanking her hair painfully.

"Don't fight me," he growled impatiently, "or you'll make me angry. . . ."

Even as she thrashed about in his powerful embrace, she

20

knew it was hopeless to fight him. All she was doing was exhausting herself. With a moan of despair, she relaxed, gazing up at him desolately.

When her struggles stilled, his voice softened, became cajoling. "Come now, clergyman's daughter," he urged, "why won't you use your head? Be . . . sweet to me, give me a little of what you've already given my brother. If you please me . . . don't you realize that I could set you up in far better style than Andrew ever could?"

Sick with humiliation, Jessica drooped her long lashes over her bloodless cheeks, trying to shut out the sight of Raeburn's avid, bewildering gaze. "Why are you doing this to me?" she sobbed in a voice heavy with defeat. "I didn't know that Andrew would—"

"Damn Andrew," Raeburn swore in an undertone, and his mouth came down brutally over hers.

She had never been kissed before, had never been touched in any way by a man, her father's profession a thin but adequate armor against the casual flirtations of the village swains, who had considered her above them. In her dreams she had envisioned sexual passion with both lyricism and distaste, an uncomfortable compound culled from the Song of Solomon and the guttural moans she heard issuing through the wall of her parents' bedroom at night. . . . Even with Andrew she had never truly imagined him caressing her. Now the earl's mouth ravaged hers, frightening her with greedy demand as his arms pressed her slim body against the hulking mass of his own and made her intimately aware of his driving male hunger. He was hurting her badly, and although she tried to tell herself that he was inflicting this pain with calculation, that his intention was to humiliate her into submission, not degrade her, she panicked. When one of his large hands closed with shocking intimacy over the swell of her breast, Jessica again began to flail wildly, all her senses outraged, certain that if she did not escape him at once, he

21

would soon subdue her in the most basic and irrevocable way of all. . . .

Suddenly he released her.

His action came without warning, just when Jessica was pushing against his wall-like chest with renewed vigor, and she lost her balance, oversetting herself. Clawing at the air, she toppled backward, and before Raeburn, lunging for her with lightning reflexes, could catch her, she fell with a disgruntled splash into the puddle.

Instantly muddy water soaked the thin fabric of her dress, plastering it to her slender body, and her black hair, freed from its sedate knot during her struggles, dangled over her breast in soggy ropes. Shaking with temper and reaction, she stared down at herself, at her murky reflection on the agitated surface of the puddle, and as she watched helplessly, one tear worked its way down her smudged cheek, marking a rivulet of white against the dirt. When the tear had dripped from her chin into the puddle, a second began its course down the other cheek. She buried her face in her hands and began to sob helplessly, sick with shame and humiliation and fury at her own impotence.

A shadow fell on Jessica as something large and solid came between her and the sun, and she glanced up with red-rimmed eyes to see the earl looming tensely over her, his mouth tight, his expression inscrutable. As Jessica's gaze moved over the towering length of him she noted with malicious satisfaction that his boots had been badly splashed when she fell; she hoped the clinging mud stained the white tops beyond repair.

While she watched, he pulled an immaculate handkerchief from the sleeve of his coat and extended it to her. "Here," he muttered, "you can at least clean your face."

She did not move. When he tried to press the square of fine bleached linen into her fingers, she let it fall unhindered into the mud beside her. She watched as if fascinated as the folded cloth slowly absorbed the dirty water and at last foundered

22

until only one white corner remained aloft like the topsail of a grounded schooner. With cool deliberation she forced under that last corner as well, then she looked up at the earl again. "I hate you," she said slowly and distinctly. "I wish you'd die."

Raeburn's hooded gray eyes became shuttered. "No doubt you do," he said in a voice that matched her own. "With me out of the way, Andrew would succeed to the title, and you'd be halfway to your countess's tiara. . . . How unfortunate for you that I have no intention either of dying soon or of sanctioning any union between my bird-witted brother and a cheap little guttersnipe, no matter how beautiful she is. Good day to you, madam." He spun on his heel and stalked away to his grazing stallion. . . .

"Miss Jess," Willa reproved sternly, "your broth is getting cold."

Jessica blinked hard, jerked back to the present with dizzying abruptness. "Wh-what did you say?" she stammered in confusion, staring about the cramped, humid kitchen as if she had never seen it before.

Willa, recognizing one of her mistress's "moods," repeated more gently, "Your broth is getting cold, and you look as if you're like to spill it all over yourself. Pay attention now, and drink it up quick, before all the goodness steams out of it."

"Yes, Willa," Jessica answered meekly, raising the thick cup to her lips. As she sipped the savory soup she admitted that its rich warmth was indeed comforting, almost—almost as comforting as Andrew's regard and solicitude had been that day when he found her beside the road long after Raeburn had galloped away. Even as he leaped from his horse he had been ripping off his coat and he had wrapped it modestly about her wet, muddied shoulders. He had pulled her into the shelter of his embrace, touching her with an extreme tenderness that had been belied by the unusual hardness of his soft

23

brown eyes, the edge in his young voice. "That bastard," he had groaned fiercely, "if I had known what he—if I could have caught up with that damned great stallion of his . . ." He had drawn her still-trembling body closer to his, cradling and protecting her, and even as Andrew held her, Jessica had felt him begin to tremble too. When she looked up questioningly at him, his face had been glowing with a strange new light. He murmured huskily, "I'll keep you safe, Jessica, I promise. I'll fix it so that he can never hurt you or insult you again. You'll be my wife. That'll show him. All you have to do is come away with me, come away with me *now*. . . ."

"Willa," Jessica said quietly, "I think I—I ought to go lie down for a while. I'm feeling very tired."

The maid nodded, setting aside the pan of vegetables she had been scraping. "Yes, I think that would be a good idea. You're not completely recovered from your cold yet, and you've overtaxed yourself today. Shall I bring a warming pan?"

Jessica shook her head as she rose stiffly from her chair. "No," she said, reaching up to unpin her black widow's cap as she trudged in her stockinged feet toward her bedroom. "I'll be all right, if only I can get some . . ." Slipping into the lumpy feather bed, she fell into a deep sleep troubled by dreams that she had thought were behind her, memories of the bitter arguments that had arisen when a girl in love with love and a boy bent only on spiting his authoritarian older brother had found that their spring-fresh sexual attraction, while intense, was not adequate to bind them securely in the face of a disapproving world. . . .

She was jolted from her restless slumber by a loud pounding on the front door of the cottage. "My God," she choked, sitting upright, "who can that—" Her hand flew to her mouth as the realization came to her. "W-Willa," she called tremulously, "don't let him—" but she was too late. The loud knock came again, and from the little sitting room

24

Jessica could hear the metallic scrape of the bolt being drawn back.

"Your Lordship!" she heard the maid exclaim, and the front door banged as if it had been pushed all the way open. Hard-soled boots strode imperiously across the uncarpeted entryway.

"Well, well, Willa Brown," she heard Raeburn's deep voice drawl hatefully, "I might have known I'd find you here. Now go fetch my sister-in-law and tell her I've come to get her."

Chapter Two

"There's no need to announce you, Graham," Jessica said drily from her bedroom door, affecting a good deal more aplomb than she actually felt. "I see that you still have not learned the art of making a gracious entrance."

She stood barefoot in the archway, masses of gleaming hair flowing like a river of ink until they curled just under the curve of her small bottom. The cold penetrating the soles of her feet was nothing compared to the chill in her heart as she gazed resignedly at the man whose image had haunted her more surely even than that of her dead husband. She had tried to exorcise him from her fevered brain, hoping that if she poured all her bitterness into her cartoons, she would at last be free of him, but each time her pen sketched his broad, compelling features, she had found she was only feeding her obsession. Sometimes she thought she would never be released from the hold he had had on her since that shocking spring afternoon by the roadside. . . . Now at last he had found her again. But a short year since she had fled him, thirteen brief months to relish her uncertain liberty before he tracked her down like one of the deer in the park surrounding Renard Chase, and now he was closing in for the kill. She faced him stiffly, like a doe at bay, her slanting green eyes wide and wary in her ashen face. She would show him no fear, she vowed proudly; though he threatened her and her child, she would never . . .

Jessica blinked hard, her heart pounding fiercely. Oh, God, her child! In that first instant of seeing him once more, of affecting cool disinterest in his sudden appearance, she had forgotten that Raeburn didn't know about Lottie. When Jessica fled from the Raeburn estate, no one but Willa had suspected that she was pregnant, that within her she had carried a new life conceived during the last night she slept with her husband, the last night he wrapped his strong young arms around her and pretended that he cared nothing about society's disapproval. . . . She had not even garnered the courage to tell Andrew. By the time he contracted the influenza that killed him, he had begun to despise both his common-born wife and himself for their misalliance, and although Jessica nursed him tirelessly and diligently throughout his illness, she had known that even if he recovered, she had lost him forever. . . .

Raeburn whirled around, his greatcoat fanning out from his body. "Jess—" he said unsteadily, breaking off the word as he stared at her dishevelment. He had obviously interrupted a nap or something, and he knew a moment's irritation that while he had been scouring the cold and dreary confines of Brighton like a madman, collaring total strangers and demanding to know the whereabouts of the young woman in the long widow's veil, she had been sleeping peacefully in her snug little cottage.

And yet, Raeburn admitted honestly, glancing about him, the cottage did not appear particularly snug, nor did Jessica look as if peace were her frequent companion. He was shocked by her pallor, her enormous green eyes the only color in a face so white and pinched that her pronounced cheekbones made her appear almost catlike. She seemed to vibrate with tension, and in her dull weeds she looked incredibly fragile, thinner, except for—except for . . . Her body had altered somehow, he thought, frowning. He studied her judiciously, until after a moment he realized what seemed different about

28

her: her breasts were larger. For a second he wondered if this change was an optical illusion caused by her unnatural slenderness, but soon his connoisseur's eyes recognized that the bosom pressing against the worn bombazine of her short-waisted gown was indeed fuller, more rounded, than he remembered. No longer were Jessica's the high, girlish breasts that he had felt under his hungry hands one bright afternoon less than two years before. She was a woman now, with a woman's body, and despite her lack of color, her thinness, he thought she had never been more beautiful.

Aloud Raeburn said, "You look like hell."

Jessica endured his infuriating appraisal with iron control, knowing she dared not let him see that he flustered her. She could never best the earl in a clash of tempers, and if he realized that his presence made her nervous and apprehensive, he might begin to wonder why.

When she remained silent, he probed again. "I'd venture to guess you've dropped at least a stone since last I saw you. . . ."

Aware that her unusual silence might be as damning as a display of temperament, Jessica nodded with exaggerated courtesy and responded tartly, "And you look bigger than ever—too big to be quite natural. Are you sure your mother didn't mate with a Minotaur or something?"

Raeburn's mouth thinned. "Charming as ever, I see," he muttered tightly. His gray eyes scanned the dim parlor again, noting the drab furnishings, the threadbare rug, the pathetically small fire in the grate. He could feel the chill through the thickness of his caped driving coat. Mentally he contrasted the cottage with the elegance of Renard Chase, where logs blazed continually in every room, making even the slick marble floors seem warm. Out of the corner of his eye he saw Jessica shiver, hugging her thin arms and rubbing her bare toes together, and he snapped harshly, "Why on earth don't you quit hopping around and put on your—" He blanched, stricken. "Good Lord, Jess," he choked, "don't tell me you don't have any—"

"Of course I have shoes," Jessica replied impatiently. "They're warming on the hearth in the kitchen."

Raeburn relaxed visibly. "I'm grateful to hear that there's a fire someplace in this house. I was beginning to think . . ."

He smiled, the corners of his wide mouth spreading until they almost touched his blond sidewhiskers, and Jessica, watching him warily, was reminded that when Graham Foxe chose to do so, he could radiate a charm that was well-nigh irresistible. She had seen him use it on the most stickling of dowagers during those miserable weeks in London when he had tried to get the *ton* to accept her clandestine marriage to Andrew. In retrospect she admitted honestly that he might have succeeded in his quest had she herself not been so incredibly defensive about her position that she managed to alienate almost everyone, including her husband. But Jessica had been very young and sensitive to snubs even when none were intended, and her nature was such that when she felt herself attacked, she attacked in return. After Raeburn managed somehow to cajole one of the patronesses of Almack's into issuing a pair of vouchers for the errant couple, Jessica had capped her abortive introduction to society by tossing a cup of sticky-sweet orgeat into the sneering face of Lady Daphne Templeton, the Duke of Crowell's daughter. She had lost her temper completely when that haughty young woman asked, with a significant glance toward Jessica's waistline, whether she planned to have her children christened by a blacksmith, since she had seen fit to be married by one. . . .

Raeburn suggested lightly, "If it's warmer in the kitchen, Jess, why don't we go in there? You and I have a great many things to discuss."

Jessica stiffened with alarm, and her green eyes shot sidelong toward Willa, who was standing apart, pretending not to listen to the conversation. Both women were thinking of the

30

cradle where little Charlotte lay sleeping serenely, as ignorant of her volatile uncle's existence as he, thankfully, was of hers. Thus far, Raeburn had conducted this reunion with far more restraint than Jessica had anticipated, but if he should discover that she had kept his brother's only child from him . . .

Bobbing a deferential curtsy, Willa gushed with an obsequiousness that, Jessica suspected, must have choked her, "Begging you pardon, Your Lordship, but I've been scrubbing the floor in the kitchen, and 'tis all atumble in there right now. If Your Lordship would allow me, I'll bring the scuttle in here and build up a fine fire faster than you can say—"

"All right, girl," Raeburn said impatiently, dismissing her. "Just be quick about it. And make sure you bring your mistress's shoes and a warm wrap."

"Yes, Your Lordship," Willa mumbled, and she fled to the kitchen. In a moment she was back with the coal and the requested garments, and as Jessica stooped to tie the ribbons of her toasty slippers, she glanced questioningly at the maid, who stood just behind Raeburn. Willa shook her head slightly and pantomimed sleep.

Jessica sighed and seated herself on the sprung settee, draping her wool shawl about her thin shoulders. With an uncertain smile she motioned to the seat beside her. "Please do sit down and make yourself comfortable, Graham," she said archly. "Let Willa take your coat back into the kitchen with her, and it will be most pleasantly warm when you are ready to leave."

Raeburn glanced suspiciously at Jessica and murmured enigmatically, "Don't think you're going to get rid of me that easily, my girl." He shrugged the greatcoat from his broad shoulders and passed it to Willa, who had to carry it high against her chest to keep the tails from dragging the floor. When she had departed from the parlor again, Raeburn turned to Jessica and regarded her silently for a long moment, watching her fingers begin to plait her hair deftly and reshape

31

it into the coiled knot that seemed almost too heavy for her slender neck. He commented curiously, "How do you do that? My sister needs two maids and a half a dozen mirrors . . ."

Her task completed, Jessica folded her hands sedately in her lap and shrugged, her expression carefully neutral. "Those of us who have not been so . . . blessed . . . as Lady Claire must learn to do for ourselves."

Raeburn's frown deepened. " 'Lady Claire'?" he echoed mockingly. "Why so formal with your sister-in-law? You've never had any difficulty calling me Graham."

But you and I went beyond the bounds of formality the first day we met, Jessica thought with a stab of bitterness, recalling anew his assault on her innocence, those groping hands and bruising lips that had ravaged her dreams. . . . Aloud she said waspishly, "When I . . . joined your family, Lady Claire told me bluntly that although she was Andrew's sister, she would never be mine. After that I took pains never to encroach upon our accidental connection."

His fair brows lifted sharply at the venom in her voice. "Forgiving little thing, aren't you?" he muttered.

Jessica eyed him squarely. "My father may have been a clergyman," she said slowly, "but I have never learned to turn the other cheek."

Raeburn's gray gaze was equally direct. "I'm well aware of that," he said. After the briefest of hesitations he continued. "Speaking of your father, did you know that he has married again?"

Jessica caught her breath with a hiss. "Remarried?" she demanded hoarsely. "You mean he has already found someone to take my mother's place, after he killed her with his lust?" Her jade eyes lost their luster as she thought of her mother's body wasted in death, her emaciation made even more grotesque by her bloated belly. She had writhed in agony for a day and a night, calling out her oldest daughter's name repeatedly, before Jessica's father—who had vowed publicly never to speak to his thankless child again—relented enough to allow one of her brothers to ride his old cob to Renard Chase to fetch her. By the time Jessica and Andrew raced to the vicarage with the Foxe family physician in tow, her mother was dead, the infant still unborn. . . .

Jessica leaped to her feet and paced nervously about the tiny parlor, trying to compose herself. With withering scorn she snapped, "Well, I suppose he requires someone to care for the children who are yet at home, but for the sake of his new wife, I hope she proves barren!"

Raeburn watched her jerky movements with concern. "She is, I believe, a widow with three young ones of her own," he said quietly.

Jessica whirled on him, her pale face luminous with hatred. "You seem to be exceptionally well informed about the affairs of an unremarkable country parson," she accused, her voice growing high and shrill. "Am I to assume that your concern is in the nature of payment for services rendered?"

Raeburn stared. "What the *hell* is that supposed to mean?"

Through clenched teeth Jessica snarled, "You know what I mean! When the great Earl of Raeburn found he couldn't control the encroaching country girl with the sheer force of his personality, he decided to strike at her through her family. . . ."

Beneath a drooping lock of fair hair, Raeburn's face purpled with rage, and he swore viciously. Unfolding his long frame from the settee with surprising grace, he stood up, his broad shoulders and impressive bulk filling the little room as he loomed over Jessica. Suddenly apprehensive, she tried to back away, but his large hands snaked out to capture her arms, and he hauled her up against him, his gray eyes glittering like mica. "Listen to me, my girl," he growled, his blunt fingertips digging into the softness of her flesh, "the only reason I have ever had any congress with that sycophantic father of yours was to find out if you had contacted him to let him know your whereabouts. My sole concern was and is your well-being—"

"Liar!" Jessica shrilled. "It was because of you that he forbade me to see my own mother, denounced me from the pulpit like some—"

In a booming voice so loud that it rattled the glass chimneys on the candlesticks, Raeburn bellowed, "*I never told him to disown you!* That was his own crackbrained—"

But Jessica never had an opportunity to hear the rest of his impassioned disavowal. In the kitchen a baby squawled.

Jessica froze, staring up helplessly at the earl. The thin, hungry cry of infant outrage sounded again, and Raeburn's fair head jerked around to stare at the half-open scullery door. His hands clamped bruisingly around Jessica's arms, making her squeal with pain as he growled, "What in the name of . . .?"

Jessica twisted her head to peer over her shoulder at the doorway, where suddenly Willa appeared, her rough hands cradling a squirming, swaddled bundle high on her shoulder so that the baby's face could not be seen. Jessica could hear the smacking noise her daughter's tiny lips made against Willa's throat, and she felt her breasts swell at the sound, reminding her with aching insistence that it was again time for Lottie's feeding. Beneath spiky black lashes her fearful green eyes flicked up at the ashen face of the man who held her brutally while he gaped at her maid. Oh, God, Jessica moaned with silent, impotent anguish, what would he say now, what would he do when . . .

Willa said, "Miss Jess, I'm sorry my baby disturbed you. I promise it won't happen again."

Raeburn's grip relaxed slightly. His wide brow furrowed, he demanded harshly, "Your child, Willa Brown?"

Willa lifted her chin, her dark eyes meeting his contemptuous gaze steadily from beneath the ruffle of her mobcap. For as long as she could remember, Willa had been the object of men's lust and scorn, and at seventeen, after falling into the hands of a pack of aristocratic ruffians, she had vowed that she would die rather than suffer degradation again; but when she flung herself into the stinking waters of the Thames, Jessica had saved her, had revived her life and her soul, and since then Willa had been her eager slave. Now she said evenly, "Yes, Your Lordship, this is my baby," and Jessica, hearing this, felt her heart flip with wary gratitude at the enormity of what her friend was trying to do.

Raeburn's gaze narrowed cynically. Under his breath he muttered, "Well, I suppose it was to be expected. . . ." His voice lifted in curiosity. "Dare one inquire after the father of this unfortunate infant?"

Willa glanced quickly at her mistress, who at last had managed to free herself from Raeburn's hands. Angrily Jessica inserted her slim body protectively in the space between the maid and the earl as she insisted, "Graham, you have no right to interrogate my servant. Her private life is not your responsibility."

One thick, fair brow arched sharply upward. "On the contrary, my dear sister-in-law," Raeburn drawled, "you are most definitely my responsibility, and if this woman and her bastard are imposing on you—"

"Damn you, Lottie is not a bastard!" Jessica snapped fiercely, too incensed by his attack on her child to weigh her words. "She's—she's . . ." Aburptly her voice faded as she recognized just how close she was to revealing the one secret she had struggled for over a year to keep. Helplessly she glanced at Willa again, who gently rubbed the fussing baby's back, trying to soothe her. As Jessica watched, one of little Charlotte's fists worked loose from her tight wrappings, and she began to suck on it greedily. Jessica winced at the effort not to reach out to her.

Raeburn's hooded eyes were inscrutable, but skepticism was patent in his deep voice. "Perhaps," he suggested evenly,

"Miss Brown—or should I say Mrs., since you tell me the child is . . . legitimate—ought to take the infant back to the kitchen and feed her. I claim no authority on the subject of children, but even I can see that the brat is hungry."

Anxious to distract him, Jessica interjected, "Actually, we think she's teething. . . ."

Lottie wailed loudly, and Raeburn grimaced. "All the more reason to get it out of here," he grumbled. He frowned at Willa. "Well, girl, what are you waiting for? Go on, be quick about it!"

Willa glanced uncertainly at her mistress. "Miss Jess?" she ventured as she bounced the baby on her shoulder.

Jessica wavered, torn between her fear of Raeburn and her instinctive maternal response to her child's cries. Her hand pressing tightly against her breast, at last she said reluctantly, "Perhaps you had better take her back to the kitchen, Willa. There must be something there to soothe her . . . her pains. I-I'll join you as soon as His Lordship leaves."

Willa nodded slowly. "Yes, miss," she said, turning to carry her wriggling bundle back to the warmth of the other room. Just as she did, little Charlotte gave a final furious howl and waved her fists blindly, dislodging the worn blanket that Willa had kept draped over her head. The frayed woolen cloth fell back, revealing a mass of baby-soft curls that blazed like infant fire against Lottie's flushed skin.

Raeburn gaped, his flinty gaze riveted to the child's red hair. Jessica heard him mutter, "What the . . . ?" as he pushed her aside and stalked toward Willa, who was retreating toward the kitchen. Intercepting her, he towered over the maid like some emraged Titan, and when he ordered in a low, strained voice, "Give me the child, Willa Brown," she had no choice but to obey him.

Jessica gnawed her lip as she watched the earl lift the infant carefully into his arms. For someone who disclaimed knowledge of children, she thought irrelevantly, he seemed to hold this one with surprising skill, crooking one elbow so that the baby's head and back were cradled securely against the broad lapels of his perfectly tailored coat. Lottie calmed at once, lulled by the only masculine arms that had ever held her, except for the palsied grasp of the arthritic old vicar who had christened her. With his free hand Raeburn gently tugged the blanket away from her face, and he peered intently into her small, perfect features, the rosebud mouth, the short nose, the long lashes that were the same burnished copper as her hair. "Andrew's hair," he murmured in wonder, and as he spoke her lashes flew up, revealing wide slanting eyes that already gleamed with emerald fire.

Raeburn glanced dismissively at Willa's plain round face, her brown eyes and yellow curls, then he turned to Jessica. With eyes as bright as her daughter's, she met his gaze courageously. Through clenched teeth he asked, "A girl, you said? What is her name?"

"Lottie," Jessica mumbled. "Charlotte Andrea."

Raeburn digested this for a moment. "Exactly how old is she?"

"Six months. She was born the week after Easter."

"And it was Michaelmas when Andrew . . ." he muttered, scowling. Jessica could almost see the calculations whirling in his head. Suddenly he growled, "You miserable bitch, you must have known!" Jessica said nothing. Raeburn looked down at the baby again and his face darkened with rage. He accused, "Damn you, Jessica Foxe, if you were a man, I'd kill you for this! How could you keep my brother's child from me?" Lottie whimpered uneasily, and Raeburn's blunt fingers moved with unexpected tenderness as he soothed her, stroking her hair. She settled again, her green eyes focusing uncertainly on the bright buttons of his coat. Just for an instant Jessica saw Raeburn's harsh features soften in a poignant smile, but when he lifted his head to glare at her again, his expression was cold and unyielding.

Gravely Jessica reminded him, "She's my child too, Graham."

Raeburn retorted, "She's a Foxe, the granddaughter of an earl. How dare you keep her in this—this tenement? She belongs at Renard Chase, among her own kind."

"*I* am her kind," Jessica insisted, reaching for her daughter, whose cries had quieted momentarily. "I will be the one to decide what's best for her."

Raeburn released the baby and watched Jessica set her expertly on her shoulder. He drawled sarcastically, "And you think it's best for her to keep company with prostitutes?"

Out of the corner of her eye, Jessica could see Willa's recoil, her forthright, honest face flushing with humiliation. In Jessica's mind flashed a picture of her maid as she had been when she and Andrew fished her out of the river one foggy London night not long after they were married; Andrew had wanted to leave her on the embankment, saying that it was enough that they had saved her from drowning, but Jessica had insisted on taking the shivering girl back to the security of Raeburn House, where even Willa's garish rouge had not been able to disguise the livid bruises and contusions purpling her unhealthy ceruse-poisoned skin. . . . Jessica's temper flared at Raeburn's callousness, and bright flags blazed in her pale cheeks. She said with withering disdain, "Well, Graham, I see you've become very adept at insulting those who can't defend themselves. Why not try calling me names for a change?"

"Jess—" he tried to interrupt, but she would not be stopped.

"Why so squeamish, dear brother-in-law? You've found it easy enough to revile me in the past! Shall I remind you of some of your favorite epithets? 'Doxy,' 'vixen,' 'conniving little temptress,' just to name a few. But, of course, 'upstart drawing teacher' is the term of choice with your family, I believe. At any rate, that's the one I recall overhearing the

38

day of my husband's funeral: 'How shall we rid ourselves of the upstart drawing teacher now that Andrew's dead?' "

Raeburn was staring at her with a puzzled grimace. "Who said that?"

Jessica shrugged silently. She turned to Willa and passed over the dozing infant. "Here," she soothed, knowing her friend was still hurt by Raeburn's crude reminder of a life she had tried to put behind her, "why don't you return Lottie to her cradle? I know she wants feeding, but I do think she'll sleep for a little longer now."

"Thank you, Miss Jess," Willa murmured, fleeing from the room.

Raeburn watched the maid escape through the kitchen door; then he turned to face Jessica's accusing eyes again. "All right," he murmured grudgingly, "I'm sorry I . . . spoke slightingly of your servant; it was unworthy of me. One of the first lessons my nanny ever taught me was to be courteous to those of inferior station."

Jessica laughed sardonically. "Am I to conclude from that that you consider my family equal to that of an earl? You have never made any effort to be courteous to me!"

Raeburn's face darkened as he recalled her earlier words. "Obviously someone at Renard Chase was less than . . . deferential to you. Who was it, Jess?"

Jessica shrugged, trying to disguise her remembered pain. "At this late date, I'm not quite sure, Graham. Is it important?"

"Yes," he growled. "I want to know who dared speak so cruelly to you that the words drove you away from your home before the clods had even settled over your husband's coffin."

The image made her shudder, and to disguise her reaction, she seated herself on the settee once more and smoothed her skirt over her lap. She murmured reluctantly, "It was a woman, I remember that much. I suppose the speaker could have been Claire, or possibly her bristle-faced witch of a chaperon, Mrs. Talmadge; it matters little. I just remember

39

that from my sitting-room window I watched the crepe-hung carriages return from the churchyard, and I thought . . . I thought that despite our differences you might see fit to come to me and tell me about the service. . . ."

Her voice thickened suddenly, and she looked away. "I knew you were as heartsick as I was, and I even had some bird-witted notion that I might help assuage your grief by telling you your brother had not died without issue . . . but you didn't come to me, Graham. I sat alone in that room, with no one to comfort me except for Willa, until nightfall, when I decided to bury my pride and go to you. But as I stepped onto the landing outside the small parlor, I heard all of you discussing how to rid yourselves of the upstart drawing teacher, and I knew then there would never be a place for me at Renard Chase, even if you welcomed Andrew's child." Her face twisted, and her hands closed protectively over her belly, as if sheltering the baby she had once carried there.

Watching her, Raeburn shook his head solemnly, his gray eyes stricken. "Whatever you overheard that day, Jess, I knew nothing of it. After I finished burying my brother, someone gave me a brandy flask—to combat the cold, he said, although I seem to recall that the day was fairly temperate for autumn—and by the time we got back to the Chase, I was as drunk as a French whore. I didn't come to my senses till the next morning, when my sister told me that you and your maid had run away during the night."

"I'll wager that was welcome news," Jessica muttered.

Raeburn colored. "Welcome?" he repeated hoarsely. "Damnation, woman, if you had any idea what I've been through this past year, worrying about you, not knowing if you were alive or dead, or whether you had enough to—"

Jessica's eyes clouded as she remembered those first horrible weeks, a time when she had learned with chilling impact that in her father's house, despite their penury, she had never known true hunger before. . . . She smiled ironically, her dark head sketching a circuit of the dismal room. She said lightly, "Well, Graham, now you may be reassured. I am alive and well, my daughter and my maid and I eat with reasonable regularity, thank you, and in future we shall—"

"But how did you manage?" Reaburn demanded to know. "You took nothing with you but the clothes you wore."

"I had my wedding ring," Jessica reminded him stiffly. "I sold it."

Raeburn said grimly, "The most prudent housewife in the world could not make the proceeds from that ring last a year. What else did you sell—or was it that dubious companion of yours?"

Jessica blushed scarlet as his implication struck her, and frustrated rage burned in her at his obvious belief that no woman could earn money except on her back. . . . In truth Willa, concerned about the health of the child her mistress carried, had reluctantly offered to go back to the only occupation she knew, but before she had been forced to make that ultimate sacrifice, Jessica had discovered, by fortunate accident, that people were willing to pay for the bitterly satiric cartoons she had hitherto sketched only to vent her anger and frustration. . . .

Glancing at him from behind the curtain of her long lashes, Jessica imagined with spiteful satisfaction Raeburn's astonishment if she were to identify herself as the mysterious Erinys, with whose work the earl was no doubt familiar. But even as the thought formed in her mind, she realized she could never tell him. Too often he had been the target of her most malicious satire, he and his horses and his overblown lightskirts; his huge frame and blond hair made him ridiculously easy to caricature. . . . Aware that he awaited her answer, Jessica improvised, "I also . . . gave drawing lessons."

"To whom?" Raeburn inquired softly, his gray eyes cold and disbelieving. "To fishermen's daughters?" When Jessica refused to answer him, he sighed and said, "Well, perhaps it does not matter now. You're coming home with me."

Jessica shook her head. "No, Graham. This is our home now. The cottage may not compare to Renard Chase, but it is adequate for our needs."

"You may have learned to economize when you lived at the vicarage," Raeburn insisted, "but I tell you right now, this hovel is not adequate for my niece's needs. She is a Foxe, and she will be raised as befits her station." His gray eyes narrowed as he surveyed the room once more. "For God's sake, Jess, how could you run off like that, knowing you were increasing? Weren't you aware that any child of Andrew's would inherit a substantial income, the one that would have come to my brother had he lived to his twenty-first birthday?"

"I was never interested in Andrew's money," Jessica said wearily. "I told you that, but you refused to believe me."

Raeburn persisted. "Did it not occur to you that if the baby were a boy, he would be my heir, the next Earl of Raeburn?"

Jessica flushed. Yes, that thought had occurred to her, and she had known a moment's bitter triumph at the possibility that the son of the detested art mistress might aspire to one of the loftiest titles in the realm. But when she had imagined her child living at Renard Chase, studying at the finest schools, and mixing with the cream of society, she had begun to wonder if he would grow to despise her for her common background, as his father's people had, and that possibility had made her determined to bring the baby up on her own. She had acquitted herself of any niggling charge of selfishness by deciding that she must save her child from the contaminating influence of wealth and position. . . .

Thinking with loving adoration of her sleeping daughter, Jessica murmured quietly, "But as it happened, Graham, my little one proved to be but a girl. I'm afraid it will be up to you to provide for your own heir."

Raeburn's hard cheek twitched. Stonily he said, "And so I've done."

Jessica jerked her head upright and stared at him, oddly breathless. "What do you mean?"

His strong features were absolutely expressionless as he replied, "I am engaged to be married."

Jessica blinked hard, wondering why her stomach suddenly felt so hollow. "Married?" she echoed with a nervous titter that turned into a hoarse cough. "You, Graham? I—I always thought you were determined never to take that fatal step."

He said darkly, "As you pointed out so succinctly, a man must have an heir. With Andrew gone . . ."

"I see," Jessica murmured, staring blindly at the thread-bare square of drugget that passed for a parlor rug. She shook her head in wonder. Raeburn married, leg-shackled. The idea was incomprehensible. Raeburn was a man large of stature, large of appetite. He liked big, fast horses, and his taste in women seemed inclined along the same lines. While Jessica and Andrew were in London, they had attended a perform-ance of *Don Giovanni*, and her husband had pointed out Lucinda, the almost-too-buxom brunette singing the role of Zerlina, as Raeburn's latest *chère amie*. Of course he would never demean his family name by taking to wife anyone of less than impeccable family and reputation, but the notion of him dancing attendance on some simpering debutante struck Jessica as rather grotesque. With an effort at politeness, she asked, "So who is the lucky girl, Graham, and when may I wish you happy? I seemed to have missed the announcement in the—"

"There's been no official announcement as yet," Raeburn interrupted. "The old duke, Daphne's father, died almost a year ago, and she won't be out of mourning until the end of November. She'll be spending Christmas at Renard Chase with her brother the Marquess of—I mean Crowell now—and we'll make it official then. We intend an Easter wedding."

Jessica gaped as his words fit together in her mind, and the picture they formed was too shocking for diplomacy. "You're going to marry *Lady Daphne Templeton*?" she choked in ragged astonishment. Even her artist's imagination, with its appreciation of the unusual, the novel, could not accept that small, insipid young woman as wife to the large and flamboyant earl, even though their families had long been acquainted. Daphne was two years older than Jessica, and when they had met—and instantly clashed—she had been winding up her fourth unsuccessful Season in the marriage mart, a sorry fact that Andrew had privately attributed to her father's clutch-fisted refusal to provide an adequate dowry for the girl. Both Daphne and her brother were hanging out for an advantageous marriage, but she was far too conscious of her exalted birth to consider an offer from a wealthy cit, and among her own kind her lack of both portion and particular beauty made a proposal unlikely unless some man fell madly in love with her personality. And since she was by nature prudish and condescending . . . The last time Jessica had seen Lady Daphne had been on the dance floor at Almack's. Her light blue eyes had been alight with rage, and over her bland face, its usual prim expression wiped out by fury, an ostrich feather had dripped with the sticky-sweet almond liqueur that Jessica had flung there. . . . Jessica giggled wildly at the memory. "Graham, you've taken leave of your senses!"

Stiffening, he said frigidly, "Jessica, I advise you to be quiet before you say something you may deeply regret in future. Lady Daphne is a woman of unimpeachable breeding and demeanor. Our fathers were close friends, which I suppose is the chief reason I thought of her when . . . She has greatly honored me by consenting to become my wife. You would do well to remember that once we are married, she will not only be mistress of my house but also your kinswoman, and you should conduct yourself accordingly."

Jessica flushed, acknowledging her ill manners. Whom Raeburn chose to marry was no concern of hers. "I'm sorry if I offended you, Graham," she admitted tensely, bowing her head so that he could not see the effort this apology cost her. "I was unpardonably rude, and my only excuse is that, as I'm sure you're aware, your—your fiancée and I have not always been on the most cordial of terms. . . ."

She heard Raeburn snort, and she continued with as much dignity as she could muster, "I am truly sorry, Graham, and I promise I shan't embarrass you if I meet Lady Daphne again. But—but happily there is little chance of our encountering each other—"

"I should say there was every chance," Raeburn drawled wryly, "since the two of you will both be living at Renard Chase."

"No," Jessica said with flat insistence. "You cannot make me go back there." She turned to stare at the dying fire, and she shivered. Watching the glowing embers turn softly gray, she wondered why people claimed hell was made of flame and sulphur. Hell was cold, cold as the slick marble walls of the Palladian mansion, cold as the scornful painted smiles of the Foxes and their friends and their household. . . . Jessica repeated, "I will not go back, Graham."

She could hear the puzzled frown in his deep voice. "But why not, Jess? I'm not asking you to come back in some inferior position, if that's what you fear. You'll be treated with all honor and respect as my sister-in-law, my brother's widow, and the fact that I am marrying will not change that one jot. It is my duty—and my most earnest wish—to provide for you now that Andrew is gone, and I will continue to do so until such time as you yourself decide to remarry."

Remarry? Jessica thought bitterly. After the fiasco her union with Andrew had become, despite her love for him, did Raeburn really think she was eager to repeat the experience? No doubt that was what he hoped. He had not yet succeeded in convincing her that she ought to return to his home, and already he was plotting to rid himself of her, to foist her onto someone else. "You should be more prudent with such offers, Graham," she muttered cynically, still not looking at him, "else you may find yourself with a pensioner for life. I have no intention of ever marrying again."

At her last words, her voice dropped forlornly, her waspish resentment overpowered by the image of the future she had just outlined for herself, a life without love, without comfort, without . . . Something twisted deep inside her as she faced the prospect of never again knowing the sweetness of lying in a man's hard arms, minds and bodies joined in one perfect moment of communion. She and Andrew had rushed untried into marriage, driven by anger as much as by love, but despite the social and mental differences that inevitably drove them apart, their physical union had been fortuitous—eager, youthful enthusiasm more than compensating for their mutual clumsiness and naiveté. Jessica had cared for her husband, and she had been bitterly hurt when he obviously grew to regret their elopement; but when Andrew died, the thought that had most shattered her was the realization that henceforth she would have to sleep alone. . . .

Raeburn's large hands closed gently over Jessica's shoulders through the thickness of her shawl, and he eased her around on the settee so that she faced him. One long finger curled under her drooping chin and tilted her head upward so that he could study her pale, defiant face. He was troubled by the signs of depression bruising her translucent skin, the ashen tint that seemed a reflection of her worn black weeds, and the fire had gone out of her beautiful eyes, leaving them lackluster and bleak. For one grinding moment he felt a perverse urge to rip the ugly, tattered dress from her shoulders, kiss her fiercely until her mouth was red again, her cheeks flushed with color, her eyes glowing with their customary rage at his high-handedness. . . .

46

Rigorously he repressed that thought, and his hand dropped away from her face. He said with soft insistence, "Of course you'll marry again someday, Jess." He wondered why the words set his teeth on edge.

Jessica shook her head in a mute gesture of denial, and Raeburn continued with studied calm. "You were born to be some fortunate man's wife. Perhaps you think me callous or even cruel for saying such a thing, but I promise you I don't mean to be. You loved my little brother. So did I. After my father died, it fell to me to be the one to raise Andy and Claire, and not a day passes that I don't feel his loss acutely . . . but that doesn't mean my life stops while I mourn him. Your life must go on too."

"My life consists solely of my daughter," Jessica said stiffly, and Raeburn's expression hardened.

"As you wish," he muttered, "but in that case, you had better resign yourself to returning to the Chase with me, for that is where my niece is going to be raised . . . with you or without you."

Jessica trembled, hugging her arms convulsively. At last he had said it, had uttered aloud the implicit threat that had haunted her since her husband's death, had made her choose a hard, tenuous life of obscure poverty over the undeniable comfort of the Raeburn estate. Her green eyes enormous, she whispered hoarsely, anxiously, "You mean to take my child from me, Graham?"

He knew a fleeting moment of shame at her obvious fear, but he did not allow his expression to waver. He declared steadily, "I have no wish to part you from your daughter, Jess, but in this I must be adamant: my brother's child will be raised at Renard Chase in a manner befitting her station in life. Of course I should prefer that you live there too, but if you will not, then you will leave me no choice but to seek custody of her. I am already trustee for any moneys she stands to inherit from her father; it should be easy enough to have myself appointed her guardian as well. . . ."

"But I am her *mother*," Jessica asserted. "She needs me." With mute appeal her hands reached up to touch the bodice of her dress. "Graham," she pleaded hoarsely, "you cannot take Lottie from me. I . . . I still nurse her."

His gray eyes flicked over her full bosom covered with somber black bombazine, and he felt a sudden urgent desire to see her swollen breasts bared as she gave suck to her child. He felt his body stir potently at the thought, and he realized with alarmingly jealous surprise that he wanted it to be his child too. . . . Aloud he said with a shrug, "I believe wet nurses are moderately easy to procure these days."

Jessica paled, humiliated that she had abased herself. She squared her shoulders and faced him with hate-filled eyes. "I warn you, Graham, if you try to go through with this, I will oppose you."

With affected unconcern he declared tiredly, "That's scarcely anything new, Jess. You have always opposed me. You are the least governable woman it has ever been my misfortune . . ." He stood up deliberately, looming over her, large and intimidating, and when she shrank back instinctively, he softened his tone somewhat, a little ashamed of taking such easy advantage of his superior size and strength. He cajoled, "Be reasonable, my dear. You know it is hopeless to fight me in this; we are not evenly matched."

"But I *will* fight you," Jessica insisted doggedly, trying to garner her courage. "I will use every weapon at my disposal."

"I'm sure you will," he agreed quietly, and he sat down beside her again and took her icy fingers in his. He spoke conversationally, but his tone was sympathetic, almost—almost pitying. "If there is one thing that I have known about you from the first day we met, Jessica Foxe, it is that you are a fighter. Unfortunately for you, so am I. So . . . oppose me if you will, but in this matter I will not be swayed: you and your daughter—and your maid too, if you want her—are coming back with me to the place where you belong, the place where my brother's child will be raised as she ought to be. As soon as I can hire a coach, we are all going home to Renard Chase.''

Chapter Three

The flat-columned facade of the house rose grim and forbidding under threatening skies as Jessica peered warily out the window of the coach, and with a sigh of resignation she pulled the leather curtain shut. She had dreaded this moment for days, ever since Raeburn had found her in Brighton. She had been so distraught at the prospect of returning to the estate that she had been only partially conscious of the time they had spent in London, time during which the earl had sent word to his family to prepare for the prodigal's return, time during which he had wound up his affairs in Town and, incidentally, had also called in an expensive but discreet modiste to outfit Jessica with a new wardrobe to take to Renard Chase with her.

Jessica gazed down at her fashionable gown of lilac half-mourning, comparing it with the threadbare black dress that she had been wearing when Raeburn found her, the same dress she had worn the night she fled from his home. Half mad with anguish, she had wanted nothing that would remind her of the inhabitants of that house, and she and Willa had escaped with only the clothes on their backs. Later, when those garments had faded and frayed, Willa had advised her mistress to use part of the money paid her by her publishers to purchase something sturdy and warm, but Jessica had clung to her widow's weeds as if they were a shield, a battle-scarred banner, with each new rent and tear a further charge against the Foxes. . . . Of course she hadn't told Raeburn that. When he said grimly that he was ordering new clothing for her, she had made little comment, beyond a tight-lipped insistence that she was not ready to put aside her mourning entirely, even after thirteen months.

Jessica sighed and glanced anxiously at her daughter. The interior of the coach was extremely cold, but, wrapped in a warm new blanket of softest Kashmir wool, Lottie slept peacefully in Willa's arms, lulled by the rocking motion of the well-sprung carriage marked with the Raeburn crest. Had it really been only a little more than a year since Andrew's death? Jessica mused. It seemed to her that she had lived forever in dread of discovery. But no, only thirteen short months had passed, and now she was returning to Renard Chase, as everything she had ever feared came true. . . . She wondered drearily how long it would be before the Foxes made their move to take the baby from her. In her heart she knew it was only a matter of time.

A faint cough attracted her attention, and she turned to look at the man sitting beside her, his long legs stretched diagonally across the narrow space between the two seats, catching the hem of the rug covering Jessica's lap and crowding her tightly into the corner. Raeburn was peering at her intently, his wide brow furrowed as if he were trying to see into her mind.

"Jess, do you really hate Renard Chase so much?" he inquired quietly, his tone oddly gentle. With resignation she nodded silently, and after a moment he noted with forced lightness, "That's strange. I've always vastly preferred it to any of my other houses."

Aware that sullen rudeness would serve no purpose, Jessica made an effort to smile. "I've never denied that the Chase is beautiful," she conceded with characteristic honesty. Andrew had explained to her once that the seventeenth-century house was one of the earliest efforts of John Webb, a student of

Inigo Jones, and while its Palladian design was clearly imitative, more suited to a Mediterranean clime, the architecture was light and graceful, a symphony of white marble and airy arcades that were singularly inviting in the summer. Andrew had loved the house too, never understanding that to Jessica those tall Ionic columns had seemed like sentries bent on keeping her, the interloper, outside. . . . When she and Willa had sneaked out of the sleeping house in the middle of the night, she had heard her footsteps echoing behind her, and to her distressed mind they had sounded like the mocking laughter of all the Foxes who had ever lived there.

Raeburn said, "I think you could be happy if you'd try, Jess. In your heart you know your daughter belongs here, and I want you to feel that you also belong. Promise me you'll make an effort. That's all I ask."

Jessica smiled without humor, her memories still too vivid to make concession easy. "I think perhaps you ask too much, Graham," she muttered.

Raeburn's tone hardened, and his eyes pointedly remarked her new clothes and the color that was already returning to her cheeks due to her improved diet. "My dear sister-in-law," he said icily, "most women would be on their knees with prayers of gratitude at such an opportunity. To have one's wants so generously provided for, with no requirement in return beyond a modicum of common courtesy—surely such duties will not be too taxing for someone of your undeniable . . . resources?"

His voice lifted interrogatively, reminding Jessica of his repeated questions on the subject of how she had survived during the past year. She knew he was frankly mistrustful of her claims that she had supported her family by giving drawing lessons, and she suspected that only the patent lack of any male presence in her household had prevented him from accusing her of accepting some man's carte blanche. More than once she had been tempted to tell him the truth, disclosing her identity as the cartoonist Erinys, but each time she opened her mouth to speak, her furious denials had been silenced by the ominous realization that she needed to preserve her anonymity in case she and her child should have to flee the Chase again. She thought with grim satisfaction of her secret account in the Brighton bank. To Raeburn the sum of Jessica's assets would seem niggling, pitifully small, but to Jessica that small amount of money spelled security. On that day when the earl at last manufactured some pretext for taking Lottie from her, he would discover to his chagrin that his widowed sister-in-law was not the typically helpless, utterly vulnerable female that he assumed her to be. . . .

The carriage passed through the arched gates and onto the smooth graveled driveway, shifting slightly at the difference in road surface. The baby whimpered uneasily in Willa's arms, and the maid crooned soothingly to her. Jessica glanced warily at Raeburn. Like most men, he was not enamored of young children, and he had assumed that Lottie would travel separately with Willa in the slower baggage coach; however, when Jessica had reminded him, flushing, that she needed to stay beside her daughter in order to feed her, he had vetoed the suggestion that she too ride with her maid. The breaking weather had made it unlikely that Raeburn would then elect to make the journey on his great gray stallion while the women rode inside the elegant carriage, but still Jessica had thought that somehow he would find a way to travel apart from them. When they had all been crowded into the coach, Raeburn ignoring Willa as if she were invisible and taking only minimal notice of Lottie, Jessica wondered irritably if he feared she would try to leap from the moving carriage if he did not keep her under constant surveillance.

But when, at irregular intervals, Jessica had draped her shawl modestly over her thin shoulders before she unbuttoned the bodice of her dress to nurse her baby, her irritation was superseded by another emotion that she was unable to name.

Raeburn watched her actions with a hooded intensity that disturbed her deeply, his close gaze making her extremely reluctant to bare her breast in his presence, even for this most natural of purposes. Somehow all she could think of was that day by the roadside when his large hands had fondled her in a way no man had ever done before, and she blushed deeply, wondering if he remembered it too. . . . Inevitably her tension had communicated itself to her child, making Lottie fussy and colicky. The dreary journey out of London had begun to stretch endlessly.

"It's good to be home," Raeburn said fervently when the carriage swayed to a halt at the foot of the wide steps leading up to the colonnaded portico. He glanced at Jessica as if challenging her to dispute his exclamation, and she refrained from commenting that in winter she found the cold marble facade of Renard Chase about as inviting as an iceberg.

Silently she adjusted her bonnet, her lips pursed, her green eyes unreadable. An instant later a footman garbed in smart blue and gray livery swung open the door, and when he stepped back, bowing deeply, Raeburn looked out the door, recoiling in surprise. "Oh, damn," he muttered, "what does that woman think this is, a royal progress?" After a second he leaped down from the coach with that grace that always surprised Jessica and turned to hold out his hand to her.

Leaning forward from the squabs, Jessica saw what had startled him: a double row of servants flanked up the steps, waiting in the chilly, frost-laden wind with grim expectation, silent and intimidating. She hesitated in confusion, fighting down an urgent desire to slam the door shut again. As she wavered, Raeburn's wide mouth thinned, and in a low rumble he chided, "Buck up, my girl, I thought you had more spirit than that. . . ." With a sigh of resignation Jessica pulled her pelisse tight about her and placed her small, mittened hand in his.

Rigidly she mounted the marble steps, her chin high, her

arm tucked securely through Raeburn's. He nodded cordially to the senior members of his household and muttered again, with less humor, "Dammit, Jess, relax! Despite the way they're lined up, these are my servants, not some Paris mob, so there's no need for you to act like an *aristo* climbing into a tumbril."

"I'm not an aristocrat at all," she shot back acidly, her eyes trained on a point somewhere above the powdered head of the butler at the top of the stairs. "That's the problem. There's not a man or woman here who doesn't know that my birth is as humble as their own. They'd be more willing to accept—"

"They'll accept you as my sister-in-law," the earl growled impatiently. "That's all that matters."

"Oh, Graham, don't be *naif*," Jessica began, thinking of the thousand little slights she had suffered when she first came to Renard Chase, the tiny indignities she had suffered as the servants, taking their cue from their master's offhand attitude, reminded her in their own subtle ways that she was no better than . . .

"Graham, you're back!" a light, musical voice squealed with unfeigned delight, and as Jessica hesitated, startled, a tall girl with bright red hair rocketed out of the doorway and burst through the ranks of servants, flinging herself at the earl.

Jessica recoiled instinctively as Raeburn released her arm. She was not ready yet to meet her enemy. . . . Raeburn caught the girl easily, his massive chest absorbing the impact of her exuberant greeting as he steadied her slender shoulders with his large hands. "Easy now, Clairie," he teased, hugging her fondly, "else you'll have us all rolling around like ninepins at the foot of the stairs. Comport yourself as a lady and prove to Jess that you've abandoned your hoydenish ways since last she saw you."

"Oh, Graham"—the girl laughed, her bouncing curls gleaming ruddily in the watery sunlight—"don't you start sounding like Aunt Talmadge! She wanted me to sit in the parlor doing needlework until you called for me, but I just couldn't wait that long. I had to see you." She turned to face Jessica, and her naturally pale cheeks were faintly pink. "J-Jessica?" she ventured, as if uncertain of her reception.

Jessica struggled to school her expression, astonished by that hesitant note in her young sister-in-law's voice, so different from the imperious tone she had always affected in the past. Staring at her, Jessica realized that Claire's attitude was not the only thing that had altered considerably since she first met her. The coltish, freckled fifteen-year-old whose unruly red hair had been worn in frizzy plaits was now a young woman, tall and slim, her blossoming figure graceful in a fashionable day dress of cream-colored wool. The freckles had faded, and the startling hair, cropped, was worn in a tangle of curls, the deceptively artless coiffure that Raeburn said took two maids to achieve. Only those wide brown eyes were as Jessica remembered them, dark and velvety, and they reminded her so much of her husband that she shivered.

Raeburn sensed that shudder, and his hand caught her wrist, as if he feared she might flee. "Well, Jess, have you nothing to say?" he demanded.

Jessica continued to gaze at the girl, her emotions an unstable amalgam of pain and nostalgia. At last she murmured, "I had forgotten how very like Andrew you are . . . Lady Claire." She could not help the irony that crept into her voice as she added that title, but when she saw the girl's obvious chagrin, she wished she had maintained better control over her tongue.

"Oh, please, Jessica," Claire pleaded, "don't—don't be so formal with me. I—I want us to be sisters now."

"Sisters, my lady?" Jessica queried drily, and she felt Raeburn's grip tighten so painfully around her wrist that she winced.

"Yes, Jessica," Claire continued earnestly, unaware of her brother's action, "or at least, friends. I know I was a brat to you before, unbearably high in the instep, but—but I hope you'll let all that be in the past now. We've both lost someone we loved very much, and I'd like to think that—that . . ."

Her young voice cracked suddenly, and Jessica realized that for a girl like Claire, cosseted and spoiled since birth, reared to believe in her inherent superiority, having her every whim catered to, such an apology must be difficult in the extreme. The daughters of earls were not often called upon to humble themselves before a clergyman's offspring. For the first time in days, Jessica felt her chilled heart warm. Perhaps there was hope, after all. . . . With real gratitude for the effort the girl was making, Jessica leaned forward and kissed her lightly on the cheek. "My dearest sister," she said quietly.

From beneath lowered lashes she glanced up at Raeburn, expecting to read pleasure in his narrowed gray eyes—or perhaps mockery—at her capitulation. But, strangely, the expression she saw mirrored there was something quite different, something—unexpected. Jealousy? Jessica thought in bewilderment. Resentment because she had smiled at his sister? No, no, of course not . . .

Raeburn asked abruptly, "Where's Aunt Talmadge, Claire? There's someone else the two of you must meet." He turned and beckoned to Willa, who had stood apart, Lottie cradled expertly in her arms. "Come, girl," he barked, and Willa stepped forward between the ranks of liveried footmen, her weak chin held high as she ignored their knowing glances.

Despite the adversities of the year she had dwelt in Brighton with her mistress, the anonymity of their position had given Willa time to forget some of the horrors of the past and mend her shattered self-esteem. She had been able to pretend that she had never been anything but an ordinary domestic, lowly but industrious and virtuous. The return to Renard

Chase, where everyone from the earl himself down to the meanest scullery maid knew her history, put an end to that happy obscurity, and only Willa's deep love and profound obligation to Jessica had induced her to come with them. When Jessica, sensing Willa's reluctance, had offered her independence by sharing her small savings with her, Willa had refused, saying with a bleak smile, "No, Miss Jess. How can I leave you and the little one alone in that great house when you don't even know enough to keep your feet warm and dry. . . . ?"

"Come, Willa," Jessica said quietly, when she saw the maid hesitate. "It's time for Lottie to meet her aunt Claire."

" 'Aunt Claire,' " Claire echoed with pleasure as Jessica took her sleeping daughter into her arms and gently pulled back the blanket from her face. "I like the sound of that." She glanced impishly at her brother, her brown velvet eyes outlining his powerful body. "I think I shall enjoy hearing you called Uncle. It will make a welcome change from all this 'my lord'-ing. Will you mind very much? Somehow 'Uncle Graham' makes you sound rather cuddly. . . ."

Raeburn said repressively, "Considering that I've been aware of my new status as an uncle for scarcely a week, I've hardly had time to give the matter much thought."

"That's funny," Claire said, still teasing. "I've thought of nothing else since you sent word that . . ." Her voice faded as she turned back the edge of the blanket and gazed down at the baby's tender features, petal-smooth skin startlingly white against the flaming curls that peeked from under the edge of the soft infant cap. "Oh, Jessica," Claire whispered reverently, "she's—she's beautiful." When she looked up again, her soft eyes shimmered. "Andy would have been so proud," she said hoarsely.

Jessica felt her throat constrict, and she shivered with a spasm of some curious emotion that might have been guilt. In all her battles with Raeburn, her continuing arguments over what was best for her child's welfare, not once had she asked herself what Andrew would have wanted for his daughter. . . .

From the doorway behind them, another voice, feminine but querulous, intruded on Jessica's reunion with her sister-in-law, rapping sharply, "Claire, come here!"

Claire's shoulders slumped. When Jessica glanced around and saw the woman standing behind her, her plump form framed by the tall menservants on either side of her, her spirits sank. She did not have to meet the glare of those pale eyes squinting balefully to know that at least one member of the household had not altered her opinion of the upstart drawing teacher. "Aunt" Flora Talmadge, a distant cousin of the Foxes and Claire's chaperon when Raeburn was not at hand, regarded Jessica with open dislike. Her small mouth curled disdainfully as it had in those days when she had spied on Jessica and Andrew's clandestine meetings in the portrait gallery, giving her pudgy face the pinched, tentative expression of someone about to sneeze. Jessica noted with spiteful triumph that the woman's upper lip was still spotted from the cucumber lotion with which she bathed it nightly in a futile attempt to bleach out her grizzled ghost of a mustache.

Mrs. Talmadge's gaze shifted to her charge. "Claire, how many times must I tell you not to go out of doors without your cloak? You'll catch your death. Come inside at once!" the woman snapped, and Claire flushed hotly.

"Yes, Aunt," she mumbled, staring down at the ground like a scolded child, but before she could turn toward the door, Raeburn's large hand closed firmly over her shoulder. "Really, Aunt Talmadge," he said with quiet force, "I hardly think my sister should be chided for her enthusiasm in greeting a member of the family who has been too long absent from us. At such a happy moment, anyone could be excused for forgetting such a trifle as a cloak, unless she were already unwell. Claire enjoys good health, does she not?"

"Oh, yes, of course, Graham," the woman persisted unctuously, "as I always say in my letters, I have made Lady Claire's well-being my primary—"

Raeburn waved her to silence. "I'm sure you've been most diligent," he drawled. Then, glancing at the servants assembled on the steps, some visibly shivering beneath their smart livery, his gray eyes narrowed. "Would that someone took as good care of my staff," he muttered. "Tell me, Aunt, whose idea was it for everyone to stand on parade in the cold?"

"You sent word that we should make our guest feel welcome," Mrs. Talmadge said doggedly.

"I said to prepare for my sister-in-law's return to the family," Raeburn corrected with scathing emphasis. "That, my dear aunt, is another thing altogether, as you must well know. In such a case, too much ceremony is quite as offensive as too little. I suggest that you exercise a little moderation in future."

"As you wish, Graham," she muttered, but the glance that she shot in Jessica's direction boded ill for the future.

Raeburn turned to the butler and said, "You may dismiss the staff, Barston, with my apologies for the misunderstanding that brought them out of doors on such a day. I suggest that you have the kitchen prepare a hot negus for everyone before they return to their regular duties.

The butler's face remained carefully impassive, but his eyes reflected his surprise at this unexpected treat. "Very good, my lord. Thank you."

"Think nothing of it. Later on we'll have to arrange something festive to celebrate the return of my brother's wife and child to their home."

"Very good, my lord," Barston said again, bowing deeply, and Raeburn turned to usher the women through the door into the house. As Jessica crossed the threshold she overheard this snatch of conversation with astonishment. A celebration? She had never imagined such a thing, especially not one that would encompass the servants as well. Suddenly she wondered if Raeburn had indeed been more aware of the household's attitude toward her than she had thought, and if this was his way of winning the staff over to her. . . .

Inside, Jessica handed her mist-damped cloak and bonnet to the waiting footman and glanced around her, shivering despite the overheated atmosphere. She had not been inside this house since the day of Andrew's funeral, and she thought bitterly that the marble floors and looming columns looked as sepulchral now as they had then, the bouquets of flowers fresh from the orangery somehow stiff with invisible crepe. From just behind her, as if reading her thoughts, Raeburn murmured, "It's been a long year, Jess, full of sorrow, but the house will be happier now with a child in it."

She looked back over her shoulder and met his gaze squarely. "Will it, Graham?" she asked in a savage undertone. "Or will the gloom instead infect my daughter until she too becomes as silent and cold as a stone cherub?"

He shook his head. "I won't let that happen, Jess. I promise you that Lottie is going to be happy here. She'll be coddled and cherished by everyone, and naturally"—he hesitated for a fraction of a second—"once I am married, I hope there will in due time be a regiment of little cousins for her to play with."

Jessica smiled weakly. "Yes, of course. I was forgetting that—"

Flora Talmadge's voice cut into their private conversation with the subtlety of a bludgeon. "Graham, I knew you would be chilled after your long journey, so I've ordered a tea in the small parlor. Mrs. Foxe, I am sure, will wish to retire to her room to rest. I'll have refreshments sent up to her there."

Claire started to protest, and Raeburn said tightly, "I'm sure my sister and I can delay our meal until Jessica is able to join us in the parlor."

Jessica was uncertain whether it was a lingering side effect of her illness or merely the expression on Mrs. Talmadge's face, but suddenly she felt far too exhausted for argument. The emotional shocks of the last few days had drained her more than she cared to admit, and now she longed only for rest and quiet. Touching Raeburn's sleeve lightly, she said, "Please, Graham, there's no need to wait for me. I think—I think I'd like to retire for the night, if you don't mind."

"So early, Jess?" he asked, frowning.

She nodded. "I am very weary. If someone will direct Willa and me to our—"

"It's the suite you shared with Andy," Raeburn said. "I told you nothing would change." He glanced at Mrs. Talmadge. "You did order those rooms to be put ready for my sister-in-law, did you not?"

"As always, I followed your directions to the letter, Graham," the woman said deferentially, but her spotty upper lip was as hard as her eyes. "If Mrs. Foxe wishes to go up now, I'll summon one of the nursery maids to take the child—"

Jessica's head jerked up. "No!" she said sharply, signaling Willa to come closer. Taking her bundled daughter into her own arms, she announced with quiet force, "Lottie stays with me. She's never been away from my side."

Raeburn's scowl deepened, his gray eyes darkening beneath the thick, fair brows as he watched Jessica dandle the baby against her breast. Calmly he suggested, "You would be able to rest better if you did not have to constantly supervise the child."

"I am used to supervising her," Jessica said. "And when I'm resting, Willa can—"

"My dear Graham," Mrs. Talmadge said, a gloating smile in her voice, "perhaps you should reassure Mrs. Foxe that the staff in the nursery will take excellent care of the infant. Despite the limited time at my disposal, I personally interviewed every one of the maids, as you instructed me."

Jessica's green eyes widened. She retreated from Raeburn, clutching Lottie convulsively to her bosom. "Graham, how dare you make plans for my child without consulting me?'' she demanded.

"Jess, it's not the way you think," he began uncomfortably.

"Not the way I think? How else can it be?'' Her voice was growing high and hysterical, much to the fascination of the listening servants. "You promised me nothing would be changed, but already you've—''

Mrs. Talmadge interjected, "Graham, perhaps you ought to explain to Mrs. Foxe that no matter what her past . . . circumstances have been, it is not usual for ladies in her position to—''

Raeburn glanced down at the woman's gloating face. "Dammit, Flora, shut up!" he growled.

He turned again to Jessica, but she was looking meaningfully at her maid. "We will leave at—'' she began in a low, urgent voice, but he waved her to silence.

"You're going nowhere but to your room, Jess," he said. "After you've rested, you may inspect the nursery at your leisure to ensure that everything and everyone meet your approval. But you do neither Lottie nor yourself any good by arguing with me, especially when you are patently—not yourself.''

Jessica hesitated, an instinctive retort hovering uncertainly on her lips. Then, as she glanced from Raeburn to Mrs. Talmadge and back again, she sighed with resignation. He was right. She could not fight him, not now, not yet. The day of battle would arrive soon enough; at the moment her cause would be better served by marshaling her forces as she waited. "I will do as you wish, Graham," she said with unaccustomed meekness, and Raeburn frowned at her suspiciously.

Suddenly Claire broke the uneasy silence by suggesting softly, "Jessica, why don't you let your servant take Lottie up to the nursery? I'm sure you trust her to see that the baby is settled comfortably, and she can report back to you afterward. In the meantime, I'll show you to your room, if you don't mind. I'd love the chance for a private little coze with you. We have so much to talk about."

Jessica smiled gratefully at her young sister-in-law, warmed by her quiet tact. Indeed the girl was growing up quickly; in these awkward circumstances, Jessica admitted wryly, Claire seemed to be displaying more maturity than she herself was. . . . "Thank you, I'd like that," she said, and when she and Claire mounted the wide staircase, with Willa and the baby close behind, Jessica did not look at Raeburn again.

"Does it distress you to use these rooms now that Andy's gone?" Claire asked frankly a few days later. Her bright hair gleamed in the unexpectedly warm pool of sunlight that poured in through the high arched windows of Jessica's sitting room, and she watched fondly as Jessica burped Lottie and cuddled her for a few precious moments before sending her back to the nursery.

Jessica had conceded that the women appointed to care for her daughter could not be faulted in their diligence, and the uninterrupted nights of sleep were reviving her more than she was willing to admit, but she treasured the hours when she alone had charge of her child, and so far she had allowed only Willa and Claire to intrude upon them.

When Jessica looked up, puzzled, Claire waved her slim hand to indicate the interior of the suite and said, "When Graham sent word that you were to have your old room back, I thought at first that it was a good idea—no matter what Aunt Talmadge said—but since then I've been worried that you might be unhappy here, that it would make you sad, remembering the time when you lived here with Andy."

Jessica shook her head and leaned back in the chair. "No, Claire," she reassured quietly, with a wistful smile, "no, this room does not bother me. I will admit that when I first stepped inside again, there was a moment or two . . . But that soon passed. A year is a long time, and so many things have happened since then." She glanced sharply at Claire. "Do I sound callous, my dear? I don't mean to. It's just that sometimes when I remember being married to Andrew, it's as if—as if it had happened to somebody else." Her hands tightened gently around her daughter. "Only Lottie reminds me that it was all very real." She watched Claire anxiously, afraid that the girl would be offended by her casual attitude toward her brother's death, and in the last few days Claire's undemanding friendship had become very important to Jessica.

But to Jessica's surprise, Claire nodded sagely. "I think I know what you mean," she said. "When I look back and remember the things I said, the way I behaved, I have trouble believing that I could ever have been such a selfish, hateful brat. I was so—so stupidly jealous of you."

"You thought I had stolen Andrew from you," Jessica prompted.

Claire grimaced, her young face drooping. "Yes, that's it exactly. It seems so obvious now that I don't understand why I didn't see it then. Andy and I had always been so close. As you know, our mother died when I was born; I used to wonder if our father blamed me for her death, and that was why he was always so distant. . . . I remember asking Graham about it once, and he said no, I was being silly, and then he hugged me. Funny, but I don't remember our real father ever hugging me. In some ways Graham seemed more like . . ." She sighed. "I love Graham too, but he was always so much older than Andy and me, and after he succeeded to the title, he was away most of the time. That just left Andy and me. We used to talk about what we would do when we were all grown up, how the two of us would travel on the Continent, maybe even go to America together. . . ." Her voice faltered, and she lifted her velvety brown eyes to Jessica, pleading for understanding. "The only trouble was, Andy grew up long before I did, and while I was still in the schoolroom, he found you."

Jessica watched the girl compassionately, her heart responding to the plaintive note in her voice, the same note she had once heard in her husband's voice. Claire was so very like Andrew. . . . Jessica said, "I understand, Claire, and it really doesn't matter anymore."

"Oh, but it does!" Claire insisted, determined now to make a full confession. "You don't know what I did, Jess. I used to *spy* on you and Andy when you'd meet in the portrait gallery after my drawing lessons. I was just waiting to see him kiss you so I could run to Aunt Talmadge and tell her. But I never could catch him touching you—"

"He never did, not then," Jessica murmured.

Claire nodded absently. "I guessed he was being careful. . . . But one day after you'd gone, I saw him standing in the gallery with this funny look on his face, and I heard him say distinctly, 'Jess and I could go to America'—and I—I exploded. America was *our* dream, his and mine, and now he was talking about taking *you* there! I came out of the place where I was hiding, and I told him that I was going to tell Aunt Talmadge about the two of you. He said, 'You stupid chit, there's nothing *to* tell, and anyway, I don't give a damn about a silly old witch like Aunt Talmadge.' "

Claire paused again, breathless, and she muttered wryly, "I guess that's when it dawned on me that my brother had become a man. I was still scared witless by my aunt, while he . . ." She shrugged, and her face shadowed with remorse again. "That's when I did the thing that shames me most, Jess," she said drearily. "I was still furious with him, certain that he'd betrayed me, and I said, 'You may not care about Aunt Talmadge, but I bet you'll give a damn'—I remember how wickedly daring I felt, saying that word—'you'll give a damn when you hear that I wrote to Graham and told him you were making eyes at a vulgar little—' "

Claire broke off, blushing. After a moment she continued, "Andrew just stared at me for a long time, then he demanded, 'What have you done, you little snitch?' and before I could say anything, he snapped, 'Well, you needn't have bothered, because I'll write to Graham myself and tell him you're a liar and I'm going to marry Jess whether he likes it or not!' Within a matter of days, Graham was back from London, storming around in a vile rage, and you and Andy had run away to Scotland. . . ."

When this recitation ended, the sun-drenched sitting room was silent, except for the cooing of the baby. Jessica relaxed in her chair, eyes closed, absently stroking her daughter's fiery curls as she mused over what Claire had told her. At last she had the answer to the riddle that had puzzled her for more than a year and a half, the question of why Andrew had applied to his brother for permission to marry her, long before their courtship had progressed to a point where such an action could reasonably be expected. A little girl's malicious jealousy had precipitated that rash action and, consequently, Jessica and Andrew's equally rash reaction to Raeburn's violent opposition. Jessica had thought many times over the past year that if only Andrew had spoken to her first, had told her what he planned to do, she would have discouraged him from even thinking about marriage, much less speaking to his brother about it. And if they had not married, how much less heartbreak there would be. . . .

Claire said humbly, "I'm sorry, Jessica. Please believe me: I'd never want to hurt you now."

Jessica looked at Claire, then at the child sleeping in her arms. Lottie's hair was almost the exact color Claire's had been when Jessica first met her. When the baby grew up, except for her emerald-bright eyes, she was going to look very much like her aunt. Funny to think that in a very roundabout way Claire was responsible for Lottie's existence. . . . With a smile of ironic gratitude that Jessica knew her sister-in-law would never understand, she said, "Forget it, Claire. You were a child then. When we are little we all do things that embarrass us later, after we're grown.''

At that moment one of the nursery maids appeared at the door, and Jessica handed over her daughter reluctantly. When the woman had taken Lottie away, Jessica turned back to Claire, whose eyes had brightened as her melancholy mood passed. She stroked the skirt of her gown self-consciously. "Do you think I'm all grown up, Jess?" she asked wistfully.

"I think you're becoming a beautiful young woman," Jessica said honestly. "In a couple more years . . ."

"A couple more years," Claire echoed with a groan. "You sound just like Graham. I'm seventeen now, old enough to marry, old enough for my come-out, if only Graham would let me." She leaned forward in her chair, her eyes flashing with indignation, and Jessica could tell that she was about to be the recipient of some long-simmering confidence. Claire declared hotly, "Oh, blast Graham, anyway! For absolutely *ages* I've expected that I'd get to make my debut next spring. Everyone did. It was all planned. Since I haven't any close female relations, Graham was going to get Lady Bergen to sponsor me—she's a viscountess, widowed and rather poor, but *very* respectable, and she's done this sort of thing before— and I knew exactly the kind of dress I wanted to wear when I was presented, and the kind of flowers we'd use to decorate the town house for my ball, and all that—and now all of a sudden I have to wait another whole *year,* and it's all Graham's fault! Oh, I never dreamed he'd be such a selfish beast. . . .''

When Claire paused her gushing long enough to take a breath, Jessica frowned and inquired, "But whatever is the problem? Graham seems indulgent enough. Why has he decreed that you must wait?"

"Because he's getting married, silly," Claire retorted in exasperation. "He and that—that ape-leader Daphne Templeton have decided to wed the day after Easter, and by the time they get back from their honeymoon, the Season will be almost over. Obviously Lady Bergen can't do anything with Graham not around to pay the bills, so he says I must delay another year, and then his wife can present me." Claire snorted. "With my luck, old Daphne will be increasing by then, and Graham will tell me I'll have to wait yet another year until she's fit to sponsor me. Mustn't do anything to hazard the heir, you know. . . . Of course, Graham being the way he is, it may be a dozen years before she's fit for aught but waddling around with a belly like a whale, although after the women he's had, like that singer, why he'd want to bed a—"

"Claire!" Jessica exclaimed, blushing hotly at the images the girl's words put in her mind. "You mustn't talk that way. It isn't—it isn't suitable."

Unrepentantly Claire scoffed. "Oh, Jess, don't be missish. You know what men are like. You're a married woman."

"Yes, but you're not," Jessica said sternly, "and anything you've heard is just hearsay, idle gossip, unfit for—"

"Oh, it's more than hearsay." Claire laughed, her brown eyes taking on a sly gleam as she glanced toward the sitting-room door to ensure that it was closed. Her girlish voice became low and insinuating. "You know I love Graham dearly, Jess, and I'll be the first to admit that when he's here at Renard Chase with me, he's a—an absolute pattern card of rectitude, but I know for a fact that when he's in London, he's not nearly so—so upright. In fact, he's so notorious that the satirists draw caricatures of him! When he came down from Town the last time, a couple of months ago, one of the grooms who had gone with him brought back some of the cartoons, and he showed them to me. I didn't understand the point, exactly, but Fred explained them to me. For instance, there was this one picture of Graham as a centaur—it was kind of strange and spiteful but very funny, and it looked just like him, with even the horse part resembling his gray stallion—and he was carrying off this fat woman who . . ."

Jessica closed her eyes, wishing she could shut out Claire's eager description as easily. Oh, yes, she was familiar with that cartoon. The original was on the third shelf of her wardrobe, behind a hatbox, locked in a battered tin casket along with all her other sketches. . . . That one had been one of Erinys' earlier efforts, drawn, as it happened, not long before Lottie was born, when Jessica's discomfort and apprehension at her forthcoming confinement had made her pen especially venomous. . . . Satire was primarily a male interest, a fact which Jessica had used to protect her anonymity; consequently it had never occurred to her that Claire might have occasion to see any of her work. Despite the girl's uneasy laughter, Jessica wondered if the vicious satire on someone she loved had hurt her. To soothe the pang of remorse growing in her breast, Jessica said sharply, "I doubt your brother would appreciate your being so familiar with a groom, Claire."

Claire stared, her eyes dark and large in her pale face. "Oh, Jess," she protested huskily, "you wouldn't say anything to Graham, would you? Fred might lose his position if you . . . Besides, there's nothing *to* tell—" Her voice choked off as she grimaced curiously, and Jessica, watching the girl, wondered with ironic amusement if she were recalling that once Andrew had pleaded with those exact words. . . .

Jessica began, "Of course I won't—" but her words were interrupted by a knock at the door. She turned, frowning, as a liveried footman stuck his head inside. "Your pardon, Mrs. Foxe, but your cases have arrived, and the master ordered us to bring them up to you."

"My cases?" Jessica repeated, confused, as menservants trooped into the room lugging a succession of leather-and-brass trunks, all obviously new, obviously heavy. "What is this?" she murmured, but before anyone could venture an answer, Willa slipped into the room, back early from her half holiday, and took charge of the situation. In the uproar, Jessica had time only to cock one fine eyebrow inquiringly at her friend and murmur, "Were you able to mail the parcel?"

"Yes, Miss Jess," Willa answered in an undertone. "It took some doing, but they agreed to hold any letters addressed to 'J.F.' until the next time I come to the village."

"Thank you," Jessica said, and she stood out of the way as Willa began to order the footmen about. Soon the men had departed, leaving Jessica and Claire to gape in astonishment as Willa unlocked case after case packed to overflowing with silk and satin and muslin dresses, velvet cloaks and pelisses trimmed with fur. One trunk contained beribboned slippers to match the dresses and trim ankle boots with contrasting slashings. A second was laden with lacy undergarments of cobweb delicacy, a third with gloves and plumes and fans. Soon Jessica's bed was covered with a rainbow of rich fabrics, everything beautiful, exquisitely made, of the first stare of fashion. Claire gurgled like a playful child, and even Willa's round face glowed with feminine delight. Jessica gazed at the bounty surrounding her and she wailed, "But—but he promised!"

Claire glanced up from a jade-colored velvet frock trimmed with swansdown and stared at Jessica. "What on earth is wrong with you? Don't you like Graham's surprise? When he told me he had ordered some things for you, I had no idea he meant anything so grand."

Jessica took a deep breath. She splayed her fingers over the skirt of her gray bombazine day dress, and she was surprised to find that they were shaking. In a tremulous voice she whispered hoarsely, "Of course I like the clothes, Claire. A person would have to be blind not to. Everything is incredibly beautiful. But I told Graham while we were still in London . . . I thought he understood . . . that—that I'm not ready to put aside my mourning clothes, not . . . just yet." As she spoke her thick lashes drooped heavily on her cheeks, and she realized with wistful self-knowledge that she mourned not so much for her late husband as for the death of her girlish dreams. . . .

Brown eyes heavy with sympathy, Claire tossed aside the green dress and hugged Jessica fiercely. "Oh, Jess," she sighed, "I'm so very sorry. I know how very difficult it must be for you, even after a year. . . . But I'm sure Graham didn't mean to hurt you. He just wanted to make you happy, to make you smile again. We all know that you mourn Andy in your heart—as do we—but you can't bury yourself alive forever. You're a young woman." She loosened her hold on Jessica so that she could see her face clearly as she said with a smile, "There's to be a house party at Christmas, when Graham and Daphne announce their engagement, and with all your beautiful new clothes you could be quite—quite the Incomparable. Why, Graham says that someday soon you're sure to . . ." Her voice trailed off at the glowering expression on Jessica's brow.

With icy control Jessica asked mildly, "What does Graham say I'm sure to do, Claire—find a new husband? Is that why he's organized this house party, bought me all these frills and furbelows? Less than a fortnight back in his house, and already he's plotting to be rid of me?"

"Jess, *no!*" Claire squealed, aghast and bewildered. "You can't believe that!"

"I believe Graham Foxe would bargain with the devil himself if he thought he could be free of me forever!" Jessica grated. She wrenched away from Claire and dashed out of her room, almost colliding in the corridor with a startled housemaid. "You!" she barked, in a tone uncannily like that of the man she sought. "Do you know where His Lordship is?"

"N-no, ma'am," the girl stammered. "That is, I—I thought I glimpsed him earlier, upstairs, near the—the nursery."

With a curt nod, Jessica turned and ran to the staircase, bounding up the marble steps to the third floor in a manner

73

guaranteed to endanger anyone she encountered on her way. Her heart was thudding and her green eyes flashed. In the nursery, was he? No doubt plotting against the day when he had disposed of her, Lottie's mother, and could abandon the child to the indifferent care of someone like Flora Talmadge, as had been done with Claire. Despite his assertion that he would cherish his brother's child, Jessica had no illusions about Lottie's fate once Raeburn and his precious Daphne had filled the Renard Chase nursery with their squawling offspring, which seemed to be his intention. She knew from bitter experience what happened when a woman was continually pregnant: exhausted by constant childbearing, the mother of necessity delegated to the eldest daughter the care of the younger children, and soon that girl found herself trapped in limbo somewhere between infancy and maturity, alienated from her siblings by the authority she had to enforce, yet not respected as an adult by her elders. Little Charlotte, only a foster child, without even the rights of blood to cushion her lot, would be doomed to live as both guardian and drudge for her titled cousins. . . .

Jessica gritted her teeth. It had happened to her, but she would not let that happen to Lottie. She would stay and fight for her daughter, and if Raeburn tried to marry her off . . . Oh, God, the idea was insupportable! She wanted no man in her life.

She continued resolutely up the steps. She had resisted Raeburn when he and that great stallion of his had first swooped down on her, big and fair and wild, and she would continue to do so. She was not a fool: she knew now that his ultimate goal was to relieve his family of her embarrassing presence by finding her a new husband, and if he had not succeeded in that quest by the time he himself married, Lady Daphne Templeton would undoubtedly goad him into redoubling his efforts. Jessica supposed that she really ought to be grateful; after all, despite her indifferent origins, her present connection with the Foxe family practically guaranteed that candidates for her hand would be well born and financially secure—especially if Raeburn settled a sizable dowry on her. In the end, she would have to choose. . . . But now she intended to tell Raeburn flatly that she would never consider any match, no matter how "suitable," unless she was permitted to take her daughter with her to her husband's home.

Of course, she added grimly, there was always the feeble security of that bank account in Brighton. . . .

When Jessica reached the third-floor landing, she was panting, as much from nerves as exertion, and she started her journey down the empty, echoing hallway at a more sedate pace, strolling past vacant guest rooms and apartments that she had never seen, even before when she lived at the Chase with Andrew. The house was huge, and the only time she could remember it being filled to anything approaching capacity had been on the day of her husband's funeral. . . . She paused outside the wide nursery doors, consciously composing herself. Just as she laid slim fingers on the chased handle, the door swung away from her.

A little maid carrying an empty pitcher jerked back, startled. "Oh, Mrs. Foxe," she exclaimed with a puzzled smile, "it's a fair fright you gave me! We weren't expecting you. Is it time for Miss Lottie's feed already?"

Jessica shook her head. "No, not for two more hours. I just wanted to see my daughter."

The girl relaxed. "That's good. We've all been having such a time watching His Lordship play with Miss Lottie that I was afraid we might have forgotten the hour."

Jessica hesitated, oddly breathless. "Lord Raeburn has been . . . playing . . . with my daughter?" she asked, thinking of the way he had ignored the child on the journey out from London.

"Oh, yes, ma'am." The girl grinned, glancing back conspiratorially over her shoulder. "He came in long ago, frowning in that stern way of his, and he said to the head nurse, 'I want my niece.' Nurse, she was fair quaking for fear she'd done something amiss when she handed the little one to him.''

The maid's expression softened, and when she spoke again, it was not as servant to mistress, but woman to woman. "You should have seen him, Mrs. Foxe. You know how men are: highborn or common, they're all embarrassed and clumsy with babies, afraid to admit they like cuddling them. His Lordship was no different—but soon he loosened up, laughing and joking fit to beat all as he bounced Miss Lottie on his shoulder. He looked so—so proud. He said to nurse, 'Isn't she a beauty with her father's red hair and her mother's wonderful green eyes? Don't you think she'll set the *ton* on its ear when she's all grown up and we take her to London to make her bows?' Then he began to play games with her and sing—''

Remembering the one or two musicales she and Andrew and Raeburn had attended in London, in the days before her gaucherie disgraced them completely, Jessica interrupted in amazement, "Sing? His Lordship? But he never sings for anyone—he has a voice like a jackass!''

"Yes, ma'am," the maid agreed demurely, "but he seems to know a fine lot of lullabies. . . .''

Jessica shook her head in wonder. Standing on tiptoes she glanced past the girl into the interior of the nursery. Raeburn was facing away from her, and she could see his broad shoulders straining the seams of an impeccably cut coat of blue broadcloth as he hunched over the cradle. Candlelight played on the back of his blond head. His deep voice was tenderly crooning something that sounded suspiciously like baby talk, and Jessica could hear her daughter babble with delight. She blinked, stunned. With a pang of something that felt almost like—like jealousy—she thought, My God, he loves her, like—like a father. . . .

Stepping back from the door, Jessica said quietly to the young maid, "Since His Lordship is . . . so happily occupied, I won't disturb him now. I'll see Lottie when you bring her down to me for her feeding."

"Yes, ma'am," the girl answered, curtsying in some confusion as she observed the troubled expression on Jessica's face.

Jessica turned away and walked slowly back toward the staircase, biting her lip as she thought about Raeburn in the nursery. She wondered with remorse how she had ever deluded herself that he would neglect his brother's child, no matter what he thought of that child's mother. She ought to have known better. Despite his temper, his licentiousness, his numerous other faults, Raeburn had always been passionately devoted to the welfare of his family. Whatever the outcome of the continual battle of wills between Raeburn and Jessica, Lottie would not suffer.

Suddenly Jessica wished that she had not sent Willa that day to the village to post the latest parcel of drawings to Haxton and Welles.

Chapter Four

"Dear Graham," Flora Talmadge suggested instructively, "perhaps you, as a gentleman whose mind must of necessity be occupied with loftier matters, do not realize how very disruptive the presence of a person less than—than suitable can be to the running of a household."

Heedless of the fine cloth of his jacket, Raeburn wiped the steamy windowpane with his forearm and stared out into the bleak afternoon. From this lofty vantage point he could see over the tops of the naked oaks, westward across the rime-crusted meadow to the wood half a mile away. With ease his gray eyes followed the course of the dogcart where it had cut muddily across the brown, winter-flattened grass until it disappeared under the distant trees. He frowned expectantly at that point where the parallel tracks intersected the dark body of the forest, but when he realized that he was waiting for the cart to reappear, he turned away quickly, impatient with himself. Blinking, he saw Flora Talmadge regarding him with an air of sniffling reproof. "Forgive me, Aunt," he said automatically. "I was . . . elsewhere in my thoughts."

"Of course, dear Graham," Mrs. Talmadge murmured, and she proceeded to repeat her earlier statement.

Raeburn grimaced; he loathed being bothered with household matters. "To which less-than-suitable person do you refer?" he asked, an edge to his deep voice.

"I mean the woman who serves as personal attendant to

Mrs. Foxe. I am sure that you cannot be ignorant of her—her unfortunate background. . . ."

Raeburn nodded, his expression inscrutable. "Ah, yes, Willa Brown." For an instant he remembered the maid as he had first seen her, late one night when there had arisen in the bowels of his London town house an uproar so violent that he had dashed, pistol in hand, through the green baize door leading belowstairs, expecting to find robbers or vandals. Instead to his astonishment he had discovered the butler, deeply affronted, and the housekeeper in convulsions of outrage that Andrew was trying ineffectually to calm. The cause of these alarums was a quivering, sodden figure wrapped in a carriage robe, who lay slumped in a wooden chair while Jessica, disdainful of the satin ball gown she wore, knelt beside her. Tenderly Jessica's slim hands had bathed blood and streaky face paint from the creature's battered cheeks, and she had crooned encouragement to her as if she were a child. When from beneath ropes of yellow hair stinking like seaweed the woman had glanced up wildly, warily at Raeburn, he saw with mingled surprise and disgust that under the garish mask of her profession she was indeed little more than a child, perhaps seventeen, if that. He remembered with a pang that her bruised brown eyes had seemed to hold the sorrow of the ages. . . .

Briskly Raeburn asked, "Well, Aunt, what do you mean when you say the wench is disrupting the household? Are you telling me that our young Magdalen has taken to debauching the footmen?"

High spots of color appeared on Flora's thin cheeks, and her spotty lips quivered. "You should not be so frivolous about such matters, Graham," she said stiffly. "It is the duty of those in authority to guide their subordinates to the path of virtue."

Brushing a lock of fair hair away from his eyes, Raeburn

muttered, "By God, Aunt, I didn't know you'd turned Evangelical."

"Laugh at me, if you will, Graham," Flora retorted, her eyes taking on a spiteful gleam, "but I doubt whether Lady Daphne Templeton will be so—so lenient in the makeup of her household when she becomes mistress here!"

Despite his apparent indolence, Raeburn's bulky figure suddenly seemed to fill the room, and the furrows on his wide brow deepened. "My fiancée is a capable and sensible woman who knows that once she is my wife she will naturally have a free hand in dealing with domestic concerns," he said with quiet emphasis, his deep voice growing increasingly silky. "Much as you have taken upon yourself, Aunt, although originally when I invited you to leave those dismal rooms you lodged in and make your home at Renard Chase, I required only that you provide companionship and guidance for my young sister. . . . But whatever Daphne's personal inclination in any matter, I fancy that when she becomes my countess she will have wit enough to remember whose wishes must always be paramount in this household. Do I make myself clear?"

Flora retreated quickly from his implied threat, her face pasty. "Y-yes, Graham," she answered unsteadily, "you know I've always tried my best to—"

The note of genuine fear in her voice brought Raeburn up short, and he regarded the woman with vague remorse. Flora Talmadge might be pretentious and common, her whining sycophancy at times annoying almost beyond endurance, but she was in essence a figure to be pitied, in her own way as helpless as Jessica's protégée who, while still a child, had been sold into whoredom by her own father. A widow with only a minuscule pension, Flora might have finished her life a victim of genteel starvation had Raeburn not remembered that she was a distant relation of his late mother and called upon her when he found himself in sole charge of his adolescent half brother and sister. The airs she affected were perhaps but a feeble attempt to armor herself against the grim knowledge that her existence was utterly dependent on Raeburn's goodwill. With a contrite smile he said, "Forgive me, Aunt, you caught me at a bad moment. I should not have . . . snapped at you."

Flora relaxed visibly. "You are ever gracious, Graham."

He shook his head with wry amusement. "Gracious? No, Aunt, not I . . ." After a hesitation he continued curiously, "Tell me, I beg you, what is it that makes you distrustful of the maid Willa Brown? You were acquainted with her history when she lived at Renard Chase before. I grant you she is an . . . unorthodox adjunct to a respectable household, but I think when my sister-in-law, who of course is the daughter of a clergyman, found the girl, she was brought to mind of the parable of the Good Samaritan; perhaps we should all heed her example. . . . In any event, Willa appears most sincerely reformed in her behavior, or so Jessica believes. Have you evidence that she is mistaken in her trust of the wench?"

"I don't know," Flora said. "I can only say that I have observed behavior that is so outside the norm for women of her station that I thought I ought to bring it to your notice."

"Since Willa is Jessica's personal servant, I am surprised that you did not take your . . . observation . . . to her first."

Flora said sweetly, "But I could not do that, Graham, for I have reason to believe the maid's peculiar behavior is carried out at Mrs. Foxe's bidding."

Raeburn's gray eyes turned flinty. At last, he thought, the object of all this circumlocution. . . . He gestured toward a chair, the firelight glinting on the carved sapphire of his heavy signet ring. "Perhaps you'd better sit down, Flora. I am all attention."

The woman seated herself primly in a high-backed wing chair and tried without success to hide the insinuating gleam in her pale eyes. With a complacent sigh she said, "As much as it pains me to relate such a tale, I feel compelled to tell you that the maidservant appears to be acting as go-between for Mrs. Foxe and some man whose identity is as yet unknown to me."

A curious hollow sensation welled up in Raeburn, somewhere in the vicinity of his watch chain. He said slowly, "That's a serious charge, Aunt. I presume you have some evidence for it?"

Flora shrugged meaningfully. "The woman Willa has on several occasions made journeys into the village, ostensibly as recreation for her half holidays, but at intervals far more frequent than is usually granted for domestics. This in itself might be due to no more than the regrettable indulgence of a too-lax mistress, except that Willa Brown has also been observed carrying packets to the shop that serves as receiving office for the mail, and once or twice she appears to have picked up letters that were waiting there."

"The wench is a Londoner," Raeburn said shortly. "Perhaps she has family she writes to." Even as he spoke, he realized how lame that explanation was. The girl had never had anyone except a gin-soaked monster of a father who had sold her to the flesh pedlars for the price of a few bottles of Blue Ruin. Now she had only Jessica, for whom she would readily have sacrificed the tattered remnants of her soul. . . .

"But, Graham," Flora added triumphantly, "according to the shopkeeper, the letters come directed to"—she made a significant pause—" 'J.F.' "

Raeburn's wide mouth tightened grimly. "I see, Aunt. I had no idea you were so well informed. Dare I ask whether the shopkeeper also made note of the destination of Willa's mysterious parcels?"

"There was no name, but the address was somewhere in Clerkenwell."

"Clerkenwell?" Raeburn repeated, puzzled, as he wondered what attraction there could possibly be for Jessica in a drab district of London notable only for an indifferent school, some print shops, and a jail. Perhaps, he thought wildly, with her penchant for attending the downtrodden, she had begun corresponding with convicts? He blinked, ruffling his fair hair with his fingers, and when he looked up at Flora, he was appalled to find her watching him intently, her bristly upper lip curved into a smile of undisguised gloating. Damn the old tattlemonger, she had always hated Jess, he realized now; jealous, no doubt, of her youth and beauty and the deference she received as his brother's wife. Even when Andy was alive, Flora had tried to undercut Jessica's position in the household—always in the guise of following Raeburn's wishes—and thinking back, he was sure that it must have been Flora whom Jessica had overheard that last night plotting to get rid of "the upstart drawing teacher." It sounded just like her.

His deep voice spelling dismissal, Raeburn said curtly, "Thank you for telling me of your concern, Aunt. I shall deal with the matter personally." He nodded toward the door, and for once Flora had sense enough to take her leave immediately.

After the door had closed behind the woman, Raeburn turned to the window again. In the distance, halfway across the frosty meadow, he could see the dogcart wending its way back from the forest, laden with baskets of Christmas greenery. From the color of their cloaks, Claire's blue, Jessica's a deep rose, bright as butterflies against the dingy dead grass, Raeburn saw that Claire was driving the small buggy while Jessica clung to a great bundle of holly and ivy piled beside her on the narrow seat. He noted with mild displeasure that the groom who had accompanied the two girls to the forest was riding his hack directly alongside the cart, rather than at a discreet distance behind. Squinting slightly, Raeburn identified the man as one fairly new in his service, O'Hara or O'Shea or something like that, a good-looking broth of a lad whose line of Irish blarney struck the earl as just a trifle forced. The man seemed to know horses well, and his references had been good, but Raeburn had a suspicion that those engaging blue eyes concealed the soul of a revolutionary. . . . In the morning when Tomkins, the head groom, came for instructions, Raeburn would suggest he keep a careful watch over the new man.

Sometime later Raeburn heard the girls' voices wafting up the grand staircase as they came in at the front of the house. The butler must have been on hand to take their cloaks, for Claire gushed, "Thank you, Barston. Lud, it's freezing outside, but just wait till you see what we got for you to decorate the house with! We found *bushels* of holly and ivy, and enough mistletoe to make a dozen kissing boughs—"

As he approached the landing Raeburn heard Barston interrupt with the familiar indulgence of an old family retainer, "Now, Lady Claire, you'd best get His Lordship's permission before you make plans for that sort of thing."

Jessica agreed, a smile audible in her voice, "Yes, Claire, you know how Graham—"

"Oh, don't be such a prig, Jess," Claire retorted without rancor. "I'll bet by the time my precious big brother was my age, he'd kissed half the girls in the county!"

"By no means, little sister," Raeburn declared, his voice booming down from on high. "Just what do you take me for?" Jessica and Claire glanced up, startled, their eyes wide as they watched his descent. When he reached the foot of the stairs, he said with a grin, "When I was seventeen, I am sure I must have kissed at least three quarters of the girls in this county—and the next!"

Claire launched herself at her brother, squealing, "Oh, Graham, you are the most impossible tease!" and Raeburn gathered her close against his broad chest.

As he hugged his sister, above her red curls his gray gaze traveled across to where Jessica was exchanging her bonnet and damp cloak for a paisley shawl that the butler held out for her. As Raeburn watched her drape the triangular wrap over her thin shoulders and knot it at her breast his eyes darkened at the way her pink wool gown emphasized her bosom. Although the earl expected his women to be fashionably dressed at all times, he had never allowed them to succumb to the absurd and dangerous affectation of wearing only wispy, transparent muslin even in the dead of winter, unlike certain ladies of the *ton* who were willing to risk possibly fatal pneumonia in their quest to be thought desirable. Even Daphne, usually the most sensible of women . . . Gazing at Jessica, he couldn't help thinking how unconsciously provocative and mysterious she managed to look in her modest, utterly opaque day dress. He wondered where the couturiere who designed her new wardrobe had found those fabrics that, while warmly appropriate for the season, somehow flowed and clung like silk around her willowy figure. . . .

Jessica glanced up suddenly, meeting the unspoken question in his gaze. "Yes, Graham? You wanted me for something?"

"For . . . something," he muttered under his breath as he released Claire, but aloud he said, "I wonder if you will do me the favor of coming to my study? A matter has come up that I think I ought to discuss with you."

Claire interrupted, "Oh, Graham, we were just about to have some hot chocolate, to warm us. Can't you wait to—"

"No, Claire," her brother said sternly. "You go ahead with your own refreshments, but Jess's will have to be sent up to the study. It is imperative that she and I speak now. Privately." His emphasis on the last word was subtle but unmistakable. After a second, Claire nodded and shrugged.

Puzzled, Jessica ventured, "I did plan to go up to the nursery for a few moments, Graham, if you don't mind?"

Raeburn sighed with resignation and signaled in the general direction of the upper stories. "Of course I don't mind, my dear. Come back to the study when you can." When Jessica smiled her gratitude with bright green eyes and turned to trip up the gleaming staircase, Raeburn watched her ascent thoughtfully. He tried to remember if she had ever smiled at him before.

By the time Jessica knocked quietly on the door of Raeburn's study, a maid had brought up a tray with pots of both chocolate and coffee on charcoal warmers, and after Jessica was settled comfortably into a plump armchair, Raeburn asked her to pour. He shook his fair head when she offered chocolate; grinning amiably, he said, "No, I've never acquired the taste, except possibly for breakfast. I much prefer coffee."

Jessica declared, "Oh, I love chocolate! To me it tastes like—like luxury. I'd never had it at all until after Andrew and I were married; now I think I could drink a dozen cups a day. It's probably just as well that I can't afford to, else I'm sure I'd be quite fat."

"My dear girl," Raeburn said, frowning slightly, "if you wish, you are welcome to have two dozen cups of chocolate a day. No one is keeping accounts on your food and drink."

Jessica felt her cheeks warm. "I know, Graham. I'm sorry if I sounded ungracious. It's just that—that I cannot grow unaccustomed to the necessity of practicing economy."

The line between his brows deepened. "Is that why you ask for so little, why you make no demands? Two full months have passed since you returned to Renard Chase, and in all that time I can think of nothing you have required of me. Even the clothes on your back were a gift—and one I frankly admit I expected to have to force upon you. I was . . . most pleasantly surprised when you gave me no argument."

She thought about the day her beautiful new wardrobe arrived at the house, her indignation, her furious flight up the marble staircase to confront him. She remembered with self-deprecating amusement how certain she had been that her new garments were part of some devious and convoluted plot to take Lottie from her and turn the child into a household drudge. She was fervently thankful that something had stopped her before she made that wild and unforgivable accusation.

With a wry shake of her head, Jessica wondered if she could have been suffering from some temporary brainstorm that day, or if her depression of the past few months had been deeper than she had ever imagined. To conjure up such a fantasy about this man who was proving to be the kindest of guardians for her infant daughter, her mind would have had to be . . . troubled. She knew now that the unresolved conflicts between her and Raeburn—and whether he chose to acknowledge them or not, many still remained—would not derive from his treatment of Lottie. Regarding him through the thick curtain of her black lashes, Jessica said wryly, "Oh, I was fully prepared to argue with you about the clothes—but then I decided it would be wasted effort to do so. You are not an easy man to oppose, Graham."

"I'm aware of that, Jess. What astonishes me is that you are willing to admit it." He studied her in pensive silence. After a moment he inquired again, "Why don't you ever ask for anything, Jess? Even though we have lived very quietly since coming down from London, there must be things you need, things you want? Claire is forever pestering me for some trifle or another, and even Aunt Talmadge—"

I ask for nothing because I don't want to be burdened with obligations when the day comes that I must flee this house again, Jessica thought silently, but aloud she said, "Claire is your sister, and Flora Talmadge has a definite, useful occupation in this house. I have neither blood nor purpose that gives me the right to make demands of you."

"Jess!" Raeburn exclaimed irritably, setting aside his coffee. "Don't start that again. I thought we had agreed that you and Lottie belonged here."

With a wistful smile she shook her head slowly. "No, Graham. I never agreed to any such thing. You insisted that Andrew's daughter belonged in his ancestral home, and be-

88

cause I happen to be her mother, you have allowed me to accompany her. I suppose I'm grateful for that consideration, but I do not delude myself that it means I am needed here. You have employed an excellent nursery staff who give Lottie constant care and attention, better than I would be able to provide on my own. Were it not for the fact that she is not yet weaned . . ."

Jessica hesitated, choosing her words carefully before she continued. In a small voice she said, "When you brought us to Renard Chase, Graham, I fully expected you to—to insist that Lottie be turned over to a wet nurse. I thought you planned to force the issue, just as you forced me to put away my mourning clothes. . . . I—I am grateful that I was wrong. Thank you. The closeness I share with my child is very important to me: it gives me a sense of—of purpose."

His fair brows came together. "This . . . 'purpose' . . . seems to be very important to you," he observed thoughtfully. "I'm not sure I understand why. Claire has no more occupation than you do, and she is happy enough."

Deciding that now was not the time to tell Raeburn that his little sister was chafing at the thought of another year of enforced girlhood, Jessica pointed out drily, "Claire is seventeen years old. In case you had not noticed, I am not."

One long finger rhythmically stroked the bridge of his hawkish nose for a moment. "Oh, I'd noticed," he drawled.

Jessica's green eyes flew up to meet his gray ones, and the languid insinuation she saw there made her blush suddenly with a strange new heat. Quickly she drooped her head so that the black hair framing her face like ravens' wings covered her hectic cheeks, masking that feverish glow. She was becoming altogether too aware of him, she realized in dismay; she was looking at her overbearing brother-in-law in a new way that was neither appropriate nor—nor wise.

She could not remember feeling quite this way before. When Raeburn had galloped into her life on that bright spring day, she had been unawakened, old enough to recognize the man's overwhelming sexual aura, but not yet capable of responding to it. But since being married . . . Compared to most couples, the nights she and her husband had spent together had been few in number, but they had been sufficient to ripen her body from that of a dreamy adolescent to a woman, to imbue her flesh with a woman's needs and secret desires. The first year of her widowhood had been too traumatic, too occupied with providing for her family the basic necessities of survival, such as food and shelter, to think about other more personal but equally basic needs—but now that Raeburn had relieved her of the burden of responsibility, her body, exulting in its restored health and spirit, was demanding relief of another kind. . . . She had but to look at him when no one was aware of it, and the sight of his broad shoulders, that large but surprisingly lithe body . . . those powerful thighs . . . made her breasts tauten, and there stirred deep inside her a nagging, twisting ache that she had no wish to feel again—certainly not for the Earl of Raeburn.

She supposed that his image had somehow become fixed in her mind because he was the first presentable man she had encountered since Andrew died, but whatever the reason, she knew she had to vanquish this appalling fixation at once, before it betrayed itself in some humiliating fashion. No matter that Raeburn had once told her he "wanted" her; he would not thank her if she embarrassed him in return, especially now that he was betrothed. She must get away, and soon. The situation was not healthy.

Jessica set aside her chocolate cup and said with stilted levity, "I enjoyed the refreshment, Graham. Before I go, was there anything else you required of me—other than satisfying your curiosity as to why I'm not spending more of your money?" She smiled archly and stood up, smoothing her skirt.

Lounging back in his chair, Raeburn massaged his square

jaw as he watched her broodingly. Just when she shrugged her shawl tighter about her shoulders, her fingers working at the knot, and turned to go, he said, "There is one last thing, if you don't mind. . . ."

"Yes?" she murmured.

With deliberation he asked, biting off the words, "Tell me, Jess, just whom do you send packages to in Clerkenwell?"

For a long moment she could not speak, staring at him, her face unnaturally white and still. Only the flutter of long inky lashes vibrating over slanting green eyes showed her capable of movement. As Raeburn watched her intently he saw her lids dip shut for just a moment then open wide again. With an infinitesimal sigh she said quietly, "My congratulations, Graham. I underestimated your spy network."

The rigid control she displayed was so out of character for Jessica that he wondered if she was deliberately trying to bait him, to make him lose his temper while she remained cool, her very composure an act of defiance. Since the first day he met her, she had been able to incite and infuriate him as no other . . . In a tone matching her own, he replied, "I keep no spies, Jessica. There are only those who . . . appreciate how vitally concerned I am about the well-being of my family."

"And naturally they hasten to report to you anything of interest?"

"On occasion." He rose to his feet but did not approach her. He could sense in her slender body nervous tension leashed like a coiled spring, like a gazelle poised for flight, and he did not want to alarm her into running. He said with great precision, "Surely you must have realized that you could not use your maid to carry on a clandestine correspondence for any length of time without someone becoming aware of what was happening? The very fact of a domestic servant receiving letters is so outside the ordinary as to be quite remarkable. Even if Aunt Talmadge hadn't—'' He broke off abruptly, but too late.

Jessica nodded grimly. "I might have known Flora was behind this. She has always disliked me intensely."

"She is devoted to this family," Raeburn corrected, ignoring the conclusions he himself had drawn after his sister's chaperon had left him earlier. "She wants no harm to come to any of its members. And you must admit that your furtive actions invite speculation. . . . Tell me, Jessica: are you in some kind of trouble? Why do you not—"

"I don't have to tell you anything, Graham," Jessica said rudely, small cracks appearing in her shell of icy calm. "You have no right—"

"I have every right, and you know it!" Raeburn exclaimed impatiently. "We have been through all that before. Now tell me, why—"

"No!" She glared at him, her green eyes wide and defiant, her rounded chin lifted in an attitude of rebellion that struck her, even as she posed, as perhaps just a trifle too artificial to be effective. With bitter self-examination she wondered what there was about Raeburn that always made her behave so melodramatically, why in his presence she tended to posture and rant like a simpering adolescent making her debut in amateur theatricals. Forcing herself to relax slightly, she repeated with iron control, "No, Graham, I will not tell you."

He took a deep breath as if debating how to continue. After a moment he ventured, "You know, Jess, if you will not give me some explanation for your extraordinary behavior, I shall be forced to draw my own conclusions."

She smiled ironically. "Since the first day we met, you have always drawn your own conclusions about me—and you have always been wrong." With a shrug of resignation, she turned toward the door.

Raeburn winced. Quickly rising to his feet, he crossed the

room to her before she could touch the knob and forestalled her by laying a gentle but irresistible hand on her shoulder. Jessica halted, glancing back in surprise, uncomfortably aware of the warmth radiating from his palm through the double thickness of shawl and dress to penetrate her smooth flesh. She looked down at his hand, then up to his face. He was regarding her seriously, his gray eyes almost—almost remorseful. As if picking his words with great care he said, "You've never forgiven me for that first day, have you, Jess? Despite all the time that has passed, all the things that have happened since then, you refuse to forget the way we met."

"Did you really think that I would?" Jessica asked bluntly, raw anger stabbing her as memory came flooding back. "I was completely innocent, and without the slightest justification you humiliated me, you brutalized me, you threatened to—to rape me. I have never doubted that if you had encountered me in some more secluded spot, you would have carried out your threats."

He shook his head fiercely, his blond hair catching the waning afternoon light. "No, Jess," he said hoarsely, "no, I would never have hurt you. I do not hurt women. It's just that I was drunk, I was . . . enraged. There had been . . . letters. I thought Andrew had fallen victim to—" He broke off abruptly, hesitating until Jessica quirked one fine black brow interrogatively. With a sigh he finished. "I had been told my brother had become enamored of a beautiful slut. It would not have been . . . unprecedented."

Jessica blanched, chilly with indignation. She thought of the first nights she had spent with her husband, his eager but fumbling ineptness, his astonished delight at sensations that were obviously as new to him as they had been to her. Disdainfully she said, "Graham, you cannot hope to excuse your own behavior by accusing Andrew of—"

"I did not mean Andrew," Raeburn said quietly. "I realize now that the boy was as untried as you when the pair of you eloped to Scotland. The Foxe I referred to who cherished the fatal propensity for unsuitable women was . . . our father.''

Jessica stared, eyes narrowing as she tried to recall what she knew personally of the fourth earl, who had died when she was eight years old. She could remember nothing of the man himself; rather she could call to mind only a gleaming crested carriage with drawn curtains that had rattled through the muddy principal street of the village one day, and her mother's urgent admonition to ''Curtsy, child, quickly, in case he should look out at us.'' If villagers gossiped about the man, it had been outside Jessica's hearing. Nor did she think Andrew had spoken overmuch of his father; his much older half brother seemed to have been the chief male influence in her husband's pathetically short life. . . .

At last she said helplessly, ''I'm sorry, Graham, but I don't understand.''

''I'm sure you don't. Few people know the story.'' Gently he guided Jessica away from the door. ''Come, my dear, let us talk some more,'' he urged as he settled her back into the puffy armchair. ''There's chocolate remaining in the pot that will go to waste if you don't drink it . . . and I think it is time I trusted you with some of the family secrets.''

Jessica sipped her chocolate and waited with anxious expectation for Raeburn to begin his narrative. She was aware that he had decided to ''trust'' her with his confidence in the hope that she in turn would show a little faith in him, but her irritation at the obvious ploy seemed minor compared to her curiosity about what he intended to tell her. Silence stretched between them. Just when she thought Raeburn had changed his mind about confiding in her, he asked suddenly, his deep voice unnaturally resonant in the charged silence of the study, ''Jess, just how much do you know about Andrew and Claire's mother?''

The question startled her, for her mind had been intent on her husband's father; she had assumed that when Raeburn

94

said the man pursued "unsuitable" women, he had meant to imply that his predecessor had fallen victim to some avaricious lightskirt. Considering what Jessica knew of Raeburn's own inclinations—and apart from the things Andrew had told her, during her year away from Renard Chase she had followed the earl's adventures avidly in the society columns of the London gazettes—she could not help reflecting cynically that he showed no particular moral objection to the muslin company, only to those members of its dubious sisterhood who . . . aspired too high.

But what had all this to do with the late Countess of Raeburn?

Seeing that Raeburn awaited a response to his question, Jessica said, "I know almost nothing about your father's second wife. I've never even seen a portrait of the woman. Claire did tell me, however, that her mother died when she was born."

Raeburn's eyes were dark gray and impenetrable, reminding Jessica of fog banks on the Channel, such as she had seen during her time in Brighton. When those cloudy masses appeared thick and threatening on the horizon, fisherfolk and landsmen alike scrambled for the safety of home and hearth, anxious to be indoors when the fog rolled through the deserted streets. . . . Raeburn said baldly, "Claire is mistaken. Her mother died when the daughter was six months old. She ingested a substantial quantity of the white lead that she had formerly used to paint her face."

Jessica blinked, stunned. "A . . . an accident, you mean?"

"No, my dear," Raeburn said quietly, shaking his head. "It was deliberate suicide, of a most excruciatingly slow and painful sort. The wretched woman would have done better to find some Prussian blue. . . ."

Shuddering, Jessica set down her cup with trembling hands. "Graham, I don't understand."

"Neither did we, until after her funeral, when the moneylenders came forth like vermin from under a rock, demanding payment for her many debts." He saw the confusion sitting awkwardly on Jessica's lovely features, and he said, "Perhaps I ought to start at the beginning."

He gulped down the dregs of his coffee and grimaced, the sour taste a feeble echo of the bitterness of his memories. As he forced his tongue to shape the words smoothly, it occurred to him that he was confiding in Jessica with a frankness he had never before used with any woman, except possibly his old nanny, long since gathered to the bosom of her ancestors. The women in his life had not been chosen for their talents at conversation; even glorious Lucinda, the opera singer, with her magnificent voice, had been little used for *talking*. . . . When Raeburn tried to imagine telling his stepmother's unsavory tale to Daphne, he knew that his fiancée would refuse to listen, chiding him primly with the admonition that some secrets were better off buried with the dead. But now Jessica watched him patiently, attentively, the intelligence in her eyes belying the demureness of hands folded in her lap as she waited for him to begin.

With an effort Raeburn said, "My own mother did die in childbed when I was but a toddler. I don't remember her at all, although in the London house there is a Gainsborough portrait painted at the time of her marriage. She was my father's second cousin, blond and pretty, a most . . . appropriate bride, and although the match was arranged by my grandparents, by all accounts my parents dealt quite amicably together, until she died. After that I was raised by my nanny until I was of an age to be sent away to Eton. My father was not an especially affectionate father, and I saw him rarely, although he made a point of calling on me whenever he was in the vicinity, and he never forgot my birthday or Christmas. I'm not sure just what he did the rest of the time. I think he took his seat in Parliament now and then, no doubt because it was expected of him, but I don't know that he ever spoke on any issue. In short, he was stolid, undemonstrative, and very, very correct . . . and no one could have been more stunned than I was when, just after my eleventh birthday, he called me home from school to introduce me to my new stepmother, the beautiful teenage daughter of a Gloucester innkeeper.''

"Good God," Jessica said inadequately.

Raeburn looked skeptical. "Indeed? If there is a good God, I fear He sadly neglected that poor woman. . . .''

He braided his long fingers together, absently toying with his signet ring as he said ruefully, "Looking back over a distance of more than two decades, I realize that the person most blameworthy in that debacle was my father, a man of some forty years lusting after a girl less than half his age. Apparently he had been touring the Cotswolds, and he suddenly took a fancy to look at Gloucester Cathedral; when he stopped at an inn just outside town and saw the host's radiantly beautiful sixteen-year-old daughter. . . . He was so besotted that he offered marriage, and I suppose the girl's parents can be excused for thinking they were doing well by her, forcing her to accept him, but surely someone ought to have realized how very . . . cruel it was. She looked like a countess, tall and slim and lovely, with vibrant red hair, but whenever she opened her mouth, her West Country accent betrayed her, and she had neither education nor native wit to help her cope with the vast changes in her station, her life. She tried hard enough—at first—but she was always making mistakes. The servants used to laugh at her behind her back." Raeburn paused, grimacing. "God help me, so did I."

Jessica heard the pain in his voice. "But you were just a child."

"So was she," Raeburn exclaimed impatiently. "When Andrew was born, she couldn't have been any older than Claire is now. We became friends of a sort after she gave me my little brother, but I soon went back to school and she was left to manage alone."

"Didn't your father help her?"

Raeburn shrugged. "I think not. I doubt that he even realized the enormity of her distress. As I said, he was not by nature a demonstrative or insightful man. Once his infatuation with his young bride waned, they continued to cohabit after a fashion, but emotionally he abandoned her to her own devices in much the same way he had abandoned me. Unfortunately, because she was so utterly unsuited to the life and society in which she was compelled to live, she was easily led astray. The friends she made—or rather, people she erroneously thought were her friends—tended to be hangers-on eager to take advantage of her youth and inexperience. Aspiring cicisbeos, ivory turners . . ."

His gray eyes grew bleak, and when he spoke again he spit out the the words as if they had a foul taste. "I remember vividly the last time I saw my stepmother . . . alive. It was just before I entered Oxford. I had been living in Town for some time, but in most respects I was still grass-green, and some of my cronies decided to drag me off to a gambling hell to . . . shall we say . . . further my education. I was nervous, but eager enough to prove myself a man of the world, but when we stepped inside that . . . that establishment, the first thing I saw was my stepmother, holding the bank at the faro table. I was incredibly shocked to find her there, for until that moment I had had no idea of her . . . failing, but her appearance was even more upsetting. I had not seen her since paying a duty call when Claire was born, and in the intervening months she had aged years. She looked raddled, ill, so ill, in fact, that my friends did not recognize her. I remember with appalling clarity the look in her eyes, that wild, glazed expression you see sometimes in those for whom gaming has become a kind of—of disease. She refused to abandon the cards, even when the proprietor informed her that he could extend no more credit. Only when she saw me did she seem to come out of her spell."

Raeburn hesitated again. "Somehow I managed to get her out of the hell—although not before my friends had made ribald remarks about my questionable taste in women—and I escorted her back to Raeburn House. There I found that Andy and Claire were safely ensconced in the country, and my father had gone out of London on some pretext or another. I turned my stepmother over to the butler's care, who seemed unsurprised at her appearance. . . ."

Once more Raeburn paused; then he concluded heavily, "Within a month she was dead, by her own hand."

He leaned back in his chair, eyes closed as if he were shutting out the memories that assailed him. Jessica watched with compassion, wishing she could find words adequate to comfort him. She remained silent. After a few moments Raeburn straightened up again and opened his eyes. He regarded Jessica sardonically. "Of course," he drawled, "a poignant but innocuous explanation was found for my stepmother's 'tragic accident.' Never let it be said that the reputation of the Foxe family had been sullied by a rumor of suicide—as if we had any particular claim to morality in the first place."

"And Andrew and Claire never discovered the truth?" Jessica asked, shaken.

"What is truth?" Raeburn mocked with such irony that Jessica knew he was calling to mind the unanswered question from the Gospel. "Do we say that a weak woman committed the unforgivable sin in order to escape her creditors? Or would it not be more accurate to say that a simple country girl died because my father selfishly dragged her away from all that was familiar and abandoned her to wither in a hostile environment, like a wood violet uprooted and left out in the sun? There is more substance than prejudice in the old saw, 'Like should marry like.' In Gloucester, among her own kind, she would have married a young farmer or perhaps a merchant's clerk with prospects, and her life, while hard, would have been content, possibly even happy, as she lived surrounded by children and grandchildren. Instead, because she was beautiful and an aristocrat desired her, she died in a particularly grisly fashion at the age of twenty-two, leaving behind a baffled husband and two orphaned babies.''

Suddenly he jumped up from the chair, as if his memories would no longer allow him to rest. He stalked over to the frosty window and stared out at the bleak vistas before him. In the empty meadow stretching to the wood beneath iron-colored skies, the narrow tracks left earlier in the afternoon by the dogcart were being dusted away by a light powder of snow, the first of the season. By the time the Templeton party arrived for Christmas, the white marble arcades of Renard Chase would be glittering with snow and ice, like the palace of the Esquimau queen. . . .

Jessica watched him helplessly, even from across the width of his study feeling the tension in him, seeing the powerful muscles of his back knotted beneath the fine fabric of his coat. As the silence in the room thickened and contracted she tried desperately to think of something to say.

While she struggled to find the words, Raeburn spoke again. Still staring out the window, he said quietly, his deep voice low and clear, "I wronged you, Jess. When Andrew told me that he wanted to marry a . . . to marry you, all I could think was that the troubles were about to begin again, that my little brother was intent on repeating the disastrous mistakes of his parents. And believing that, I . . . reacted too harshly. I railed at Andrew, played the autocratic big brother, and when he would not be swayed, I attacked you instead, never dreaming that you were different from my poor stepmother, that you were something . . . quite out of the ordinary. For that I am truly sorry, Jessica. My actions were unforgivable, I know. My only excuse is that . . . that I thought I was protecting my family.''

His pain reached out to her from across the room, and

without hesitation she rose and went to stand beside him at the window, her slender, graceful figure dwarfed by the tall bulk of him. He did not look at her immediately; rather he stood with his hands rammed deep into his pockets, spoiling the cut of his superbly tailored coat, as he squinted out at the stark landscape. His wide forehead was furrowed above fair brows and ice-gray eyes, and his mouth was compressed into a thin, inflexible line. As Jessica gazed up at him, noting the austerity of his expression, she remembered with a pang all the times she had sketched those handsome features in an attitude of grinning, unrepentant debauchery, all the times she had made him the target of her most vicious satire. During her year in Brighton, it had been easy for her to imagine Raeburn as her *bête noire*, the occasion of all her trials, the source of all her woes. In her troubled mind—and now she realized with painful clarity that during those agonizing months she had indeed been profoundly depressed—the Earl of Raeburn's image had grown and distorted until she saw him as some kind of mocking devil, the epitome of all the worst faults of his class, bent on tormenting her for her insolence in daring to love his brother. Whenever "Erinys" dipped her pen into the inkwell and began a visual attack on some evil of the society, whether it be brutal treatment of horses or the Prince of Wales's unseemly capers, somehow the chief villain in the sketch had always looked like Raeburn. . . .

Jessica cringed inwardly. For every sin that the earl had confessed against her, she had wronged him a hundred times over.

Her fingers worked nervously at the knot of her shawl as she struggled against the impulse to unburden her soul, reveal her identity as the anonymous cartoonist. She knew she dared not. Despite his frequent forays into the fleshpots of London, the governing passion of Raeburn's life was the maintenance of his family's welfare. If he found out that Jessica had held the Foxes up to public ridicule, he would never forgive her.

His disgust might even prove to be so great that in retaliation he would carry out his threats to take Lottie from her. She could not risk that. No matter how much she longed to ease her guilt by speaking frankly, she must remain silent.

Suddenly Raeburn turned away from the window. The sleeve of his coat brushed againt Jessica's hands clasped over her breast, and his eyes darkened as he gazed at her. Her heart racing, Jessica smiled uncomfortably and quickly looked down, closing her eyes against the compelling sight of him, annoyed with herself for reacting to his nearness. She was a widow, for God's sake, she reminded herself irritably; not some schoolroom miss giggling over the dancing master. . . . But despite her efforts to remain in control, a faint blush appeared on her cheeks, deepening when Raeburn caught her chin in his large hand and gently tilted her head upward so that her slanting green eyes stared back at him from behind starred lashes.

He watched the color flowing just under the surface of her ivory skin, tinting her complexion with a delicacy made even more subtle against her jewellike eyes, the blue-black luster of her hair. When he saw her pink tongue flick nervously across her lips, he felt a wave of desire, startling in its intensity, wash over him. "Beautiful Jessica," he murmured huskily, "at least my poor brother had *you*. . . ."

Jessica trembled at his touch, the male scent of him heavy in her nostrils, the warmth of his fingers on her face somehow radiating to her extremities. She was woman enough to know that he would like to kiss her, to make love to her, and despite his claims to the contrary, she did not think he respected her position enough to draw back if she encouraged him, as he would have done as a matter of course with his highborn fiancée. To Raeburn she would always be the upstart drawing teacher. . . . Because she knew that if his mouth touched hers, she would be lost utterly, unable to deny him anything, seduced by her own hunger into an act of sheer

102

madness, she could not allow that to happen. Drawing back as far as his hold on her would allow, Jessica said brightly, "Thank you for confiding in me, Graham. Now I understand why you wish to marry Lady Daphne. With her breeding and background, she will make a most *suitable* bride for you."

At the mention of his betrothed, he forced his hand to fall away from Jessica's face, wondering why he found it so difficult to conjure up the features of the woman he had chosen out of duty. Blinking hard, he drew himself up to his most imposing height and noted briskly, "I can't tell you how glad I am that you approve my choice, my dear. I too am sure that Daphne and I will deal excellently together." He paused momentarily, and when he spoke again, his tone had grown sharper. "I have enjoyed our convversation, Jess, but you and I do seem to have strayed rather far from the subject which I wished to discuss with you. So I must ask you again: with whom do you correspond in London?"

Jessica's face grew pale. For a moment she had been lulled by the soft enchantment of Raeburn's deep voice, and she had forgotten that he was a man who never abandoned any chase before its conclusion. This Foxe was a hunter, and now she—or rather, her secret—was his prey. Taking a deep breath, Jessica said, "Although I value the confidence you placed in me, Graham, I fear I cannot return the favor, not—not in this matter. It is private, concerning no one but myself, and I have no intention of telling you about it. After your many kindnesses, I dislike having to refuse you, so I must request that you do not question me again."

He studied her in grim silence, his eyes coldly intent, but when he spoke, his voice sounded almost—almost hurt. "I had thought you were beginning to trust me, Jess. I am not trying to play the tyrant; my concern is only for your welfare. I know you must have endured much during the past year. If there is some man . . ."

Silently she shook her head, making stray tendrils of her

black hair flutter about her face. When she did not speak, he expelled his breath with a hiss and muttered harshly, "Very well, my girl, if that's the way you insist it must be, so be it. But do not think for a moment that the matter is forgotten. We will discuss it again later." He paused, thinking hard. "In the meantime, Jessica, since you seem so anxious to have some kind of occupation, some purpose, to justify your presence under my roof, I shall give you one: as you know, in a few days my fiancée and her brother Lord Crowell and a few other persons will be journeying here to Renard Chase to spend the Christmas season with us. I should like you to handle the arrangements for their visit. Despite her best efforts, Aunt Talmadge is quite hopeless at such matters—she tends to go overboard with ceremony and then omit essentials like food and adequate linens—and Claire is too inexperienced—"

"But I have no experience at all in these things," Jessica interrupted, startled. "I've never tried to run a house the size of this one!"

Raeburn shrugged. "Perhaps not—but you have good sense and good taste, and you have proven yourself adept at . . . coping with adversity. I am certain you will have no difficulty in making my fiancée welcome in her future home."

Jessica regarded Raeburn enigmatically, shaking her head at his blindness. The question was not whether she could make Lady Daphne welcome; the problem was that Raeburn's intended was unlikely to consider Jessica welcome in her future home. . . .

Chapter Five

Footmen bore away the plates soiled with the remains of the sweet course—currant dumplings in wine sauce—and laid out the savory of oyster patties and—Raeburn glanced grinningly at Jessica—chocolates. Jessica was too busy discreetly directing the activities of the servants from her position next to Claire at the opposite end of the long dining table to notice the earl's quick look, but at his side, Lady Daphne Templeton observed it and frowned. Raeburn, returning his attention to his betrothed just in time to catch that fleeting expression of displeasure in her light blue eyes, asked solicitously, "Is something amiss, Daphne? May I get you anything? More coffee, perhaps?"

"No, thank you, Graham," she answered sweetly, smiling up at him. "You know your hospitality is above reproach."

"Oh, hardly that, my dear," Raeburn denied. "You have Jessica to thank for the fact that the fish was not boiled to mush nor the pheasant overdone. I believe she had a most edifying discussion with the cook and at last somehow managed to convince that good woman that charcoal inhibits digestion. . . ."

"By God, yes!" Daphne's brother William Templeton, Lord Crowell, declared from his seat at Claire's right hand, just opposite Jessica. He picked up his wineglass and waved it toward Jessica in a vague gesture of salute, to which she responded with an equally vague smile, not yet certain that she liked the young duke. He was about twenty-four, with the same small stature, medium brown hair and sallow complexion his sister had, but unlike her, he was already running to fat, and Jessica thought privately that the fleshy folds around his pale eyes made his face look piggy. He said, "I congratulate Mrs. Foxe on the cuisine, but frankly, Raeburn, any change would be an improvement. I still remember the last time I stayed here, some two years ago, for the hunt. We kept running out of food, and what there was was burnt to a crisp. It's only because I already love you like a brother that I must tell you that when you invited us here for Christmas, I hesitated before accepting. Were it not for the fact that your cellar is without peer . . ."

Jessica glanced sidelong at Flora Talmadge, who sat in the middle of the table, staring resolutely at her plate, as she silently suffered the man's rudeness. Jessica could see hot, embarrassed color rouging Flora's bristly cheeks, and despite her own conflicts with Claire's chaperon and the woman's admitted failings as a housekeeper, Jessica felt a surprising wave of outraged family loyalty at Lord Crowell's insolence. Didn't he realize that Flora had been in charge of the household during his last visit—or was he simply too confident of his inherent superiority to care that he was hurting a subordinate? Jessica said clearly, "My lord, you give me too much credit for the changes here at Renard Chase. I have only come onto the scene in the past few weeks. Mrs. Talmadge is the one who has labored so diligently over the years to make this establishment a comfortable home for my brother-in-law and his family."

Flora glanced in astonishment at her unexpected champion, but she looked away quickly, biting her lip. Lord Crowell squinted across the table at Jessica, uncertain of Jessica's mockery and hardly daring to believe that he had actually been chastised by the beautiful but encroaching female his sister disliked so intensely. A clumsy retort quivered on his thick lips, but before he could speak, from the head of the table Daphne's voice injected with insinuating clarity, "Well, Mrs. Foxe, I collect I have much for which I must be grateful to you and Mrs. Talmadge." Daringly she laid her hand on the table beside Raeburn's in a gesture of invitation as she added, "I know your efforts will ease my happy task of making a home for my husband, his sister, and myself once we are married. . . ."

Since the moment Daphne Templeton first stepped into the marble entry of Renard Chase and laid her cold blue eyes on Jessica, Jessica had been aware that the two of them were in a state of armed truce, affecting cordiality because Raeburn, observing their meeting, had made it tacitly clear that he would permit nothing else; but Jessica had also known with wry insight that the other woman would cut her deliberately any time she thought she could do so without arousing her future husband's wrath. After careful consideration Jessica had decided that the most effective method of dealing with those snubs would be to shrug them off indifferently—by no means always an easy plan, especially not for one of her volatile temperament, but so far she had adhered to it with near-religious devotion. But now at her side she could feel Claire bridling at the way Lady Daphne had purposely omitted Jessica and Flora's names from her list of family members— and although she was touched that the girl wanted to leap to her defense, she knew she must try to prevent an argument that would only serve to alienate Claire from the woman who would have charge of her social life until she herself married. . . .

Jessica reached out to touch Claire's arm in warning, but Raeburn interceded smoothly, squelching his sister and turning to smile at his fiancée with deceptively cool indulgence, "Yes, my dear, I'm sure we shall all be quite happy with Flora and Jessica and little Lottie rounding out our family circle." His long fingers closed firmly around hers, and when, after the briefest of hesitations, Lady Daphne nodded her head in submission, his smile warmed and he brushed his lips across her fingertips.

Shrinking back in her chair, Jessica winced. Despite her sternest efforts to control her expression, she could not prevent the shudder that ran through her slim body at the sight of the earl making restrained love to his well-bred fiancée, and she had to close her eyes to keep from crying out with pain. When she thought she had enough control over her volatile emotions to endure watching them exchange small, affectionate caresses, she raised her long lashes again, praying that no one had noticed her momentary weakness.

But as her green eyes moved casually over the diners, as if checking on their comfort, they collided and were held by the feral yellow gaze of the third guest at Raeburn's table, a tall, gaunt man of some forty years. His thinning sandy hair was carefully combed to hide his bald spot, and the quality of his clothes indicated a tailor aspiring with questionable success to be judged the first crack of fashion, disguising the poor cut of his work with flashy materials. But then, Jessica thought acidly, the man himself was much like that. He was an artist of doubtful qualifications, hiding his indifferent skill with his pen by churning out crude, often libelous sketches of his betters for the less prestigious London gazettes: John Mason, self-appointed social commentator and satirical cartoonist—and chief rival for the popular position now held by the anonymous artist Erinys.

Jessica knew his work and despised it, not necessarily because it was poorly executed, but because it was so pointlessly cruel. All too often Mason chose as the target for his lampoons the innocent, the defenseless: once-powerful men robbed of strength and wit by senility; former beauties wasted with disease—as if the mere fact that those people had once been admired now made them fit victims for his vicious attacks. Whenever Jessica saw Mason's cartoons, she hated him for degrading a literary and artistic form that had been recognized as a useful weapon against social ills since the days of Juvenal. At least the satires of Erinys, while biting and occasionally even venomous, had indicted only those whose misfortunes were the direct result of their own willfulness and folly. . . .

Except, perhaps, she admitted with a swallowed groan, the man she loved, the Earl of Raeburn.

With outward control Jessica met Mason's knowing gaze evenly, wondering, not for the first time, how he had come to be associated with the young duke and his simpering sister. Mason was decades older than Crowell, his aspect and address as mediocre as his background, hardly the kind of man one would expect to find on intimate terms with a haughty, aspiring Corinthian. While it was certainly not without precedent for people accomplished in the arts to be "adopted" by easygoing members of the aristocracy, to be fawned over and treated to sort of an informal patronage, John Mason's talents were not, at least in Jessica's opinion, so notable as to merit such lionization. Nor, for that matter, did she think that Lord Crowell was the type to value even the most exalted artistic achievement; for all his high position, the young man struck her as a self-indulgent Philistine, determined to waste what was left of his inheritance in crude pleasure.

Forcing a smile, Jessica asked, "Mr. Mason, is there anything you require for your comfort? You've been very quiet all throughout dinner. I hope everything was to your taste."

"Yes, Mr. Mason," Claire chimed in, belatedly remembering her nominal role as hostess, "you must tell us if there is anything we can get for you."

"Thank you, my lady," the man replied with oily smoothness, bowing deferentially in the girl's direction, "but I think I should indeed be hard to please were I less than satisfied with the hospitality you have shown me. Your gracious condescension, the beauty of Renard Chase itself—I find your home quite unequalled among the great houses of the realm. . . ."

Claire hesitated, uncertain whether the man's unctuous raptures were meant sarcastically, but before she could frame a response, from the head of the table, Raeburn drawled, "Then I gather you are familiar with the . . . great houses of the realm, Mason?"

"I have been privileged to visit some of them, my lord," Mason said tightly, a line of white circling his compressed mouth.

Beside him, Lord Crowell, raising his newly filled wineglass to his lips, said airily, "Oh, Johnny's been everywhere." He frowned into the glass. "Sees everything . . ." he muttered after a moment.

"Indeed," Raeburn drawled again. "In that case we shall all have to be on our best behavior, lest we find ourselves figuring in one of your cartoons."

"Graham!" Lady Daphne choked indignantly. "Mr. Mason would never be so reprehensible. . . ."

The man hastened to protest, "My lord, I assure you I would not dream of trespassing against your hospitality in such a deplorable fashion."

Raeburn nodded, his hair gleaming like gold in the abundant candlelight. "Well, then, Mason, I am indebted to you for your forebearance. Would that everyone displayed such . . . sensibility."

At the grim note in his voice, Jessica felt herself grow cold, but she had no choice but to sit helplessly, without visible reaction, while Mason agreed. "Yes, my lord, you have been the victim of a certain scurrilous penster in recent months, have you not?" He turned slightly in his seat to regard Lord Crowell. "You possess quite a few of those drawings, don't you . . . Billy?" Jessica noticed one of Raeburn's brows lift curiously at Mason's insolent familiarity.

110

The rosy flush in Crowell's cheeks darkened. "Damned impudent hack," he mumbled thickly, and Jessica could not help wondering which cartoonist he meant.

"Graham," Lady Daphne said urgently, tugging at the rich fabric of his sleeve, "I hardly think such a subject can be fit for—for the ears of your young sister." She directed a significant glance at Claire, who listened eagerly.

When Raeburn also looked at his sister, the girl met his gray gaze with a smile of mild defiance. She giggled uncomfortably, "Oh, don't mind me. I know all about the sketches. I've even seen a . . ." Her laughter stilled when Raeburn's eyes turned icy.

Lady Daphne looked shocked. "Really, Claire!" she gasped; then she turned reprovingly to Flora. "Mrs. Talmadge, I should think that as Claire's chaperon you would—"

Flora blinked, flustered, her rough cheeks pinking at the rebuke. She began to scrape back her chair nervously. "Forgive me, I—I didn't think—"

"Oh, Aunt, no!" Claire protested with a willful whine. "You can't drag me away just when things are becoming interesting."

"Claire . . ." Raeburn murmured forcefully.

"Why don't we all go?" Jessica suggested in a mild undertone, her tact masking profound relief. "I'm sure the gentlemen would like to be left to their port."

Claire sighed ungraciously as she was recalled once again to her role as hostess. "Oh, very well," she grumbled, nodding to the footman who pulled back her chair. She rose lightly to her feet. "Ladies, if you will accompany me . . ."

In the drawing room, Raeburn's women retired quickly and silently to their accustomed places, as they had done each evening since the Templetons arrived, their normal conversation stifled by the presence of outsiders. The silver tea urn grew cold as Flora Talmadge settled at her tapestry stand in the corner, where she sewed tiny, meticulous stitches in what would eventually be an exceedingly drab representation of the ennoblement of William Foxe, the first Earl of Raeburn, for his valor at Culloden. Claire flung herself onto one end of the settee and burrowed behind the mottled covers of the latest romance from Leadenhall Street. Somewhat more decorously, Jessica sat at the other end of the sofa and reached for her drawing portfolio. She had begun a portrait of Claire and little Charlotte, hoping to capture the similarities the two girls shared despite the difference in their ages, their vixen-red hair, their glowing smiles. . . . Unfortunately, her infant daughter was a remarkably uncooperative subject, preferring to crawl around inquisitively on the Aubusson carpet in Jessica's sitting room, and Jessica had to content herself with making lightning sketches during those fleeting moments when Lottie was still. Now she wanted to study the drawings and decide which she could incorporate into her final painting.

Her hand paused in midair as she glanced in Lady Daphne's direction. That young woman had taken a chair close to the hearth, where an oak log crackled cheerily, and she stared at the fire, her mouth drawn up in thought, her near-colorless eyes reflecting the flames ruddily. Jessica, who was chilly despite the shawl she had draped over the long lace-puffed sleeves of her wool evening dress, could tell that Lady Daphne was grateful for the warmth penetrating her thin muslin gown, and she asked herself with genuine bewilderment why Raeburn's fiancée seemed willing to court pneumonia in order to appear provocative. Surely she must already be utterly confident of the earl's regard. . . .

Watching the woman plait her fingers in a gesture of restive boredom as she glanced surreptitiously toward the door from the dining room, Jessica felt an unexpected pang of pity for her. Lady Daphne might be all that Raeburn required of a wife, compliant, wellborn, impeccably educated in those matters of taste and etiquette that she would need in her role as his countess, but she seemed to have no personal resources or interests to occupy her mind; she seemed incapable of doing aught but waiting for some man's instruction. Jessica wondered what the woman would do after she and Raeburn were married, when the honeymoon days were over and the earl resumed his various pursuits of business or politics—or opera singers—and left his bride to fend for herself at Renard Chase. Running the household would use up part of her time, of course, but if Raeburn failed to get her with child right away, Jessica feared that Lady Daphne would succumb to the ennui that had proved so fatal for his stepmother. . . .

But all that was no concern of hers, Jessica told herself sternly, refusing to allow her mind to dwell on uncomfortable images of Raeburn and his countess, her undersized body swollen with his child. . . . She glanced back impatiently at Claire and Flora. Jessica knew that Lady Daphne was no great favorite of either of the women, but they had both been following their own pursuits with a determination that bordered on deliberate rudeness. She wondered if they had delegated her by default to entertain the guest. With an inward smile Jessica acknowledged that Lady Daphne would welcome her attention least of all. After a momentary hesitation, she sighed and picked up her portfolio.

Just as she set it on her lap and began to untie the grosgrain ribbons, the door from the dining room opened, and the three men walked noisily into the room, bringing with them the fruity aroma of port and the tang of pipe tobacco. Lord Crowell's round face was flushed with wine and irritation as he declared impatiently, "I don't care what you say, Johnny, I still think you've taken leave of your senses! A *woman*—impossible!"

Mason snapped, "Listen to me, Billy, when I tell you my reasoning—"

"Gentlemen," Raeburn interrupted, "I thought we had agreed that we would spare the ladies this conversation." His expression was unusually grim, but he forced his hard mouth into a welcoming smile as he turned to address his fiancée, who glanced up eagerly from the fire. Jessica, watching the other woman's sullen face with perceptions heightened by her own tortured emotions, saw the way Lady Daphne brightened with anticipation when Raeburn approached her, and she suddenly questioned painfully if she had been wrong about the relationship between her brother-in-law and his betrothed; if, despite the earl's harping about the "suitability" of their union, on Lady Daphne's side at least it was a love match. . . .

Before Raeburn could speak, Lord Crowell sank heavily into an armchair and addressed his sister laughingly. "Guess what, Daph, for once I've got the better of Johnny!" He glanced nervously toward the artist, who stood warming his hands before the hearth. "Cleverest fellow in the world, Johnny is about most things, but this time he's fallen into a regular mare's nest, and he's too stubborn to admit he's wrong. . . ."

Lady Daphne smiled stiffly as she shifted her gaze to her brother's florid face, and Jessica wondered if the young duke often drank too much. He was only twenty-four, but the lines of his face were already puffy and blurred by overindulgence, and despite his jovial manner, he struck Jessica as the type who would turn mean when foxed. . . . He could not be any great joy to live with. "What on earth are you talking about, brother dear?" Lady Daphne asked lightly.

"This cartoonist, 'Airy' something, the one who's been picking on your intended there—Johnny's trying to convince us that the person behind all the dirty work is a *woman*!"

Jessica gasped, choking on her heart, but fortunately her stifled outburst was matched by the shocked protests of the other women in the room. Flora Talmadge blinked in confusion, while Claire, dropping her book onto the settee, tittered nervously. Lady Daphne wrinkled her brow pensively and at last judged, "Oh, Mr. Mason, although it pains me to say so, I'm sure you must be in error."

The cartoonist looked down at her with an air of distress. He sighed. "My lady, as much as I mislike offending your tender sensibilities, I am indeed afraid that some debased member of your gender has committed these unconscionable attacks upon her betters. . . ." When he saw the skepticism on Daphne's face, he bowed and continued instructively, "As you know, in keeping with my profession, I am blessed with a certain knowledge of art and those who practice it. When the first of those . . . regrettable anonymous drawings made their appearance in London last winter, I considered it my sacred duty to see if I could determine their source, in the hopes that I might be able to spare further pain to their victims—many of whom I am honored to number among my acquaintances. Unfortunately, the publishers, in their avarice—for among a less enlightened segment of the populace, the cartoons have achieved a certain popularity—were most unwilling to stop printing the drawings or to reveal anything about their origin. Therefore I was forced to try to deduce from internal evidence the identity of the . . . culprit, I'll call her, for I hesitate to apply the word 'artist' to one who so perverts the noblest aims of that ancient craft. . . ."

As Jessica listened anxiously to Mason's pompous and selfserving oration she was torn between tears of fright and laughter at his affectation. His cadaverous chest seemed to swell with each new and hypocritical word, until he began to remind her, with his long skinny shanks, of some water bird, a heron strutting through the marshes, and she was amazed that Raeburn, who usually had little patience with humbugs, did not denounce Mason for his own vicious caricatures of the *ton*. Perhaps the earl's forebearance derived from his rigid standards of courtesy, which prevented him from verbally attacking a guest under his roof—or else, Jessica thought apprehensively, like Mason, Raeburn was resolutely determined to ferret out and wreak revenge on the unknown artist.

"There are a number of clues discernible to the trained eye," Mason continued loftily to his now-enrapt audience, and he began to illustrate his points with gestures worthy of the most blustering of Drury Lane hacks. "Perhaps most obviously revealing is the very pseudonym itself: 'Erinys,' one of the Furies, the avenging spirits of Greek mythology—a *female* spirit." Jessica noticed Flora clamp her hand over her mouth in awe of such erudition.

"And what does this Fury presume to avenge," Mason went on, "to what causes does her maudlin pen aspire? I'll tell you: the so-called plight of undutiful wives rightly cast off by their husbands; the alleged mistreatment of animals; the employment of orphans and foundlings in factories where, instead of falling into a life of vice and sloth, they may happily be taught a useful occupation. . . . Weak-minded and *womanly* concerns all. And in every case this—this 'Erinys' seems to blame these highly debatable ills of society on those persons to whom we should look for guidance and example: His Noble Highness the Prince of Wales . . . our gracious host himself—"

At this point Raeburn was at last moved to drawl lightly, "Really, Mason, I am most flattered, but don't you think you're applying the butter just a trifle . . . thickly?"

Claire sniggered, and even Flora had to stifle a giggle. Mason, lost in the sound of his own voice, took a moment to interpret what Raeburn had said, and when he did, he flushed above the points of his thickly starched neckcloth. "F-forgive me, my lord," he said stiffly. "If I seemed too . . . zealous, it is only because in addition to my natural indignation at the insolence of this scurrilous and ill-starred satirist, I am also offended that a woman would dare to trespass in what is rightly a masculine domain."

"By that I collect you mean the world of art?"

"Indeed I do, my lord," Mason said. "Although the delicacy of the feminine hand may impart to it a certain skill at draftsmanship, no woman is blessed with the intelligence and insight that distinguishes all true artistic accomplishment. . . ."

Raeburn glanced past Mason to Jessica, who sat beside Claire on the settee, her raven head bent so that he could not see her face, her slender body rigid with tension. He noticed that one of the ribbons of the portfolio lying in her lap had become twisted so tightly around her hand that it cut into her flesh, inhibiting the flow of blood, making her fingertips lividly white. He stared at the glossy darkness of her hair until his gaze seemed to penetrate her consciousness, and slowly, slowly she lifted her head to look up at him. Her mobile features seemed unnaturally still, her skin ashen, but when her slanting green eyes met his, they glowed turbulently, alive with anger and defiance and—Raeburn scowled— even pain.

Pain? he repeated in silent amazement. Jessica was something of an artist herself: was she actually hurt by Mason's idiotic pontificating? Raeburn almost snorted in disbelief. The man was an obsequious ass, certainly, but Jessica had never given a farthing for anyone else's opinion, and usually—in fact, all too often—she had been more than eager to contradict those with whom she disagreed. . . . But now she was enduring Mason's near insults with uncharacteristic forebearance, and the effort was showing.

Suddenly Raeburn wondered if Jessica was being quiet for his sake, declining to argue with Mason because the man was Raeburn's guest, or at least, a friend of his betrothed's family. Raeburn had asked Jessica to forget whatever complaint it was that she had nursed for so long against his fiancée—and certainly it could be argued that Daphne was the injured party; after all, she was the one who had been left standing in Almack's with orgeat dripping down her chin—and try to make her welcome at Renard Chase. Jessica had agreed with unaccustomed humility, and since then she had worked diligently, dealing with the servants with skill and tact that bordered on the astonishing, considering her utter ineptitude when she first married Andrew. In more ways than the physical, her trials of the past year had matured her. . . .

Raeburn sighed. Now if he could only induce Daphne to treat her future sister-in-law with equal amiability and respect . . . Aware that he was offering only a feeble sop to Jessica's hurt feelings, Raeburn said with deceptive mildness, "You know, Mason, I fear I must contradict your statement that women are incapable of scaling the artistic heights. Was it not just in our father's day that Angelica Kauffmann's work as a painter was so highly admired by Sir Joshua Reynolds and others that she became one of the founding members of the Royal Academy?"

Mason blinked, rebounding with a thud off the steel in his host's deep voice. Nodding, he said, "I had no idea you were so knowledgeable about art, my lord."

Raeburn shrugged. "The Foxes have been collectors in a small way for generations . . . and, of course, our own dear Jessica is quite talented with her brush."

"Yes, Mr. Mason," Claire interjected eagerly, joining the conversation for the first time. "You must see the painting Jess is doing of her little girl and me—"

"A painting?" Raeburn echoed, his brows lifting sharply as he met Jessica's gaze. "I didn't know you were working on anything like that."

Jessica bit her lip. "It's not finished yet. It was supposed to be a Christmas present." *A piece of myself I can give to you,* she thought wistfully, staring with ill-disguised hunger at his beloved face; *a gift of love, a feeble reflection of that which I dare not give.. . .*

From her seat by the fireside, Lady Daphne rose and shook out her muslin skirt. "My dear Graham," she said archly as she stepped over to the earl and slipped her arm through his, "don't you think we have grown uncommonly serious and gloomy tonight, especially considering the season? If I may be so bold, I'd like to suggest we adjourn to the pianoforte and sing Christmas songs. Surely that is a more appropriate pastime than arguing about painters or some scurrilous scribe who ought to be quite beneath our notice. . . ."

"Good idea, Daph," Lord Crowell, perking up from the torpor into which he had fallen when the conversation turned "arty," mumbled thickly from the depths of his armchair, and the others hastened to agree with him.

Raeburn patted his fiancée's small hand and answered gallantly. "As always, your every wish is my command, my love. Some music sounds like a delightful suggestion. If you will play, I think I can be induced to turn the pages—but not even for you will I sing!"

"Thank heaven!" Claire declared as she rose to join the general exodus to the music room. "Daphne, now that you're to be part of the family, I warn you you'll have to learn to suffer silently on those memorable occasions when my big brother waxes musical. . . ."

The mood of the group had changed utterly, and they trooped en masse from the parlor, leaving Jessica still sitting on the small sofa, weak with relief, hardly yet daring to believe that she had escaped undetected from Mason's uncannily accurate conjectures about Erinys. As much as she despised the man's work, he obviously had a keenly perceptive eye. . . .

From the door Raeburn glanced back. "Jess," he asked in concerned tones, "are you not joining us?"

Jessica shook her head as if to clear it, and as she stood up a strand of black hair came loose and dangled across her smooth cheek. Noting the meticulously neat coiffure of the woman who clung to Raeburn's arm, Jessica tried to brush the errant tendril back into place. "No, thank you, Graham," she said softly. "I'm not much in the mood for singing now.

You and—and Lady Daphne and the rest of the family enjoy yourselves, though.''

Raeburn frowned at Jessica's wan features. She was obviously depressed and upset about something. Her casual use of the word "family" made him wonder suddenly if she were missing her brothers and sisters—if not her father—none of whom she had seen since returning to Renard Chase. She never talked about them, but surely now that it was Christmas . . . He suggested gently, "Are you lonely for your other family, Jess? If so, it would be easy enough for someone to take you to the village."

She blinked in patent confusion. "What?" Shaking her head, she murmured, "Forgive me, Graham, I was miles away. I'm sorry I'm behaving like the skeleton at the feast. I think I'd better go on up to the nursery and check on Lottie. I—I'll see you all tomorrow." She smiled briefly and fled through the dining room door, leaving her portfolio behind her on the settee.

Firmly Jessica closed her apartment door behind her, shutting out the masculine voices that wafted upward from the direction of the music room. She recognized a raucous rendition of the "Gloucester Wassail"—"Come, butler, come fill us a bowl of the best, then we hope that your soul in heaven may rest"—and she could not help noting that the men's roistering discord was in marked contrast to the clear phrasing of the musician who accompanied them. Whatever else Jessica might think of Lady Daphne Templeton, she conceded honestly that the woman seemed to be an accomplished pianist, no doubt a most suitable skill for the future Countess of Raeburn. . . .

From across the room Willa glanced up from her sewing and surveyed Jessica with inscrutable brown eyes. "You look tired," she observed laconically. "I've laid out your night things. I'll help you undress."

Wearily Jessica trudged into her bedroom, giving herself up to Willa's silent efficiency, but after she had changed into a ruffled negligee of green silk, she found that she was far too restless to relax, and she wandered back into the sitting room. Willa followed, noting the deep depression that seemed to weigh down her mistress as she slumped into an armchair. The revelry that was only just audible from downstairs seemed to mock Jessica's mood, and she tipped her head backward in a gesture of fatigue, one slim hand reaching up to rub her brow, the pressure of her fingertips a weak balm against the headache tension had planted behind her eyes. Without a word Willa took her station behind the chair and began to massage her temples with smooth, competent strokes.

Even as Jessica relaxed under Willa's skilled ministrations she wondered at the woman's silence. She realized with a pang that her growing fondness for Claire had made her less dependent on her maid for companionship, and she sincerely hoped she had not unwittingly offended her old friend in some way. For days now, Willa had been behaving . . . strangely, as if preoccupied with something other than her duty. She was watchful and wary in Jessica's presence, and she had begun to disappear at odd hours. The previous afternoon, when the women had ventured out into the snow to watch Raeburn and the other men of the house party skating on the pond behind Renard Chase, the usually conscientious Willa was nowhere to be found, and Jessica had had to recruit one of the housemaids to carry her fur rug for her. When Flora Talmadge, noting the substitution, frowned a reproof and remarked on Willa's absence, Lady Daphne had looked bored, and Claire had suggested with a teasing smile that perhaps the girl was off somewhere pursuing a flirtation. Jessica could only shrug lightly. Nothing would have pleased her more than to think that her friend had found some good, kind man to care for, but there was no way she could make herself believe such a happy discovery was behind Willa's uncharacteristic behavior. Jessica knew the gleaming look of love, and that light was conspicuously absent from the maid's round face.

Jessica's hand, displaced by Willa's, dropped away from her forehead and skimmed down her cheek and throat to stroke wistfully over her breast. Not all her flagging spirits derived from her fear of Mason or her concern for Willa. Jessica knew she was suffering a very real sense of loss because she had begun to wean her daughter. Ironically, the wrenching break she had feared had been forced upon her not by Raeburn but by time. Lottie was over eight months old now, alert and inquisitive and utterly fascinated by the strange new implements the nursery maids were using to feed her. Even as Jessica smiled tenderly at the sight of her child's tiny fingers clumsily learning to manipulate cup and spoon she felt jealous anguish that she was no longer vitally necessary to her daughter's continued existence. Just now when Jessica had gone up to check on little Charlotte, the maid had rebuffed her with a polite but firm, "Hush, she's asleep," and Jessica had grasped the painful fact that except for twice a day now, when the baby was brought down to her for her morning and evening feedings, the maids were more important to the child than she was.

And soon even those two feedings would no longer be necessary. . . . Lottie would become the exclusive responsibility of the nursery staff, and such she would remain until she was of an age to acquire a governess. Her contact with her mother would consist of short, stiff duty visits conducted under the stern gaze of a nurse, with all the protocol of a royal levee, and if Jessica dared venture into the cloistered confines of the children's quarters on the third floor, she would be made to feel an intruder.

Jessica desperately needed to talk to someone, to be reassured that she was not truly losing her child. "Willa," she asked, reluctant to break the silence, "do all mothers feel this

122

way, know this—this pain as their children begin to grow away from them?''

"I wouldn't know, Miss Jess," Willa said tersely. There was no break in the motion of her soothing fingers, but her very composure was a reproach. "I never had a mother."

Jessica's eyes screwed shut, and she cursed her tactlessness, her clumsy words that dredged up tortured memories Willa must pray to forget utterly, memories of her wretched childhood and her drunken brute of a father. Jessica's thoughts returned longingly, gratefully, to her own mother, the love they had shared when she herself was little more than an infant. Poor Willa, never to have known such love. . . . From the deepest recesses of her mind Jessica could conjure up a vision of bright green eyes smiling tenderly down on her cradle, a soft voice crooning a lullaby. That, of course, had been in the days before hunger and worry and too many babies in too short a time had dimmed those shining eyes and turned Jessica's mother into a near-mindless drudge incapable of any emotion save weary indifference. Jessica stared down at her clenched fists. At least she was fortunate enough to remember her mother as she once had been. Her father's unceasing lust had robbed her younger brothers and sisters not only of their mother's presence, but also of her love while she yet lived. Jessica hoped their new stepmother was kind to them.

She sighed bitterly. Brooding was a futile exercise in self-indulgence, and it accomplished nothing. She recalled with surprise Raeburn's passing reference to her family. Far more often than she had thought anyone suspected, she envisioned the home she had broken away from when she eloped so scandalously with Andrew; she could not help wondering how her brothers and sisters fared, whether any of the older girls were married now, perhaps already expecting children of their own, or if the boys had been apprenticed in some worthy trade. She blamed their estrangement on her father, and she knew she would never forgive him for the hypocritical denunciation he had made from the pulpit, admonishing her—but, significantly, never Andrew—for her so-called "surrender to the tyranny of the flesh." She was realistic enough to admit now that wherever the fault lay, after all this time there was no point in attempting to reestablish contact with her siblings. They were strangers, utterly divorced by the life she lived in a world as alien to them as the court of the Grand Turk; if she were to borrow the crested Raeburn carriage and descend on their quiet village like Lady Bountiful, rustling with silk and lace, she would only embarrass and upset them. No, it would be far kinder if she simply stayed away.

Her bright eyes dulled, grew bleak. She was alone now, more alone than she had ever been before in her life. She had lost her husband, her family; her child was growing away from her. Now for some mysterious reason even her closest friend seemed wary of her confidence. Of all the people in the world that Jessica loved, there was only one whom she felt certain she could depend upon in time of trial—and even he owed his first loyalty to another woman. . . .

Jessica's troubled ruminations were interrupted by a soft knock on the door. As soon as Willa answered it Claire flounced into the room, Jessica's portfolio in her hands. Her red curls tumbled merrily about her face as she declared with a bright smile, "Oh, good, you're still awake! The party seemed to drag on forever; I think Daphne must have played every carol written since the Restoration! I wanted to talk to you, but I was afraid you might have gone to bed already. In the drawing room you seemed . . . tired or something. Are you unwell?"

Jessica shrugged with forced levity as she motioned to the chair beside her own. "I have a slight headache, that's all."

"Oh, you poor thing," Claire said sympathetically, "headaches can be the very devil, can't they?" She hesitated, frowning at Jessica's pallor. "You ought to be in bed, and I

124

shouldn't be bothering you. I only came by to bring you your sketchbook. I noticed that you had left it downstairs. I knew you would never dream of doing so, so I showed your drawings to Mister Mason—just to get his opinion, you understand. Doesn't he strike you as rather an odd friend for Lord Crowell to have? There's something about him, I'm not sure what, unless it's those yellow eyes of his. . . . But he seems to have made a conquest of Aunt Talmadge, and he did appear most impressed with what you'd—''

When she saw Jessica staring mutely at her with wide, shocked eyes, Claire broke off, then stammered lamely, ''I—I'm sorry if you didn't want me to do that, Jess. It's just that I thought you'd be interested in what a real artist had to say about your work.'' Still Jessica did not speak, and Claire misinterpreted the reason for her silence. She said awkwardly, ''Forgive me. You need to rest. We—we can talk later.'' She turned as if to leave.

Jessica shook herself out of the catalepsy that had gripped her momentarily, that freezing terror of discovery. What difference did it make if Mason had seen her sketches? They revealed nothing. Those gentle portraits of her daughter and Claire bore little resemblance to Eryinys' spiteful caricatures. She was allowing her guilt to overcome her good sense.

Jessica gazed up remorsefully at Claire. The girl had obviously been longing for a chance for a quiet coze, and now she thought that Jessica was angry with her. Jessica shook her head. ''Oh, Claire, don't run off like that. I know you meant well; it's just that I'm a little . . . sensitive about my drawings. Please sit down and talk to me. A chat will do my headache far more good than bed. I beg you, stay and keep me company.'' She glanced at Willa, who had resumed the mask of the well-trained servant, retreating to her corner where she picked up her sewing basket and began hemming new diapers for Lottie. ''Would you care for some refreshment?''

At Jessica's overture, Claire brightened. With a mock groan of repletion she settled into the armchair next to Jessica's and giggled, "Lud, Jess, no more food, please! I shall become as fat as—as Lord Crowell if I continue eating the way I have these last few days. I can't imagine what wizardry you have performed on the cook, to make her quit burning everything the way she usually does. Whenever Aunt Talmadge has tried to instruct the woman on proper methods of roasting and baking, for some reason she seems to resent the interference. . . ."

Jessica's fine black brows lifted as she considered Flora's probable manner of "instruction." If the cook had any spirit at all, she would undoubtedly feel goaded into doing exactly the opposite of whatever Flora told her. . . . Aloud she suggested, "I rather imagine that Cook is indeed somewhat sensitive to any challenge to her authority. It's only natural. After all, the kitchen is her realm, her domain, just as the drawing room is yours. Anyone from the family who ventures belowstairs is crossing a border into foreign territory, and they may not necessarily be . . . welcome."

"But you seem welcome enough," Claire said, a puzzled line forming between her velvety eyes.

Jessica smiled ironically. "That's because I am one of them." She thought of the deference with which the cook and her helpers had received her lately, a marked contrast to their thinly disguised scorn when she first came to the Chase. In the past year and a half, their attitude had reversed itself completely. Sometimes Jessica wondered if the staff accepted her now because she was Lottie's mother—for her tiny red-haired daughter had engaged the affections of all the household—or if the change had been in herself. Had the servants decided to welcome her because she in turn had ceased to regard them with wary and defensive hostility? She shrugged mentally and added with gentle emphasis, "It's abovestairs that I am out of place. . . ."

Claire exclaimed impatiently, "Oh, Jess, don't say things like that! I thought you'd got over feeling that way. You're very much a part of this family, and you're far more of a lady than—than old Daphne, for all that her father was a duke."

Jessica sighed. "Thanks, Claire. But you really shouldn't speak that way, you know—"

"I don't care!" the girl declared, shaking her bright curls defiantly. Just for a second her expression reminded Jessica irresistibly of Lottie on the verge of bawling, and she felt her heart swell with love for her daughter's young aunt. Claire said, "Daphne Templeton is a pretentious prig, and she makes me sick when she starts talking about the way *she* is going to organize *my* debut . . . if I ever get to have one. You'd think she was one of the patronesses at Almack's, the way she declaims on the 'proper behavior for a girl of my station.' As best I can figure out, that means it's all right to be rude to the servants, and she talks as if Graham had snatched her up before she even came out, when everyone knows that she was on her fourth season when her father died. . . ."

Claire paused, grumbling under her breath. "What Graham sees in her . . . when I asked him, he just mumbled something about Daphne being 'suitable'. . . ." She hesitated again; then she admitted grudgingly, "Oh, I suppose you're right, Jess. Daphne Templeton is Graham's choice, for whatever reason, and if she'll make him happy, he's welcome to her. I just hope no one devises a plan to match me up with that brother of hers!"

Jessica stared, but her instinctive gasp was suddenly drowned out by the clatter of Willa's sewing box hitting the floor, scissors and pins scattering all about. Jessica jerked around. "Willa, what on earth are you doing?" she demanded.

The maid was already on her knees, reaching for a bobbin of thread that had rolled beneath her chair. "Forgive me, Miss Jess," she said, not looking up. Her voice quivered.

"The basket slipped off my lap. I-I'll try not to be so fumble-fingered again."

Jessica watched Willa awkwardly gather up the strewn sewing implements, her movements distracted and clumsy. "Truly, it doesn't matter," she tried to reassure, but the maid did not seem to hear. When Jessica returned her green gaze to Claire, they exchanged a baffled shrug.

After a moment Jessica recalled Claire's earlier words and asked carefully, "Just what did you mean by your remark about marrying Lord Crowell, Claire? Has—has the man been making advances to you? I cannot believe that Graham would sanction such behavior, even in his future brother-in-law."

Claire's face drooped. She muttered, "Oh, Jess, please don't—don't say anything to Graham about this. I mean, His Lordship has done nothing that . . . it's just that sometimes he . . . looks . . . at me, and it makes me . . . afraid. . . ."

"Afraid?" Jessica echoed. "How do you mean?"

The girl shrugged helplessly, staring down at her hands. "I don't know. But I—I keep remembering how Graham has such an obsession about marrying 'suitable' people, and who could be more suited to me than a duke? I've heard he doesn't have much money—but that wouldn't matter much because Graham says I do—and he must be respectable enough if he's the brother of the woman Graham himself is taking to wife. . . ."

She inhaled deeply, then burst out, "But I don't like Lord Crowell! The man's a pig! Most of the time he seems amiable enough, but every now and then, especially after he's been at the port, I see this—this expression in his face, and it worries me." After another hesitation she lifted her chin proudly, and in her soft brown eyes Jessica could read a strange mixture of fear and defiance. Claire said, "I may only be seventeen, Jess, but I know what that look means. I've seen it before. And I tell you now that I would prefer to die than to have to

128

let someone like Lord Crowell touch me, whatever his rank. I know what I want in a man, someone strong and slim with bright blue eyes and a way of talking that makes you feel—'' She broke off abruptly.

Jessica watched with dawning suspicion. "Claire, who are you talking about?"

"Oh . . . no one in particular. Doesn't every girl dream of a handsome gallant?" The girl laughed with unconvincing archness. Her light voice hardened. "It's just that—that when the time comes for me to find a husband, if Graham tries to wed me to a man like Lord Crowell, I'll ask . . . Well, if I really have all this money, I'll find someone who pleases me and elope to Scotland, the way you and Andy did."

Jessica winced. "For God's sake, Claire, what on earth are you saying? Whom do you mean?"

"Oh, no one, Jess! Honestly, I didn't mean anyone special! It's just that I've always thought it must have been so romantic, running away with the man you loved."

Jessica groaned, covering her face with her hands as she remembered much that she had tried to forget. "Romantic?" she snorted.

Claire, watching her with dismay, misinterpreted her distress and stammered, "I'm s-sorry, Jess. I know it must—must hurt you, to think about Andy. But at least the two of you shared something that was exciting and—and beautiful."

Jessica's hands fell away, revealing green eyes that gleamed with bitter fire. "My God, the authors of purple romances have much to answer for!" she declared huskily. Suddenly she found herself spitting out words that she had kept locked inside her for almost two years. "I assure you, Claire, romantic was the one thing that ill-starred adventure was not! It was uncomfortable, bounding over roads that had yet to be repaired after the spring rains, and it was expensive, haggling with insolent ostlers for the privilege of hiring a carriage at twice the normal rate, because they knew quite well where

Andrew and I were bound. We dreaded each second we had to stop along the way, for fear Raeburn was in hot pursuit—"

Claire interjected thoughtfully, "As I recall, Graham was so deep in his cups that he could scarce have mounted his horse, much less chased anyone. . . ."

Jessica nodded in acknowledgement, remembering how she had been able to taste the brandy on his hard mouth when he kissed her. . . . She muttered, "Yes. Well, Andrew and I had no way of knowing that." Gulping down a deep breath she said darkly, "When sheer exhaustion at last forced us to stop in our flight, the first inn we came to refused to take us in. I can still recall the way the landlord looked at me, when Andrew attempted to tell him that I was his sister. . . ."

Her voice trailed off, and glancing at the girl who listened avidly, she decided not to describe the dingy, sordid tavern where they had finally taken shelter, the leering inmates and the strange hands that tried the bedroom doorknob in the middle of the night. She shook her head wryly. "And when we did at last reach Gretna Green . . . Trust me, Claire, when I say that there is nothing romantic about being married in a blacksmith's shop. If you have been raised to believe that a wedding means taking your vows in church, wearing lace and singing hymns, pledging yourselves before God and all your friends—then by contrast, leaping over the anvil seems sacrilegious and silly and . . . and degrading."

Claire wrinkled her nose, and Jessica could see that the girl still did not understand the essence of what she was trying to tell her. "But, Jess," she asked innocently, "could the lack of music and bridal finery really matter so much, as long as you became Andy's wife?"

Jessica smiled thinly, sardonically. "But that's just it, Claire," she said. "Andrew and I knew that we were married— under Scottish edict, all that is required is a declaration in the presence of witnesses—but despite the law, when we returned to England, society looked upon me not as Andrew's true wife, but as the parson's brat, the conniving harlot who had seduced him. . . ."

Claire's white skin grew whiter, showing up the faint freckles that were almost invisible. "Oh, Jess," she said miserably, "surely you don't mean that—"

Jessica's patience was rapidly vanishing in the face of the girl's persistent naiveté, and she knew that a second longer, and the words she had tried to avoid would be ripped from her throat. She could not do that to Andrew's sister, whom she loved. Slowly she crossed the room to the window, where she pulled back the drape and stared out into the night. Moonlight glimmered on the freshly fallen snow like antique satin, and she was astonished to see the same light gleaming on the pale hair of the large, solitary figure whose restless strides slashed the virginal blanket raggedly, like a dull knife.

"Please, Claire," Jessica rasped, trying to speak normally as she gazed down at him, wondering what agitation had driven him out into the cold and the dark to wander about like a damned spirit. "Please, Claire," she repeated, "I don't want to talk about this anymore. I—I only want you to understand that you must not even make jokes about eloping with a man. Such talk is . . . unseemly."

Behind her Claire recognized the dismissal in Jessica's words. She murmured contritely, "I'm truly sorry I distressed you. I didn't mean to. I was—I was just . . . curious." She stared at Jessica's rigid back, then with a sigh she turned to leave. After a second, Jessica heard Willa close the corridor door firmly behind the girl.

As Jessica watched Raeburn's aimless meandering below she wondered with a certain dread what he would make of Claire's probing questions. She prayed the girl would not repeat them elsewhere, just as she hoped fervently that they had been prompted by nothing more critical than adolescent inquisitiveness, and not some crackbrained notion of . . .

Jessica trembled with apprehension. She knew that Claire

was growing up far more rapidly than her brother credited, but still . . . She shook her head impatiently. No, of course not, she was imagining things. Claire had not left Renard Chase since last fall, there was no man nearby for whom she might have conceived an ill-advised *tendre*. Had Jessica thought there was any real danger that Claire might have formed such an attachment, she would do everything in her power to scuttle it before Raeburn found out; if such a step became necessary to quash the girl's romantic fantasies, Jessica would overcome her own scruples and tell her the rest of the story of her short marriage. She would betray Andrew in order to save Claire.

Despite the pain such revelations would cause her personally, Jessica knew that if it were required, she would not hesitate to tell Claire bluntly that Andrew's passionate, all-consuming love for her had died a very quick death. When her husband realized that the only way he could overcome the ostracism of society and regain the position he had occupied since birth was to join with the others against her, his wife, he had willingly taken their side. When the *ton* made it clear that they regarded Jessica as little better than a whore, Andrew concurred with their judgment and began to treat her accordingly. . . .

Jessica watched Raeburn hungrily as he strode along the slushy drive, the lines of his powerful body lithe and compelling even through the masking folds of his long greatcoat. In the moonlight she could just make out the little cloud of steam his hot breath formed around his mouth, and she remembered with an almost physical ache the feel of that breath, that mouth caressing her face, her skin. . . .

She must not let herself think of him in this way, she chided herself angrily; he was not hers. . . . She supposed she ought to be laughing at the cruel irony of it all, that despite the way he had assaulted her on the day they met, in the end, after she married Andrew, Raeburn himself had been the only one who had not despised her, the only man who had tried to defend her against the strictures of society—but she had not understood. She had thought him as bad or worse than all the rest, and afterward when she lashed out at those who had rejected her, she had made him the target of her crudest revenge. The shreds of her lacerated self-respect had blinded her to his worth, and they had not fallen away from her eyes, revealing the truth, until now, when it was far, far too late.

With steps weighted with remorse, she turned away from the window, dragging the drapery after her, her fingers strangely reluctant to release the plush velvet. The movement flashed an irregular triangle of yellow light that reflected on the snow below, attracting the attention of the man who walked there, and he turned iron-colored eyes upward to stare at her window. He was still standing there, his booted toes buried in the edge of a snowbank, his hands clenched deep in his pockets, long after the curtain had dropped back heavily into place.

Chapter Six

"Mrs. Foxe," Lady Daphne called softly, one white hand snaking out of the library door to capture Jessica's arm with surprising strength as she passed by in the corridor. "I wonder if I might have a word with you?"

Jessica hesitated, puzzled. Up till now, Raeburn's fiancée had avoided speaking to her whenever possible, the discreet silence almost a palpable barrier between them. She said uncertainly, "I'm sorry, my lady; perhaps another time. I was just on my way to see my daughter for a few moments before I have to change for the excursion this afternoon."

Daphne's mouth thinned, as if she were unused to being opposed. She said curtly, "I'm sure the nurse can attend to the child's needs for now. It is imperative that we talk, you and I." She drew Jessica into the musty room that was lighted only by the fire in the grate, and after closing the door firmly behind her, she waved to a chair. "Sit down, please."

Jessica remained standing. "Lady Daphne," she protested, "when we return from the woods, it will almost be Lottie's bedtime. Nowadays the hours I have to spend with my child are extremely limited, and I—"

The other woman interrupted impatiently. "I hardly think a few moments will encroach greatly upon your—your maternal duties. I must speak to you privately. More than once I have sent my maid to request that you call on me, but each time the . . . person who serves you has said that you were otherwise occupied." She frowned slightly, obviously amazed at the very idea of such a snub.

Jessica heard that brief but telling pause before she mentioned Willa, and it angered her. How easy judgment was for someone like Daphne, who had never known hunger or privation of any sort, had never been brutalized to satisfy some man's perverted whim. . . . Jessica resented the woman's smug sanctimony, and she could well imagine how Willa, deeply sensitive behind the bland facade of her round face, would have reacted to her imperious summonses. Now that Jessica was busy with household affairs, her hours of privacy in her quarters, especially those fleeting moments when, her friend serving as sentry, she was able to work on her cartoons, were increasingly rare. Raeburn's surveillance had made the correspondence with Clerkenwell difficult, just as John Mason's uncanny insight had made her fearful of exposure. The man seemed to be showing an unusual interest in her as a person—were the idea not so ludicrous, she might almost think he was pursuing her—but Jessica avoided him whenever she could and continued to cloister herself behind closed drapes with her battered tin casket and her drawing materials, driven to recklessness by the ever-growing certainty that her days at Renard Chase were numbered.

Surprisingly she now found that her greatest obstacle was the effort necessary to summon up the rage and sense of social injustice that had inspired her pen in the past; instead of vitriolic caricatures, her fingers had a distressing tendency to sketch small, affectionate portraits of the man she loved, portraits she had to kiss and consign to the fire. . . . While she labored, she always instructed the vigilant Willa to deal with interruptions as she saw fit—and if it pleased the girl to rebuff Lady Daphne's rather haughty personal maid, then so be it. . . .

Jessica could not suppress the faint gleam of triumph that flickered in her green eyes at the realization that for once she had caught out her punctilious rival in a breach of etiquette, but her voice remained steady as she suggested mildly, "My lady, I regret that the many demands upon my time of late have discommoded you. But if I might be so bold, I'd like to point out that since you were the one who sought an audience with me, it was incumbent upon you to arrange your schedule to suit my convenience."

Daphne's sallow cheeks reddened at this observation, and her jaw dropped, quickly closing again as she bit back whatever retort she had been about to make. Watching the soft white fingers that clenched and twisted the muslin of her skirt until the flimsy fabric was in danger of being shredded, Jessica suddenly wished grimly that she had held her tongue. She was deliberately baiting the woman, and she had promised Raeburn she would try to get along with his betrothed. The unaccustomed reticence Daphne had heretofore displayed was but a fragile parole against the future, one that could hardly be depended on if Jessica herself did not observe it. With a sigh Jessica said, "Since I am here now, perhaps you'll tell me what you wanted to talk to me about."

Lady Daphne regarded her warily until she at last recognized that the truce was still in effect—for the moment, at any rate. She nodded brusquely and said, "Sit down."

Jessica bristled at her manner. She thought irritably, You'd think she owned the place; then, cringing, she reminded herself that in a few short months, when Lady Daphne became Raeburn's countess, she would do just that. . . . With reluctant resignation, Jessica settled onto a straight, high-backed chair, holding herself stiffly. She had no idea what Daphne wanted, but the physical discomfort of her tense posture was a constant reminder that she must not relax her guard either. Outwardly placid, she gazed at Lady Daphne, waiting for her to speak.

Now that the amenities had been resumed, Lady Daphne seemed in no great hurry to break the uneasy silence. Her light blue eyes narrowed as they skimmed over Jessica's slim figure, evaluating her, studying her with impersonal curiosity as if to deduce her origins—as if, Jessica thought acidly, she were a porcelain figurine produced without a trademark. The silence thickened and lay as heavily on the air as the dank smell of old paper and library paste that the crackling fire could not dispel. Still Daphne did not speak. Jessica began to suspect that she was being challenged in some way, that Daphne was daring her to speak first, like a child attempting to outstare its fellow. Losing patience with juvenile games, Jessica made a restless gesture and said tightly, "My lady, if you have nothing you wish to say, there are some rather pressing household duties that require my presence just as soon as I have seen my daughter. . . ."

Daphne's smug smirk told Jessica instantly that she had given her the opening she sought. "Of course; your duties," the woman murmured. "You have been supervising the operation of the household since your return here, have you not?"

Knowing full well that Daphne was as cognizant of the arrangements as she herself was, Jessica shook her head. "I've helped out only for the last couple of weeks. Graham thought Mrs. Talmadge might need some assistance . . . for the holidays, you understand."

Daphne nodded approvingly. "Then you do realize that your position is only temporary?"

"Naturally," Jessica said. "I've never imagined nor wished it to be otherwise."

Daphne's thin lips twitched into a semblance of a smile as she declared archly, "Mrs. Foxe, you have no idea how you have eased my mind. I was fearful that Graham had led you to believe you would be allowed to remain in charge permanently, certainly an enviable position in a residence of this grandeur. I thought that most remiss, even rather cruel, of him." She paused for emphasis, and her voice grew husky.

"For of necessity, once we are married, the situation will . . . alter completely."

Subtle as a bludgeon, Jessica judged drily. She said, "You need have no fear, my lady; I will gladly turn over the keys to you anytime you wish. I have no desire to encroach upon even the slightest of your perquisites. They hold no appeal for me."

As that prim little speech left her lips Jessica's long black lashes fluttered down over her cheeks, and she directed her gaze down at her hands, folded with deceptive demureness in her lap. She repeated in sardonic silence, No, my fine Lady Daphne, your rights do not appeal to me—except for the one that I suspect entices you least: the right to sleep with Graham Foxe. . . .

Lady Daphne looked frankly skeptical. "Are you quite sure?" she probed. "I should think any woman would be delirious with joy at the prospect of having control of a property such as Renard Chase." She glanced about her, admiring the interior of the dark library, the scrolled ceiling highlighted by the wavering firelight, the high arched windows, and her expression softened. Suddenly Jessica recognized the look she had seen on Daphne's face in the drawing room several nights before, the look that she had thought was love: so it was, of a kind—but it was not, as Jessica had achingly misinterpreted, an affection, a longing for the man with whom Daphne intended to spend the rest of her life. Rather it was a desire for his house. . . .

Daphne murmured, "I know I have admired Renard Chase since the first time I saw it, some years ago when I stopped here overnight with my father and brother. I was very young, but I remember even then wondering what it would be like to be mistress of all this."

Her fingers stroked pensively over the Jacobean embroidery embellishing her chair. She seemed to have forgotten to whom she was speaking. She mused, "Odd though you may think me, sometimes I regret that our sex is so unsuited to the independent life; it seems unfair that even an ambitious woman has no alternative to marriage, when men are so . . . so . . ." She shuddered delicately. "Yet I suppose the indignities a married woman is forced to endure may well be worthwhile if in return she gains such a prize as this." Her gaze retraced the room. "So lovely," she breathed. "By comparison, Crowell Hall . . . it wants renovation, you know, and like our father before him, William declines to spend his competence on anything but drink and—"

She broke off abruptly and peered sharply at Jessica, who gave no sign of having heard that revealing slip. After a moment Daphne relaxed and gushed brightly, "But Renard Chase: the magnificence of its architecture, its size and elegance, the richness of the furnishings, the paintings . . . I ask you bluntly, Mrs. Foxe: how can any woman *not* covet it?"

Jessica listened with dismay to what she guessed must be one of the most revealing speeches Daphne Templeton had ever made. She wondered what impulse had made her speak so candidly to a woman she claimed to despise. Jessica could hardly pretend to be surprised by Daphne's acquisitive and expedient outlook on marriage—it was, after all, the accepted fashion for her class—but still she found infinitely painful the revelation that the future wife of the man she loved regarded him only as a . . . an indignity that had to be endured. Despite the conventions of a society marriage, such an attitude seemed a recipe for disaster. Poor Graham, she thought with wistful sorrow; you're a man of lusty appetites. Will it truly be worth it, do you think, on your wedding night when you have to bed your unwilling but oh-so-suitable bride?

She was finding the conversation increasingly unendurable. Anxious to end it, she said urgently, "My lady, I don't understand why you tell me these things. I am no threat to you. I have no interest in usurping your position as mistress of Renard Chase."

Daphne's thin mouth tightened. "You have lived on your own since your husband's death, Mrs. Foxe. Until Graham found you and brought you here you enjoyed a freedom most women can only dream about. Are you now trying to convince me that you no longer have a taste to be mistress of your own household?"

"Of course I'm not saying that," Jessica responded, her thoughts harking back nostalgically to her tiny cottage in Brighton, where, despite the squalor of their surroundings, she and her dependents had lived in unprecedented liberty, answerable to no one. She said fervently, "More than anything else in the world I should like once more to be in charge of my own life—but, I repeat, I do not seek my independence at your cost. You are entirely welcome to Renard Chase!"

It is only its master that I want. . . . The words reverberated unspoken in Jessica's brain; then she chided herself sternly. Stop it! she thought: you are fast becoming as puling and maudlin as a heroine in one of Claire's romances. With a deep, racking breath, Jessica said huskily, "Lady Daphne, I still do not understand what it is that you fear from me. How can I possibly threaten you or your position? I am only the widow of Graham Foxe's brother; you are going to be his *wife.*"

For several moments Daphne gazed at Jessica with a blind and vacant expression that indicated her mind was elsewhere. She seemed to be trying to come to some crucial decision. At last her sparse lashes quivered and she again looked sharply at Jessica, her thoughts framed. Flashing a smile of patent insincerity, Lady Daphne said coolly, "I think you misunderstand the situation, Mrs. Foxe. I do not fear you—there is, after all, no way that one such as yourself can harm me—but I do regard you as something of an . . . annoyance."

She leaned forward in her chair, and her voice roughened

with insinuation. "I will pay you the compliment of speaking frankly: I do not like you and you do not like me. That is hardly extraordinary considering our utterly disparate stations and backgrounds, but in normal circumstances our lack of charity would be of little significance because the two of us would be most unlikely ever to meet. . . . Unfortunately, the circumstances can hardly be called normal. Because my fiancé's late brother was enticed into a rash marriage, which can only be regarded as a shocking misalliance, you and I must now meet as equals, relations—and I do not think either of us is overpleased with the situation."

"You are too kind, my lady," Jessica drawled, secretly amused at the woman's candor. If Daphne had hoped that her words would make her uncomfortable, she had failed. "What you say is all too true—but I confess I still do not understand the point you are endeavoring to make."

High spots of color painted Daphne's cheeks as she said tersely, forcefully, "The point, Mrs. Foxe, is that despite Graham's regrettable indulgence regarding you, and despite the fact that he was willing to acknowledge your brief marriage to his brother, I consider you encroaching and common, an upstart of decidedly dubious morals, and a most unwholesome influence on the mind of an impressionable young person like Claire—or, for that matter, on the children I of course expect someday to have. Bluntly, I do not want you in my house after I am married."

It was Daphne's casual mention of children that cut through Jessica's studied indifference, engendering in her breast a fierce and blinding anger. To imply that she would harm any child of Graham's . . . The truce had well and truly expired, the battle was resumed with a vengeance, and nothing could make her sit quiescent under an assault such as that. Her hands clenched the arms of her chair and she took a deep breath to steady herself to return the salvo.

"Fair enough," she murmured evenly, green eyes sparking. "I had been expecting something like this. . . . My dear Lady Daphne, let me return your compliment and say that I consider you a cold, pretentious prig whose insensitivity and affectations will undoubtedly make life at Renard Chase a continual misery for those unfortunate enough to fall under your authority. Believe me, I have no desire to subject myself or my daughter to the kind of treatment we will certainly suffer if we must live under the same roof as you, and I assure you that we will go from these premises as quickly as we can, today if possible. We require only enough time to pack."

With the air of one who had burnt her bridges, Jessica settled back into her chair and regarded her opponent steadily. She noted with surprise that the triumph she had expected to read in Daphne's face was lacking, replaced by an expression of puzzled uncertainty. "Go?" Daphne echoed, blinking. "Alone? Now?"

"Of course now," Jessica retorted sharply, impatiently. "Did you think I would remain here and endure your insults in silence?"

"I had rather thought that . . . I was going to suggest an alternative."

"An alternative?" Jessica asked, momentarily distracted. "What do you mean?"

"I thought perhaps—" Daphne began bravely enough, but under Jessica's piercing green gaze she soon floundered. "You are, after all, attractive in a way that appeals to men . . . if a reasonable portion were made available . . . despite your unfortunate . . . a husband might yet be found. . . ."

Jessica stared. She had suspected for months that the ultimate aim of the Foxe family—even Claire, although her motives were kinder—was to marry her off, but to have it spelled out so crudely. . . . She closed her eyes and trembled with revulsion, sickened by the very thought of being wed to any man but Graham, having to submit to the embraces of someone she did not want. Groaning, she demanded, "Is this some scheme you have concocted yourself or is"—her voice grew husky as she faced the ultimate betrayal—"is it Graham's idea?"

Daphne scowled, confused by Jessica's lack of enthusiasm. "Mine, I suppose—but I should think you would be delighted at the prospect of a good second marriage. Any woman would. I am not proposing that someone unsuitable be foisted off on you. After all, by dint of your alliance with my fiancé's late brother, you are a family connection—"

Jessica snapped sarcastically, "How kind you are, my lady! I don't suppose it ever occurred to you that I have no wish to marry again? Well, I don't—and I won't! I shall take my child and my servant and leave this house as quickly as it may be arranged."

Daphne shook her head in genuine bewilderment. "You think to manage without male protection? Is that possible? Where will you go? How will you live?"

"I am not without resources," Jessica said with obscure dryness.

"You mean you already receive some allowance from your late husband's estate?"

"No," Jessica responded quietly, enjoying a moment of smug satisfaction at the thought that she, the despised plebeian, knew how to cope in circumstances that would leave her wellborn rival utterly helpless. "No, that is not what I meant." She stood up abruptly. "If you will excuse me, I think it is time we terminate this interview. You will want to prepare for the outing this afternoon, and I must return to my room and make my plans."

Lady Daphne bit her lip, suddenly apprehending that this private conversation had been a most unwise move. She had thought only to put the upstart drawing teacher in her place, and instead she had precipitated a scene that Raeburn, who seemed to cherish an unreasoning affection for his sister-in-law and her brat, was bound to resent deeply, when he heard of it. . . . She watched her rival cross the room to the door, her tall, slender figure moving with a confidence and grace that bordered on insolence in one of such common breed. But Jessica Foxe was not common, Daphne suddenly acknowledged with painful, jealous insight; she was something quite out of the ordinary—and Raeburn's anger was bound to fall heavily on anyone responsible for driving her from his home.

With a quavering smile of appeasement, Lady Daphne said lightly, "Mrs. Foxe, I beg you, don't fly up in the boughs over our—our little chat! I didn't mean to anger you. Of course you must not think of leaving Renard Chase, not now! Why . . . it's almost Christmas!"

Jessica hesitated at the door, one slim hand on the knob. When she looked back at Lady Daphne, who regarded her with dread, her eyes were opaque as jade. "Christmas," she drawled slowly, her mouth turning upward in a sardonic smile. "Why, so it is. . . . I had almost forgotten. Well, then, my lady, I reckon I must wish you the joy of the season." The bitter humor in her voice lingered in the library long after the sound of her footsteps had faded away.

"Here now, Jess." Raeburn laughed, wheeling his gray stallion away from Lord Crowell, who was talking to his sister and Claire, and moving back along the line of vehicles to the second sleigh, "everyone else has offered an opinion. Tell us, what do *you* think of the log we've selected?" His eyes glinted with a warmth that belied the frosty air.

Beneath her voluminous cape Jessica shrugged and smiled uncertainly, the slight movement of her mouth tickling her cheeks against the rich sable that trimmed the hood. "Well, it's—it's big enough to fill even the fireplace in the great hall, of course," she ventured, glancing at the large oak tree that workmen had felled and were now stripping of branches, "but won't it be far too green to burn?"

"A Yule log is supposed to be green," Raeburn explained with good-natured impatience. "It lasts longer that way, and the longer it burns, the more good luck it brings. I thought everyone knew that. Haven't you ever had one before?"

Jessica shook her head. "My father always claimed Yule logs were heathenish."

"That father of yours would make one of Cromwell's roundheads seem a veritable beacon of enlightenment. . . ." Raeburn snorted.

Jessica's forehead wrinkled delicately as she suggested, "Graham, it might be that he is simply too proud to admit that we could never afford—" She broke off her words, blinking with an astonishment that was repeated in Raeburn's expression as suddenly she realized that for the first time in her life she had actually defended one of her father's animadversions. For a moment she pondered the significance of that unprecedented event.

Beside Jessica, John Mason asked, "Then your father is still living, Mrs. Foxe?"

"Of course, sir," Jessica answered tightly. Her newfound tolerance did not seem to extend to the artist, and she thought she had exercised commendable restraint ever since circumstances forced her into close proximity with the man.

She had come away from her interview with Lady Daphne shaking with a burning desire to leave Renard Chase, that very day if possible, but as soon as she reached her own room, Willa had pointed out the rashness of such a scheme. "No matter how much Her fine Ladyship infuriates you, you cannot disappear into the night as you did that other time," her friend had pointed out calmly. " 'Tis the dead of winter now, Miss Jess, and you have a little one to think about. . . ." Reluctantly Jessica had admitted the truth of Willa's words: she was a woman now, not an impulsive girl, and no longer could she evade troubles by simply running away. With a moue of resignation she had begun to change into something suitable for the excursion into the woods.

Jessica had almost pleaded a sudden megrim when she saw the seating arrangements for the short journey. Raeburn and Lord Crowell had chosen to take their horses, and the grooms, footmen, and carpenters required to cut down the tree once it was selected followed along behind on an old sledge that also carried the hamper of refreshments and extra fur rugs. That left Jessica, Claire, Lady Daphne, and John Mason—Flora Talmadge had not been invited—to ride in the two small sleighs. Daphne immediately chose Claire as her partner, claiming it would give her the chance for a quiet coze with her future sister-in-law—"We need to discuss the gown you're to wear when you're my bridesmaid, my dear!"—and Jessica had been forced to share the cramped confines of the second vehicle with a man she both feared and detested.

"Your father?" Mason prompted again, when Jessica, who had sulked all during the drive out to the woods, refused to answer him. "I believe he was a clergyman, was he not?"

"He still is," she said shortly, aware that she was behaving childishly. "His living is a village some miles south of here."

"I see," Mason murmured. "It must be gratifying to find yourself once again situated with your loved ones close at hand."

Jessica bridled. "I hardly think my family can be of much interest to you, sir," she said stiffly, glancing sidelong at him in a way that should have quelled the most obtuse of men.

"On the contrary, Mrs. Foxe," Mason murmured; "anything to do with you is of considerable interest to me. . . ." Before Jessica could react to that provocative statement, he continued smoothly, "Forgive me if I seem overly inquisitive, but I am by nature fascinated by all that goes on around me. The first requirement of an artist is that he be observant—and, surely"—he paused, and, leaning closer, his yellow gaze skimmed over Jessica in a way that brought hot, embarrassed color to her frost-white cheeks—"any man could be excused for taking a very personal interest in a woman as beautiful as yourself."

Jessica's green eyes flew open in horror, and she stared at Mason's gaunt face. "Sir," she gasped, "you are presumptuous! I have never given leave for you to address me so familiarly."

"Does one need leave?" he asked imperturbably, and bony fingers gloved in lavender chamois fumbled for Jessica's hand.

Recoiling in disgust, she gritted through clenched teeth, "Mr. Mason, if Lord Raeburn should notice your effrontery—"

A shuttered look came over Mason's sallow face, and he retreated into his own corner of the open sleigh, but his eyes remained focused balefully on Jessica's hot face. "Oh, come now, my dear woman," he drawled scornfully, "surely you are on . . . intimate enough terms with our host to recognize that for all his unquestioned intelligence, he is not particularly given to *noticing* things! I, on the other hand, make it my practice to be always aware of what is going on about me— and I never forget anything, as some have learned to their regret. . . . If you have any doubts about my powers of observation, you might ask Lord Crowell."

Automatically Jessica glanced toward the lead vehicle and the young duke whose plump body sat uncomfortably on the spirited mare Raeburn had provided for him. Daphne was still chatting with her brother about something, but Claire's attention seemed to have wandered, and she was gazing wistfully at the party of workmen who had denuded the great tree trunk of its branches. When the big drayhorse proved skittish, Tomkins, the head groom, barked out an order and one of his subordinates quickly grasped the bridle before the horse could rear; skillfully he controlled the animal, guiding it into position as they prepared to shift the log onto the flat bed of the sledge. He was an attractive lad, Jessica's artistic eye noted with impersonal appreciation, and for a fraction of a second her attention was diverted by the way the muscles rippled across the young man's shoulders as he tugged on the heavy harness. . . .

"Mrs. Foxe," Mason said sharply, and she returned her gaze to him. Recalling his previous enigmatic remark, she asked, puzzled, "What did you mean about Lord Crowell?"

He shrugged coolly, but when he spoke, there was a definite undertone of menace in his quiet voice. "It can be of no importance to you, madam; do not trouble yourself about it. However, it might be advisable for you to remember that it never pays to underestimate me. . . ." His mouth curled up in an unpleasant grimace that could only be described as a smirk as he elaborated. "Your distinguished brother-in-law underestimates me: he thinks me a pompous nonentity—and yet, in the few short days I have stayed at Renard Chase, I have already observed a number of things that the good earl would undoubtedly find most . . . disturbing were they to be brought to his attention."

Jessica felt the muscles of her face stiffen painfully with the effort to remain politely expressionless as dread welled deep in her throat. She wondered if she were dreaming, if this were a nightmare of some kind; it seemed impossible that this conversation, with its undercurrents of threat and malice could truly be taking place out here, in the snow, with the frosty evergreen-perfumed air biting at her nostrils. "I—I cannot imagine what you are talking about, Mr. M-Mason," she stammered.

"Can't you?" he inquired, watching her intently. Jessica shook her head, refusing to answer his leading question, and after a moment he sighed. "Perhaps I am being unfair. I should not tease you because your feminine intuition has failed you, especially since I have come to value your . . . regard." He paused tantalizingly, then he made a small, significant nod toward the first sleigh. As Jessica followed his gaze he said under his breath, "Considering the obvious closeness of the relationship between you and young Lady Claire, I am surprised that you have not noticed with repugnance that she seems to be directing her affections toward a person most unworthy to receive them."

At the realization that he did not seem to be referring to her secret identity as Erinys, Jessica's relief was profound but short-lived, counteracted at once by his ominous reference to Claire. Shivering at his confirmation of something she had suspected for weeks, she demanded, "Who is it?" She noted with odd detachment that she did not for an instant doubt the validity of Mason's statement. The man was too concerned with his own self-interest to risk making slanderous charges that he could not support; even his cartoons, crude and cruel though they were, always grew out of at least a kernel of truth. "Claire's seen no one but the family for months. Where could she possibly have found someone to fall in love with?"

"Perhaps . . . the stables?" Mason suggested.

Jessica choked. "The stables!" Then she quickly stifled her gasp of dismay lest it alert anyone else in the party to the extraordinary conversation taking place in the rear vehicle. "You mean she has formed an attachment for one of the *grooms*?"

"It is not unprecedented," Mason drawled, his smile twitching slyly. "Think, Mrs. Foxe: the highborn maiden, her beauty just now blossoming; the servant, a lusty young animal with broad shoulders and that engaging manner so peculiar to the Irish . . ."

Under the curtain of her lashes Jessica glanced toward the groom who had attracted her attention earlier: O'Shea . . . Fred O'Shea, that was his name, she suddenly remembered from the occasion when he had escorted Claire and her on their search for holly and mistletoe. At the same time she also recalled that she had caught those Celtic blue eyes of his surveying her figure with a boldness and self-assurance that had bordered on insolence. And now Claire . . . "My God," Jessica groaned, "Raeburn will kill her."

Mason leaned closer to Jessica, until she could feel his breath moist on her face, and his hand groped for hers once more. "Yes, I expect His Lordship would be most violently angry. . . . In fact, I'd suggest that perhaps it might be prudent of you to ensure that he does not have occasion to learn of this sorry—"

"Jess, Mr. Mason!" Claire interrupted, calling out gaily as she turned in her seat to stare back at the second coach. "What on earth can the two of you be discussing so earnestly? I declare, you seem quite in another world!"

Jessica jerked away from Mason, blushing guiltily as the other members of the party followed Claire's gaze. She knew that to them the whispered conversation must have appeared to be some kind of flirtation, and she watched stricken as Lord Crowell, who had finally moved away from the forward sleigh, chuckled ribaldly and winked. When her eyes passed over Daphne, whom she expected to be primly disapproving, she was surprised to find that lady nodding with smug approval. She dared not look at Raeburn.

In embarrassment Jessica returned her gaze to her friend, whose red curls bounced in innocent splendor beneath her fur-lined hood. Claire grinned back in amusement. Unable to speak, Jessica then glanced helplessly at Mason, who shook his head surreptitiously. "We'll talk later," he murmured under his breath, and as she settled back against the cushions Jessica wondered how three small words could carry so much threat.

Just how much of a threat she had no idea, until late that evening. After dinner, when the women rose to leave the table, Raeburn stopped her. "Jessica," he called, a note of unusual formality in his deep voice, "I would very much appreciate your meeting with me in my study in, say, twenty

151

minutes. A matter has come up that requires some . . . discussion between the two of us.''

"Of course, Graham," Jessica replied, puzzled, and her confusion had not yet abated when she sat in a puffy armchair, sipping a cup of chocolate. He stood stiffly before her, massive and powerful, his hands plunged deep into the pockets of his blue velvet jacket, and she had to tilt her head far backward on her slender neck to watch him as he announced baldly, "John Mason has applied to me for permission to marry you."

Jessica stared. "He—he *what*?" She croaked, almost tipping her cup into her lap.

"He has asked leave to court you," Raeburn repeated, peering down at her. "Didn't you know? I was given to understand—Daphne indicated that she thought—that his request would not be entirely . . . unexpected."

With trembling fingers Jessica set her chocolate on a side table. Ever since that disturbing conversation with Mason, she had anticipated that he would demand some kind of payment as blackmail for his continued silence about Claire's intrigue with the Irish groom: she had thought he might ask for money or, more likely, considering his sycophantic nature, some kind of entrée into the loftier circles of the *ton*—although how, Jessica had wondered ironically, he deluded himself that one such as she would be able to arrange those introductions . . . But *marriage*? Had he conspired with Lady Daphne to gain that "reasonable" dowry she had hinted at so unsubtly earlier that day? The man was mad!

"Unexpected?" Jessica echoed. "Of course it's unexpected! How dare he presume that I . . . Well, I trust you told him exactly what you thought of his—" Shivering with disgust, she broke off, unable to frame the words. Tightly she gripped the arms of the chair, trying to compose herself, to regulate her breathing, as she waited for Raeburn to assure

152

her that he had consigned Mason and his loathsome proposition to perdition. . . .

Raeburn said nothing.

When his silence penetrated her troubled brain, slowly, fearfully, Jessica lifted slanting emerald eyes to meet his gaze. Aghast, she saw the hot color creeping upward over his hard jaw, and her eyes widened in disbelief until they were almost round. Oh, God, was he also a party to this arrangement? "Graham," she whispered thickly, gutturally, forcing the sounds upward through a throat that suddenly felt as if it were filled with hot glass, "Graham, you did not tell him you—you approved his suit, did you?"

Her expression tormented him, but resolutely Raeburn's face remained rigid, his lips hardly moving as he acknowledged, "I did not reject him out of hand, if that is what you mean."

"Oh, Graham, how could you!" she cried in dismay, staring at him as if she had never seen him before. He was doing it, she thought in anguish, the very thing she had lived in dread of these past months; he was ridding himself of her unwanted presence by palming her off on the first man, no matter how disagreeable, who showed an interest. . . . She realized now with sickening insight that she had never until this moment truly believed that he would try to force her into another man's arms—if not because of that nameless attraction between the two of them, then at least for the sake of Andrew's memory.

"How can you betray me so?" she rasped, searching his stern face for some sign of remorse at what he was suggesting. "I was your brother's wife. I *loved* him. John Mason is old and—and unattractive, both in person and personality, and now, after Andrew, you expect me to—to agree to share his bed, submit to his—his . . ." She screwed her eyes shut against the vision that assailed her, Mason's skinny shanks protruding obscenely from beneath a long nightshirt, his greedy fingers clutching clumsily at her breasts, her . . . She shook so hard that she was afraid she might vomit. "Graham," she pleaded weakly, tremulously, "I beg of you, do not do this to me," and she dropped her face into her hands.

Raeburn stared down at her bent head, consternation marring his broad features as he took in the defenselessness of her posture, her attitude. In all the time he had known her, he had never before seen her so dispirited, even abject, and he did not think he liked her unprecedented state of mind. The Jess he knew and admired had always been tenacious, a fighter, refusing to concede defeat long after any sane person would have abandoned the field. Often her obstinacy had infuriated him almost to violence, and in the beginning he had wondered how Andrew kept from strangling her—until it had dawned on him that she might be different with Andrew, that in the most intimate moments of their marriage she might have shown his brother a softness, a tenderness that Raeburn, whose life, for all its passion, had been singularly devoid of the gentler emotions, could only guess at. . . .

His gray eyes narrowed as he gazed at Jessica, noting the way the firelight shimmered iridescently on her blue-black hair and shadowed the deep cleft between her breasts, and he knew that he was jealous, resentful of everyone who had some prior claim on Jessica's affections. He was jealous of poor Andrew, envious of his dead brother's pathetically few months of happiness with his wife; amazingly he realized he was even jealous of little Lottie, because that tiny red-haired sprite was the recipient of all her mother's unstinting love and devotion. But most of all, Raeburn admitted with a stifled groan, he was violently and unreasoningly jealous of not just John Mason, but all the other men who would ever see and want Jessica, men who were free, who had no previous entanglements that prevented them from honorably courting her, wooing her, and—someday, for some incredibly fortunate man—winning her. . . .

Hearing the strangled sound Raeburn made, and unaware of the struggle going on inside him, Jessica lifted her eyes to his and whispered hoarsely, "Graham, I know you wish to be rid of me, but please, please do not force me to accept Mr. Mason."

He gaped at her, wondering how she could be so blind. With a tremendous effort he kept his voice steady as he reassured, "No one is trying to get rid of you, Jess, or force you into anything against your will. We only want you to be happy. Although I wish most sincerely that you and my future wife could deal together more amicably, I am not so unobservant or insensitive that I don't realize that—"

"*Happy*?" Jessica retorted, answering the one word that had penetrated her shocked mind. Suddenly she jumped to her feet and found herself so close to Raeburn that she had to arch backward to keep from colliding with the hard wall of his body. "You think I would be *happy* with a man who—who . . ."

Raeburn chuckled uncomfortably, trying to swallow his distaste at the very idea of the middle-aged artist living with Jessica, maintaining rights over her person. . . . Dammit, he thought angrily, he was acting the dog in the manger with a vengeance, an attitude he had always detested. No matter what his personal opinion was, he must remain neutral, try not to influence her, lest he prevent her from finding future joy elsewhere. He said stiffly, "The decision is yours alone, Jess, but on reflection you might discover that you could live in surprising harmony with Mason, despite the difference in your ages. After all, the two of you share a—a mutual interest in art. . . ."

In her paper-white face, Jessica's slanting eyes widened until they threatened to fill the universe. "A . . . a mutual . . . interest in . . . in art." She gasped at the unconscious irony of that remark as a giggle tickled the back of her mouth. "With . . . with *John Mason*?" She felt herself begin to shake with tension, and tendrils of her black hair slipped loose from the restraining hairpins and dangled tremulously over her temples, brushing her distended cheeks. "M-mutual interests," she repeated again wildly, aware that she was on the verge of hysteria. "Oh, Graham, if you . . . only . . . knew!" Painfully the words forced their way through her constricted throat, each breath more difficult than the last—and then there were no words as the laughter overwhelmed her.

Raeburn watched in dismay, baffled by her reaction that seemed all out of proportion to the remark that had triggered it. "Jess, for God's sake, what's wrong?" he demanded, self-control flooding back into him as Jessica's so obviously ebbed. Her face only inches from his, she blinked up at him owlishly, and her mouth moved as if she were trying to shape words, but the only sound issuing from between her lips was a series of harsh, mirthless guffaws that chilled him like the scrape of fingernails on slate.

Suddenly he remembered the mysterious correspondence she maintained with someone in Clerkenwell, the convict or whoever. In the face of Jessica's obstinate refusal to explain herself to him, Raeburn had been forced to draw his own conclusions about those letters and packages, and he had at last decided, with undoubtedly more than a soupçon of wishful thinking, that they were part of some charitable endeavor on her part, another of those unfathomable caprices that drove her to succor lame ducks like Willa Brown.

But now he wondered sickeningly if his first suspicion had been right after all, that there had been some unknown man keeping her during that shadowy period in Brighton, some man to whom, out of a sense of obligation, she continued to write clandestinely. Since returning to Renard Chase, Jessica had never once even implied the existence of such a person, yet, knowing the desperation she must have suffered during that year . . . Raeburn felt himself grow chilled with a cold that had nothing to do with the snow on the ground beneath his window. Good Lord, she couldn't be secretly *married*, could she? He shook himself mentally. No, of course not; such an idea was worthy of one of Claire's Minerva novels! Yet, could it be that Mason's proposal had aroused in her such violence because she had already given if not her hand, then her heart elsewhere?

Still Jessica laughed. Raeburn caught her thin shoulders in his large hands and shook her lightly. "Compose yourself, Jess," he ordered in quelling tones; "tell me what's the matter! I only want to help you. Why won't you trust me?" Her eyes were glazed, and she hardly seemed to hear him. Unwilling to resort to slapping, the traditional specific for hysterics, he shook her more vigorously, and his strength made her head snap back hard on her slender neck, loosening her chignon. The motion seemed to jerk her back into awareness. She winced with pain, and the shock of it altered her laughter to racking coughs that subsided with difficulty, until all that remained of her hysteria was her stertorous wheezing.

His hands still heavy on her shoulders, she regarded him accusingly. "You made my neck hurt," she whimpered, too drained and exhausted by that storm of emotions to care that she sounded childish.

"I'm sorry," he murmured, one hand reaching up beneath the heavy curtain of hair slipping free from its pins to massage her nape. Long fingers moved caressingly along the back of her neck, rubbing and prodding, as he searched out the muscles knotted achingly under her silky skin. He could feel the tension in her like a living thing, a snake coiled and ready to stirke. "Relax," he urged soothingly, his free hand sliding down the smooth curve of her back to circle her waist and pull her closer. "Relax, Jess, and just trust me. I promise I won't hurt you, ever again. . . ."

As she stared up at him, mesmerized by the husky balm of his deep voice, her tongue flicked over her dry, parted lips, moistening them, and when his arms tightened irresistibly around her, crushing her breasts against the hard wall of his chest, she watched without thought of protest as his mouth came down hungrily over hers.

She closed her eyes, for the moment mindful only of the feel of his lips and teeth and tongue, his arms, his body, the very size of him that somehow exhilarated at the same time as it overwhelmed. She could savor the brandy still hot in his mouth, smell the musky maleness of his skin as she had done that spring day by the roadside so long before, but she was no longer an innocent girl to be frightened by the intimacies of taste and odor. She was a woman now, one who had gone too long without a man, and she needed much, much more than his kisses.

"Oh, Graham." She sighed with satisfaction when she broke away to catch her breath, leaning her dark head against his chest, her arms wound around him. Her body still tingled where he had stroked it, and even through successive layers of coat, two waistcoats, shirt, and singlet, she could hear his heart thud under her ear. His hands moved restlessly over her.

Suddenly groaning, "My God, what are we doing?" he caught her hands and disentangled them from around his waist. Gently he pushed her away from him. "Please, my dear," he reproved, "we mustn't. We'll regret it later." His voice sounded clouded, like that of a man who had been dragged too soon from a dream.

She was still too drugged by the beguiling pressure of his body against hers to understand. Bewildered, she stared up at him with bemused green eyes. "Graham, I—I don't . . . what are you saying?"

He clenched his hands behind his back and retreated from her. "I'm going to marry Daphne," he said stonily.

Jessica blinked and stammered. "D-Daphne? But . . . but what about . . . y-you and me? We—"

"There is no 'we'!" he interjected sharply. "There is only . . . Daphne and me. I am committed to marrying her, and I cannot go back on my word. You'll have to forgive me, Jess. I never should have kissed you, but you're very beautiful, and I've always . . ." He squared his broad shoulders in a conscious gesture of denial. "I lost control—not that that is any excuse. You are my sister-in-law, and I owe more respect to you . . . and to my brother's memory."

She felt her cheeks flame at the insulting ease of his rejection. She was knowledgeable enough to recognize that only seconds before, he had been as aroused as she, but now, while she still ached with frustration, still struggled to control her ragged breathing, he could stand there so pompously and declare . . . Adjusting the bodice of her dress, she snapped waspishly, "Wouldn't it have been more to the point to call up Andrew's spirit *before* you tried to seduce me?"

Raeburn's eyes narrowed to slits of flint as his gaze moved slowly over her body, noting her high color, her black hair that tumbled about her face in a most abandoned fashion. He paused deliberately at her bosom, where even the stiff bombazine of her gown could not disguise the betraying tautness of her full breasts. "My dear Jessica," he drawled with hateful emphasis, only a faint throatiness in his deep voice denying his apparent composure, "had *I* not chosen to call a halt to the proceedings, I think I would have found that precious little *seduction* was necessary. . . ."

Jessica blanched. Gasping as if he had struck her, she watched the corners of Raeburn's wide mouth curl upward into a smile of mirthless mockery at her discomfiture, and she knew that in a moment he was going to laugh. With a squeal of mortification, she turned on her heel and fled from his study, raven hair flying loose behind her—and as she ran out into the corridor and slammed the door behind her she cannoned directly into the arms of John Mason.

"My dear Mrs. Foxe!" the man exclaimed as his bony

fingers steadied her. "What on earth has happened to you?" He spoke with the same oily deference he always used, but his yellow eyes were flicking with undeniable acuity between Jessica and the still-reverberating door to Raeburn's study. He seemed to miss no detail of her dishevelment. When she did not speak, he murmured, "You appear . . . agitated. I trust nothing untoward has happened to . . . alarm you?"

Jessica stared blankly at his gaunt face, her green eyes wild and unseeing, filled as they were with the lingering images of Raeburn's scorn. "W-what?" she stammered.

Still holding her shoulders, the artist continued smoothly, "Or perhaps I am mistaken and it is something pleasant that excites you, some happy news? Has His Lordship told you of my offer? Could that be it, my dear . . . Jessica?"

She blinked hard, and her vision cleared. She became aware of Mason's grip on her, the tremor that shook him as his hands begun to fondle her upper arms. "P-please, sir," she said with unsteady formality, keeping her voice low lest Raeburn overhear as she tried to pull away. "I regret . . . I hardly think—"

"Then don't think!" he gritted, all traces of his affected amiability vanishing from his sallow features at the first sign of rejection. His voice softened to a hiss. "Don't think about anything but accepting my proposal. There's too much at stake here, and if you turn me down, I promise I shall tell your exalted lover all about you and your little secret, and then you shall learn what regret is all about . . . *Erinys*!"

Jessica stared at him in amazement. That vile little man— and despite his physical stature, she did regard him as a little man, base and petty—was trying to *blackmail* her! He thought her so craven that she would submit to one such as he rather than risk the truth becoming known. The man must be mad! But as Jessica gaped incredulously at Mason, into her turbulent thoughts came two fragments of remembered dialogue— Lord Crowell mumbling sullenly into his wineglass, "Oh,

Johnny sees everything," and Mason himself bragging maliciously, "It never pays to underestimate me"—and she realized that she had stumbled upon the answer to a question that had puzzled her ever since the Templeton party arrived at Renard Chase: the reason why the young duke endured the insolent familiarity of a man he obviously detested. Jessica wondered curiously just what guilty secret Mason had ferreted out about Daphne's brother. She wondered how many other members of the *ton* were paying for his silence. . . .

Unaware of the thoughts buzzing through Jessica's mind, Mason smiled triumphantly. "My dear Jessica," he repeated, tasting the name. "Oh, yes, I know I am going to enjoy dealing with you. . . ." As if to emphasize the impregnability of his position, he released one of her arms, and after pausing to brush a strand of his sandy hair back into place over his bald spot, he deliberately groped for her breast.

The flesh that had swelled in welcome at Raeburn's touch recoiled instantly from Mason's violation, and Jessica's temper flared. Twisting and writhing, she spat, "Oh, God, I loathe you!" as she freed her other arm from his grasp. Fury giving her strength, she swung her hand in a wide arc and slapped him with a force that almost toppled him. As he staggered backward, cursing her, she made good her escape, galloping toward the marble stairs as if some demon pursued her, and she did not quit running until she had reached the serenity and security of the nursery on the third floor.

Chapter Seven

The great clock in the hall had just struck one—or one-thirty or possibly half-past midnight; Jessica had lost count, agitated as she was by the day's events—when she heard the light, hushed sound of slippers on marble in the corridor just outside her sitting room. Looking up from the watercolor on which she had been working fitfully in a futile attempt to sooth her overwrought emotions, she listened with care. Only the family lived in this wing, and she wondered apprehensively if perhaps someone had taken ill and one of the maids had been dispatched for help; then she tensed as she became aware of the deliberate, almost furtive quality of those footsteps. Whoever was out there had no business being abroad in the middle of the night.

Because the culprit was obviously feminine, she felt no real sense of threat, and before she rose to investigate, she automatically went through the procedures she observed whenever she had to leave her work. Although her attention was still concentrated on the noise in the hallway, she swiftly rinsed her brush and dried it on a linen napkin and set lids on the tiny pots of paint that she had mixed; then, wiping her fingers, she pushed back her chair and stood up from the spindly escritoire. With a languorous stretch she slipped her hands under the heavy fall of hair at her nape and lifted it so that her inky tresses flowed unconfined down the back of her woolen night robe. After she had adjusted the robe, cinching the sash tighter about her slim waist, she picked up her candlestick and silently opened the sitting room door.

When she looked out, the corridor was empty and quiet, so still that she might have thought she had imagined those footsteps, were it not for the glow she could see reflected ahead of her on the grim portraits and shining white walls of the picture gallery at the end of hall, a circle of amber lamplight that sunk jerkily out of her view as the person she was following descended the grand staircase. After a moment's hesitation, Jessica flew silently to the top of the stairs. In her haste she bumped into a console table where someone had set out a great kissing bough to be hung in the morning, and one of the apples was knocked loose from the basket of evergreens and mistletoe and fell with a thump to the floor. Jessica froze, clutching her candle. Certain that she had alerted the person she pursued, she listened painfully, but the only sound she heard was the rustle of her satin bed gown about her trembling knees. Taking a deep breath, she continued more slowly along the gallery, and with trepidation she peeked over the rail.

From her vantage point she had an unobstructed view of the main hall with its pillars and statues and archways opening onto the various salons and dining rooms, all distorted and unfamiliar at this foreshortened angle, in the shifting light. But she had no difficulty recognizing the top of Claire's red head as, with a quick glance to either side, the girl—who, damningly, still wore her *eau-de-Nil* dinner dress despite the lateness of the hour—ducked into the unobtrusive green baize door that led to the back of the house, the kitchens and cupboards and pantries, and from thence out to the service yard—and the stables.

As the door closed on Claire's lamp, plunging the great hall into near darkness, Jessica groaned aloud. So Mason had been right, after all. . . . Not for one instant did she try to delude herself that Claire's ultimate destination might be the kitchen, perhaps for a cup of warm milk to help her sleep. Oh, no, the girl was sneaking out of the house like a scullery maid, creeping off to the dark, earthy seclusion of the stables to meet her lover, the Irish groom with the bold blue eyes— and if Raeburn ever found out about this vulgar little intrigue, he'd strangle her with his bare hands. . .

Jessica shivered at the thought of Raeburn's wrath. She had been its victim on one far-too-memorable occasion, but she knew that the violence he had shown her that day by the roadside would be as nothing compared to the rage that would erupt should he discover his beloved little sister tumbling about in the hay with a servant. . . .

Abruptly Jessica broke off that train of thought, disgusted with herself. Why was she automatically assuming that Claire's relationship with Fred O'Shea had already gone too far? No matter how the situation might look, she knew her sister-in-law better than that! She had only to look in the girl's warm brown eyes to read the innocence that still shone unsullied there. Claire was ripe for a flirtation, of course, and, like Andrew before her, willful enough to act rashly out of defiance of her oldest brother's steadfast refusal to admit that she was fast becoming a woman, but she had far too much inherent integrity to embark on a sordid affair just to spite Raeburn. By condemning her on circumstantial evidence, Jessica was wronging the girl, behaving as badly as Flora Talmadge had when she spied on her and Andrew, as badly as John Mason was behaving now.

Jessica shivered. Oh, God, John Mason! It was disaster enough that he had discovered her secret identity, but still she did not feel as threatened by his attempted blackmail as he had obviously expected she would. In fact, she admitted ironically, she had almost felt relieved when she realized that disclosure was inevitable. Painful though unveiling would of necessity be, that pain might prove strangely cathartic, cauterizing her wounded heart, and in any case she would endure whatever punishment Raeburn meted out because she knew she justly deserved it for the suffering she had caused the man she loved. No, in this respect Mason had grossly underestimated her, for she was a grown woman who had outfaced enemies far more dangerous than he—and besides, she added drily, she had lost her good name years ago.

But Claire . . . Claire was still little more than a child, vulnerable, an unmarried girl with the extremely frangible reputation peculiar to all virgins. If Mason found proof—not just suspicion, for he would not dare risk Raeburn's ire without evidence—that Claire was consorting with Fred O'Shea, he could destroy her. At all costs, Jessica must prevent that from happening.

Bunching up the hems of her robe and gown in one hand, Jessica raised the candlestick high and scampered down the stairs.

When she stepped outside and saw the stable, the wide, whitewashed door was slightly ajar, and on the frozen ground outside, the light from Claire's lamp made a slanting yellow streak that wavered and stilled as someone hung the lantern on a nail. Cold began to seep through the thin soles of Jessica's slippers, and teeth chattering, she pulled her robe closer about her. She blew out her candle and depended on the chill illumination of the crystal-bright stars overhead to guide her as she sidled silently toward the door, still praying that she was mistaken in her errand.

As she approached the half-opened door she could smell the penetrating but not altogether unpleasant odor of hay and dung wafting out warmly, and tilting her dark head against the damp wood, she listened carefully. She could just make out the sound of a horse nickering sleepily inside. With sinking spirits, she also heard the barely concealed amusement in the groom's rich brogue as he declared complacently, "Well now, me darlin' girl, and I thought you told me you'd not come."

"I—I shouldn't be here," Claire admitted nervously. "If anyone finds out . . . Oh, Fred, you'll lose your position!"

A shadow moved across the beam of light, the distortion giving the silhouette of O'Shea's well-built body a height it lacked in fact, and Jessica could see that the man was standing with hands on hips, apparently facing the besotted girl. She had no difficulty visualizing the cocky smile that must be lighting his handsome face, the glint in those engaging eyes that were startlingly blue under curly black hair.

"Now, now, love, and who's to find out about us?" she heard him reassure softly. "Tomkins? That bandy-legged old rooster sleeps like he was rocked in the arms of Blessed Mary Herself. . . ."

"B-but the other grooms might—" Claire ventured hesitantly, and O'Shea snorted.

"Don't worry about them. They're all tucked in their beds like the good Christian souls they are, and even if one of them saw us, he'd keep quiet. There's not a lad among them who'd dare cross me. . . ." There was a moment's pause, and Jessica could see the shadow on the ground move as if he reached for something, but after a second he stood straight again and continued quietly, soothingly, in a tone he might have used to gentle a skittish filly. "Don't be like that, Clairie. Be . . . friendly to me. We have hours to get to know one another. There's none to see us or hear us, no one to make a fuss because His Lordship's dainty sister is dallying with a stableboy."

"But I'm not—not dallying!" Claire gasped, obviously shaken and bewildered. "N-not the way you mean! How dare you say such a thing to me?"

O'Shea's voice grew harsher, more impatient. "Isn't that why you're here, girl? Haven't you come to me because you fancy a little tumble with a real man, not one of them fine lords with their fat bellies and soft white hands?"

"No, of course not!" Claire declared. "I've never—I would never—"

Jessica's relief at the girl's gullible innocence was quickly superseded by fear when she heard terse anger creep into the groom's tone; clearly he thought that he was being teased. She noticed inconsequentially that his brogue faded as his wrath increased.

"Well, then, milady," he mocked curtly, "perhaps you'd best explain to me exactly what it is that brings you to me in the middle of the night. I'm only an ignorant Irish peasant and I'd hate to think I misunderstood."

Claire stammered unhappily, "I—I came because you a-asked me to. I never thought . . . I—I thought you were my . . . friend, that you wanted to talk, the way f-friends do. Living out here in the country, with Aunt Talmadge in charge, I don't have many other friends, except for Jess, and she's always occupied with one thing or another around the house, and for weeks now, since the day you rode out with the two of us t-to gather holly, it seems as if you're always busy too, that there's never any chance for us to . . . to chat."

O'Shea's voice was grim and disbelieving. "You're saying you came out here to . . . talk, is that all? What about the time we discussed running off to Scotland?"

Scotland! Jessica repeated, shuddering. So Claire's clumsy questions about Gretna Green had had a point, had they? Had she actually led a servant to believe that she would *elope* with him? The girl's stupidity was almost criminal—and yet she seemed to be perfectly sincere when she said, "But, Fred, that was just a joke, wasn't it, like the time you showed me the cartoons about Graham? I—I enjoy your jokes. I like the way you make me laugh."

After Claire's ingenuous statement, a long and ominous silence stretched between the couple just inside the stable door. Jessica, her fingers and toes growing numb in the frosty air, listened warily. She considered breaking in on them, if only for the redolent warmth of the stable, but she admitted that as long as Claire seemed able to deal with the situation, she was extremely reluctant to make her presence known, lest she precipitate a scene that might alert other members of the household to the girl's gross indiscretion. If only Claire would make her excuses to O'Shea and retire to her quarters, where Jessica could deal with her privately . . .

But the enactment of such a prudent sequence of events seemed doomed from the beginning, for suddenly the groom growled, "So I make you laugh, do I? The rich, exalted Lady Claire Foxe thinks the Irish stableboy is beneath her notice, just someone to tease, like a dog. . . ." Before Claire could respond, he swore crudely and declared, "Well, my fine lady, I'll make you laugh, all right. When you're lying beneath me, I'll make you laugh and cry or anything else I damn well please. I'll make you beg me to take you. I'll make you . . ." His voice trailed off deliberately, and suddenly the little shaft of light from the doorway blazed clearly as he lunged out of its path.

From inside came shuffling sounds of struggle and the thud of a body wrestled to the packed earth floor. Claire squealed gutturally, and her frightened, almost childish whimper stabbed at Jessica as Lottie's cry would have done. Galvanized into recklessness, Jessica wrenched open the heavy wooden door and plunged inside.

After the darkness outside, she was momentarily blinded by the bright lamplight, and blinking hard, she stumbled forward and collided bruisingly with a wooden partition, striking her cheek hard against a peg hung with tack, knocking down two bridles and a long leather crop whose loop wound snakelike around her bare ankles before she could trip out of the way. Disoriented by the blow, as her eyes adjusted to the light she reeled in confusion, first noticing the double row of narrow whitewashed stalls where sleek horses, roused from sleep by the commotion, shifted about nervously. Then a flutter of bright blue and the rending sound of silk attracted her, and she ran down the aisle to an apparently empty stall where behind a bale of hay she found two figures twisting and flailing wildly on a heap of sweet-smelling straw.

Claire, pinioned beneath O'Shea's muscular body and writhing frantically to keep his knee from between her legs, spotted Jessica first. She gasped hysterically, "Help, for God's sake—" before her words were crammed back into her mouth by the groom's work-callused hand. Intent on his purpose, he did not become aware of Jessica's presence until she leaped at him and began pummeling on his shoulders. When he rocked back in surprise, heedless of her own safety she grasped the neck of his coarse woolen shirt and jerked with all her strength, almost strangling him as she dragged him away from Claire.

"Mother o' God!" he choked at this unexpected counterattack, and swearing crudely, he twisted round to defend himself against Jessica's battering fists. She slashed at his face with her nails, and he reached up brawny arms to capture her wrists and hold them out of range. In the process his rough fingers caught the sleeve of her robe and ripped it half out of the armhole, revealing the satin bed gown beneath.

As he turned on Jessica, cursing her, he lifted himself completely from Claire, who rolled free of him and staggered to her feet, gasping. "Oh, Jess," she wailed, too caught up in her own fright and despair to notice that her rescuer might still be in peril. Miserably she pulled the edges of her torn bodice together over her breast. With trembling fingers she tried to brush away the bits of straw and dirt that clung to the dress. "If you hadn't come, he—he was going to—"

Sternly Jessica calmed herself. She eyed the groom with contempt as she said grimly, "I know what he was going to do." Impatiently she tried to pull away. "Let go of me, O'Shea," she grated.

"And let those sharp little nails of yours get at my eyes?"

170

He chuckled drily as he steadied himself. "Do you take me for a bedlamite?"

Jessica shrugged as nonchalantly as she could with her wrists still restrained. "I can't see what harm you think I can do you—although it's obvious you must be suicidal, to risk Lord Raeburn finding out what happened. . . ."

"Now, now, Mrs. Foxe," he cajoled, watching her out of glinting blue eyes that narrowed assessingly as her struggles stilled. For a moment they seemed at an impasse; neither spoke, and the only sound was Claire's labored breathing and the blubbery snorts of the horses as they settled down once more. Then he released Jessica's hands and planted his fists firmly on his hips, in that swaggering stance he had affected before. His mouth turned up in a sardonic grin, and when he spoke, she noticed that his brogue had returned thicker than ever. "Is it sure you are that you're knowin' the truth of what happened, darlin' Mrs. Foxe? What if I were to tell you that Her young Ladyship asked me to meet her here, cool as you please—"

Claire squawked in protest, and Jessica declared scornfully, "O'Shea, if you think you can get me to believe blarney like that, you're a fool—and if you plan to tell your Banbury tale to the earl, you're a damn fool, or else just plain mad!"

The man seemed to consider her words for a moment. "I don't think so," he judged at last. "I'm not afraid of any man, much less an overfed aristocrat like His great Lordship, and even if I was, don't you think it's worth the risk? I expect the fine Earl of Raeburn would pay through the nose to keep the world from finding out about his teasing trollop of a sister. . . ."

"Trollop!" Claire wailed in anguish, staring at the groom with velvety brown eyes glazed with shock at his betrayal. "Oh, Fred, how can you . . . but you told me . . . I—I thought you . . . we—"

She broke off abruptly. Outside, from the direction of the

house, they could hear a deep voice rough with masculine impatience call, "Jess, where the hell have you gone?"

At the sound of Raeburn's shout, O'Shea tensed, and Jessica saw Claire go white with panic. The girl rose on tiptoe as if poised for flight, but she seemed uncertain what to do. "Oh, God," she gasped hysterically, "what am I to do? If Graham discovers—"

Jessica glanced toward the door opening out into the starry darkness. She could hear heavy footsteps approaching. With a furious jerk of her head she waved the girl back out of the light. "Don't be a ninny, Claire," she hissed under her breath. "Get out of here before Graham finds you!"

"B-but Jess, what about you—" Claire began remorsefully.

"Dammit, do you think I can't handle a man like O'Shea? I said *get out*. Go the back way!"

The girl stared at Jessica a few more seconds; then she sobbed chokingly and fled down the length of the stable to vanish into the shadows.

"Jessica!" Raeburn shouted, nearer.

When Jessica watched Claire narrowly make good her escape, she panted as if she were running each step of the way with her—as indeed she wanted to be. The patent anger in Raeburn's deep voice filled her with dread, but she knew she would have to face him if she hoped to divert his suspicions from his sister. Tugging her torn robe into place on her shoulder, Jessica flicked her head to one side to toss her long raven hair down her back. "You'd better go too," she said coldly to the groom. "I'll make up some excuse about why I came out here."

"No, Mrs. Foxe." He laughed humorlessly as he squared his brawny shoulders. "I've never yet hidden behind a woman's skirts, and I'll not start now. I've been waiting for this chance for weeks, ever since His Lordship told Tomkins to keep a watch on me, like I was a thief after filchin' the silver. . . . I swore then that—"

172

Jessica never knew the exact phrasing of O'Shea's vow, for at that moment his words were choked off as the Earl of Raeburn bellowed her name once more, just outside. Before she could step away from the groom, Raeburn yanked open the stable door and burst inside.

"Jess!" he called as he squinted blindly against the light, and his deep voice reverberated off the beams and partitions, once more rousing the horses. "Dammit, woman, don't hide from me. I heard you stumbling around in the house, and I know you're in—"

"I'm right here, Graham," Jessica said quietly, her even tone masking her apprehension as she watched his gray eyes blink painfully. She surveyed him warily, remarking his uncharacteristic dishevelment with dismay. She recognized his trousers as the satin evening breeches he had been wearing at dinner, but with them he wore white-topped riding boots and a frilled linen shirt that dangled unbuttoned over his broad chest, revealing the triangle of dark blond hair that ran down his flat stomach and disappeared into his waistband. He must have been preparing for bed when he heard her bump into that table and overset the kissing bough, she decided, and in his haste to investigate the noise, he had grabbed whatever clothing was close to hand. His ridiculous appearance augured ill for his frame of mind. "I'm right here, Graham," Jessica said again; "there's no need to startle your cattle."

His eyes at last adjusted to the lamplight, Raeburn stared at Jessica—and the man beside her. For a moment he stood petrified, as if cut from the same pale, cold marble as Renard Chase; then life seeped back into his bloodless cheeks. O'Shea was watching the confrontation with avid interest, but he recoiled instinctively when Raeburn's gray gaze touched him. With a disdainful sniff Raeburn dismissed him and turned back to Jessica. His eyes moved slowly over her, with insulting deliberation, and she saw his hard mouth thin implacably as he regarded her usually sleek hair that tumbled about her shoulders as if she had just risen from bed. Unable to face him, she drooped her head disconsolately, her tresses falling forward to mask the high, guilty color painting her elegant cheekbones, but she knew there was no way to prevent him from observing her heaving breast and the torn sleeve of her robe. His nostrils flared slightly when he saw the bits of straw that clung damningly to the hem of her nightgown. Nearly choking on the lump in his throat he sneered, "You whore."

She said nothing.

Her silence seemed to enrage him. "What, no excuses? You're not going to try to convince me that you've come out here to the stables in your bedclothes for a little timely tutoring in animal husbandry?"

Jessica winced at his sarcasm, but her only visible reaction was an almost imperceptible lift of her chin as she remarked quietly, "I might have known that as usual you would readily believe the worst about me, Graham. That's hardly surprising. You've always seemed to derive such pleasure from your misapprehensions."

Something about her tone, some indefinable element of . . . disappointment made it difficult for Raeburn to look directly at her emerald eyes. Instead he shifted his gaze once more to the roughly dressed man beside her, and his jaw tightened. He had been right about O'Shea from the beginning, and he should never have listened to Tomkins' recommendations: the Irishman was crafty, intelligent, and capable, but with those ambitious blue eyes fixed firmly on the main chance; an undeclared egalitarian who would take advantage of any opportunity to strike a blow against his superiors. . . .

And what more deadly, more personally devastating blow, Raeburn acknowledged with a groan, could there be than to seduce their women, taking their scented softness beneath that lusty, well-muscled body and plunging . . . Raeburn shuddered with disgust at the image. How could she, after Andy? How *dared* she? Jessica, Andrew's Jessica . . .

His Jessica.

Painfully he looked at her again, somehow regal even in her torn robe, her head bowed like a vanquished queen, and he admitted that he loved her, loved her and wanted her—and hated her for turning to someone else. Determined to wound her as she was wounding him, he observed scathingly, "Poor Jessica, you should have been more frank with me this evening, my dear. Had I realized you were so very . . . desperate for affection, I might have made more of an effort to oblige you. . . ." His deep voice lowered to a hoarse, accusing growl. "Or is it only the stench of the stable that excites you?"

At that she jerked up her head, the abrupt motion flicking her hair back away from her face, and as she stared at Raeburn in anguished indignation he saw for the first time the deep bruise that purpled her cheek.

He caught his breath with a hiss. "I didn't know you liked to play rough," he muttered thickly.

Their eyes met and locked, commingling their mutual pain, and unwisely O'Shea chose that moment to speak. He regarded the earl's discomfiture with a certain triumph and chuckled goadingly, "Now, now, me lord, don't discompose yourself. We're both men of the world and we know how women are. . . ."

The temper that Raeburn had kept so rigorously in check when he faced Jessica now went skyrocketing out of control at the sound of the groom's cocky, lilting accent. "You bastard," he grated, turning on the man, "you goddamned insolent bandy-legged little Irish bastard." His gray eyes narrowed into slits of steel as he glanced at the straw-covered floor and noticed the riding crop that Jessica had knocked down earlier. Quickly he snatched it up and stalked with inexorable intent toward O'Shea, one hand already raised to strike. "I'll teach you to put your muck-covered fingers on one of my—"

Suddenly the groom's overweening audacity failed him, as he realized that he had drastically underestimated Raeburn's reaction to his taunts, that for all his fine clothes and fancy ways the earl was no soft, lily-cheeked aristocrat who would stand idly by and watch . . . "Me lord!" he squawked, quailing at his hulking approach. O'Shea stumbled backward, but before he could retreat out of Raeburn's range, a large hand crushed down over his shoulder, catching the neck of his shirt in a strangling grip, and the leather-covered shaft of the short whip flexed and whistled through the air. In the stall nearest them one of the horses danced and snorted nervously, disturbing the remainder of the already jittery animals, and in the charged atmosphere O'Shea's squeals of pain were almost drowned out as the leather thong laid bloody welts across his back.

"Graham, for the love of God!" Jessica cried in protest, gaping in wide-eyed revulsion as the crop slashed again and again. The groom was young and strong, with supple, well-trained muscles, but Raeburn was half again his size, and his every blow was fueled by a fury and frustration he had kept bottled up too long. Jessica looked on sickened as O'Shea groveled at Raeburn's feet, whimpering, his tanned, brawny arms useless against the lash except as a feeble protection for his head. Fetid ordors of blood and sweat rose up to choke her and further excite the horses, and as she watched helplessly she saw a dark, humiliating stain seep through the coarse fabric of O'Shea's trousers.

"Graham, stop it, you're killing him!" she shrilled, and Raeburn hesitated for a fraction of a second, his arm upraised to strike yet again. "Please . . . stop . . . it," she begged hoarsely, spacing the words between painful gulps of air. He stared at her with eyes opaque with rage, lusterless, obsidian. "Don't . . . please don't . . ." she said again, trying to gauge his uncertainty. As he stood frozen she took a deep breath and stretched on tiptoe to reach for the riding crop.

At her movement Raeburn groaned, "You little slut!" and with all his great strength he brought the lash down across her arm.

She could not breathe. As if choked by opium vapors, she blinked and watched with the distended time-sense of the drug as the curling thong of the whip coiled about her wrist, first constricting then cutting the white flesh; she saw the strip of leather unwrap and slide away, blazing a track of livid white that almost magically swelled and pinked under her gaze. When drops of blood beaded and burned like liquid flame along the center of the welt, she lifted her green eyes to meet Raeburn's—but before she could look at him, from the shadows of the stable behind them they heard the sleep-thick voice of Tomkins, the head groom, demanding gruffly, "What in bloody 'ell is the matter with these—*Your Lordship*!"

In the shelter of her room Jessica bathed her wrist and bandaged it awkwardly with a strip of gauze torn from a diaper she had filched from Willa's workbasket. She had to use her teeth to hold the clumsy knot as she tightened it, and by the time the dressing seemed reasonably secure, she was sweating with exertion and pain. Limply she sank into an armchair and waited for Raeburn to come to her.

She knew he would come. She would have known it even had she not seen the promise in his eyes in that fraction of a heartbeat between Tomkins' appalled gasp and her own wail of mortification, between the groom's stunned intrusion on that scene in the stables and her own harried flight. As soon as Tomkins stumbled bewildered onto the shocking tableau formed in the circle of yellow lamplight by the earl, his sister-in-law, and the servant cringing on the ground at his feet, Raeburn had drawn himself up, very much the master, the man in control, peering down his long nose and daring his subordinate to question the rightness of his judgment; Jessica in her torn nightclothes had been the one who felt sullied and shamed by Tomkins' curious scrutiny. When she flushed and moaned with dismay, turning to run, Raeburn had made no attempt to stop her, but she had known as plainly as if he had spoken the words aloud that there was unfinished business between them.

Like an aristocrat awaiting the creak of tumbril wheels outside the Conciergerie, she waited for Raeburn's knock, and when it came, muffled but insistent, she levered herself out of her chair and trod silently to the door, her eyes trained steadfastly on the Aubusson carpet. She turned the knob and stepped back, still not glancing up; when he closed the door behind him and leaned against it, she noticed that the white top of one of his boots was flecked with blood, and she stared at the reddish-brown stain until he said softly, "Look at me, Jessica."

Slowly her eyes traveled up the long, strong length of him, the powerful legs encased absurdly in tall boots and skintight court breeches, the broad chest bare under the flapping lapels of his ruffled shirt. With a longing that bordered on pain, her gaze moved over his wide shoulders and the muscular column of his neck, lingering on the hard line of his jaw and his thin yet sensual mouth; then she looked into his eyes.

Even in the subdued light of her sitting room his fair hair gleamed coolly, but his gray eyes were dark and unfathomable as he regarded her in turn. She expected scorn, but his voice remained oddly neutral when he commented, "Thanks to Tomkins' timely entrance, your lover will survive."

"Fred O'Shea is not my lover," Jessica averred quietly. "I have no lover."

"No?" She watched his brows slowly come together in a skeptical scowl as he looked down at her. "I find you in the stable, in your nightclothes, rolling about in the hay with a groom, and you expect me to believe that you are innocent?"

Jessica said tiredly, "I never expect you to believe anything except what you want to believe, Graham."

"Even when the evidence against you seems overwhelming?"

She shrugged lightly. "Especially then."

For a long moment silence stretched between them, as taut as her nerves. She wondered why Raeburn didn't do what he came for, order her to leave his home and never darken his threshold again. As she waited for him to speak she noticed strands of her long black hair dangling over her eyes, and with an unconscious dipping twist of her head, she flicked them back over her shoulder. The movement uncovered the dark bruise on her cheek, and Raeburn observed it with a frown. With a delicacy surprising in one so large, he reached up to stroke the tender contusion. "You never explained how you came by this, Jess," he said. His steely eyes narrowed, and something threatening flared deep inside them. "Did O'Shea hit you?"

The warmth of his palm cupping the sensitized skin of her cheek unnerved her, making speech difficult. "No, Graham," she said huskily, looking away. "The man had . . . nothing to . . . to do with it."

"Are you sure? Don't defend him if he hurt you." Lightly his fingers splayed across her face, ruffling her inky lashes, and the pad of his broad thumb caressed her lower lip. The small, seductive movement made Jessica flush with strange heat, and to still his hand she captured it with her own, the one that was bandaged.

When Raeburn saw the gauze dressing around her wrist, he stiffened. "Oh, God," he groaned, "who am I to accuse anyone else of harming you? A whip . . ." He winced as he inspected the wound, the droplets of blood that had seeped through the crude wrapping. "Are you all right, Jess?" he asked jerkily. "I'll help you redo this if you like. I know it must hurt like hell."

Not as much as my heart, Jessica thought miserably, shaking her head, and something of her agony showed in her expressive features.

Raeburn gritted his teeth and said remorsefully, "Forgive me, Jess, I beg you. I did not mean . . . you know I would never . . ." His voice died away as he bent his fair head to kiss the bandage.

At the touch of his lips against her arm, she trembled violently. "Yes, Graham, I know," she reassured; "it was an accident. You were . . . incensed."

He thought she shivered from pain, and he recoiled, almost colliding with the door. He relaxed his considerable weight back against it and stared down at her, regarding her inscrutably. "What an enigma you are, Jess," he noted, his bass voice heavy with wistful irony; "often I think how much you seem to have changed in the past two years, how different from the girl in the shabby dress whom I met by the roadside—and then, sometimes, I wonder if you've altered at all. You were beautiful, naive, gauche, incredibly defensive. Now . . ." His gray eyes surveyed her comprehensively, pausing at the swell of her breasts beneath the loose covering of her torn night robe, and he drawled, "You're still beautiful, of course, more so than ever—although you do seem to retain a penchant for shabby garments—and you appear remarkably self-assured for someone of your age. Unfortunately, that polish of sophistication looks to have been acquired at the cost of your very appealing naiveté, your . . . innocence."

Jessica refused to be drawn in by the unmistakable query in Raeburn's words. She parried, "That's funny, Graham. I always thought my . . . innocence . . . was the virtue that appealed least to you."

Wryly he acknowledged the adroitness of her response, peering absently at the shadowed ceiling and sighing. "Did I call you 'defensive,' my dear? Now you defend everyone but yourself. Why, Jess?"

She gazed at him hungrily and remembered all the times she had wronged him, her love, her greatest ally. "You told me yourself that I had changed," she answered quietly. "Perhaps I no longer consider myself worthy of defense."

Raeburn jerked his head around to look at her once more. His eyes flashed as he grated, "What are you saying, Jess? Are you telling me that my suspicions are correct, after all, that the tender and virtuous dedication you have shown to your daughter, to everyone in the household is a sham? That since Andrew's death you have become some kind of—of whore?"

Jessica stared, her heart in her throat. His gentleness since coming to her room had disarmed her, and now she was dazed by the force of his attack. *Whore,* she echoed despairingly; one word that spelled out the utter hopelessness of her love. Jessica had managed to save Claire from the consequences of her naive folly, but in doing so she had convinced Raeburn that she herself was a slut, guilty of all the vile crimes he had ever charged her with—and she could not defend herself without condemning the girl, sacrificing the one person at Renard Chase who had shown her friendship and affection. . . . *Do they know you are my brother's whore?* What a fool she was! She could not blame this predicament on Claire. From the first day he came galloping into her life, that blunt, pithy monosyllable had capsulized Raeburn's opinion of her, and there was nothing she could do to change it, ever. It was, as she had told him, what he in fact wanted to believe. To a man of his upbringing there were only two kinds of women: ladies, like Daphne Templeton, and whores. And since Jessica could never fit the accepted mold of a lady . . .

Oh, what was the use? Hadn't she learned that lesson long ago from Andrew? Why did she worry about O'Shea or Mason or the cartoons; why was she fearful of losing Raeburn's favorable regard, when the truth was that she had never had it in the first place? She wanted Graham Foxe desperately, so what purpose could be served by denying herself his passion, the false and seductive simulation of his love, when there was no chance this side of the grave that she would ever earn love itself?

Thinking, *Just this once I shall have what I want*, she touched him.

She slid her white hands across the broad expanse of his chest, slipping them under the dangling lapels of his shirt and twining her slender fingers into the mat of crisp dark blond curls that covered his skin. She could feel his heart pound under her fingertips. Standing on tiptoe she half closed her eyes and leaned closer, pressing his massive body back against the door with her own slight weight. She felt him shift his legs farther apart to balance himself. With her lips she began to explore the sensitive hollows at the base of his throat. The scent and taste of him drugged her, making her dizzy.

"Jess," he said hoarsely, grasping her shoulders in his hands and pushing her just far enough away so that he could see her face. Her lashes fluttered upward, allowing him a glimpse of emerald eyes that were already clouding with desire, and in her cheeks a rosy tint budded and blossomed. He repeated thickly, "Jess, what are you doing?"

"Don't talk," she murmured, smiling whimsically as she broke free of his grip and nuzzled her face against his chest.

Except for the tolerant and intuitive Paphian who had initiated him into the mysteries of manhood on his seventeenth birthday—an enthusiastically received gift from several of his fellow underclassmen at Oxford—Raeburn had never encountered a woman who assumed the dominant role in their love play, his character and physique so naturally making him the aggressor, and now as Jessica kissed and caressed him, he did not know how to react. He felt flattered, aroused . . . bewildered. Far more accurately than she could have known,

182

Jessica had analyzed Raeburn's feelings about women, and now he was baffled by one who seemed to fit into no known category; he was not sure that such passion was . . . suitable . . . but oh, God . . . A wave of desire almost shocking in its intensity pulsed through him. He felt sweat break out on his brow; coherent thought was becoming increasingly difficult. From deep in his throat he groaned, "I don't understand you, Jess. I don't . . . understand. . . ."

Near faint with desire, she reluctantly raised her head. "I am yours, Graham," she said breathlessly, knowing at last that it was true. No matter how she fought him, since that first day two years before, Raeburn had been the one influence, the one reality in her life; what she had experienced with Andrew had been but a pale presage of that which was to come. . . . She lay against him, sure her knees were about to buckle. Even through the layers of her robe and gown she was achingly aware of his insistent need. "From the beginning," she murmured simply, as if explaining something to a child, "there has been only . . . you."

Gasping at the sensations aroused by her slim white hands, he stared down at her, the top of her head gleaming ruddily in the firelight. He was not sure what madness drove her, and he knew he had to give her one final opportunity to retreat. He touched her hair, and she craned her neck to look up at him. "Jess," he asked deeply, "are you certain?" Her answering smile was subtle and full of her newfound knowledge. With a strangled sound, he scooped her up into his arms and strode across the sitting room to the inner chamber and the friendly darkness of her waiting bed.

"Light the candle," she whispered as he set her on her feet beside the bed, and when he looked surprised, she stretched on tiptoe and brushed her lips lightly across his. "Please, Graham," she said; "I want to be able to see you."

Before he could put his arms around her to deepen the kiss, she stepped back and began to untie the sash of her robe. His fingers itched to perform that simple task for her, but she retreated farther. Puzzled by her mood, he nodded curtly and disappeared into the sitting room to fetch a spill of twisted paper from the basket beside the fireplace, and when he carried the light back into the bedroom, her robe and gown were piled in a heap on the rug, and Jessica lay naked between the creamy linen sheets, waiting for him.

He shrugged out of his shirt and sat down on the edge of the bed beside her to pull off his boots. When they had joined the other clothes on the floor, he swiveled around so that he faced her, and she made no demur when he slowly drew the sheets away from the upper portion of her body. His eyes glowed with the radiance of heating steel as they skimmed over her. Even in the warm candlelight her skin was very white, little darker than the bandage on her wrist, and its pallor was emphasized by the blackness of the long, shining tress that lay over her shoulder and curled softly between her full breasts. He gazed cravingly at her, the rounded firmness that belied the extreme slenderness of her waist. She shivered slightly, and he saw that the rosy-brown nipples, larger than he had expected, were already hard and swollen, whether from the chilly air or her arousal, he could not tell. He lowered the sheets further, revealing the sleek but narrow curve of her hips and thighs. Her belly was flat, but around the navel he noticed faint silvery stretch marks that disappeared into the blue-black triangle of hair that covered the soft mound of her desire.

Jessica, who had welcomed his inspection up till this point, suddenly felt self-conscious about those lingering reminders of her pregnancy, and instinctively she tried to shield them from his view with her hands. At that furtive and very feminine gesture, Raeburn smiled. Capturing her fingertips in his own, he pushed her hands gently aside and bent to trace the stretch marks with his lips.

Jessica jerked convulsively. "Graham?" she murmured uncertainly, stretching out beseeching hands to him.

"Christ, but you're lovely," he rasped when he raised his head. "More lovely than I could possibly have imagined. . . ."

Satisfied with his words, she relaxed. Her mouth curved upward to match his. "I'm cold too," she urged softly. She ran her nails experimentally along the powerful muscles of the thighs that strained his tight breeches. "Please come to bed."

Quickly Raeburn divested himself of the last barrier to their union, giving Jessica a fleeting but heart-stopping glimpse of hard masculine perfection before he slipped beneath the bedclothes with her; then there was only the tilting of the mattress and the slide of flesh on flesh, petal smooth and hair-roughened, cool and radiantly hot. He was so large, his massive body filling her welcoming arms in a way that was familiar yet tantalizingly new, and when his great weight pressed her down seductively into the sheets, she closed her eyes with a sigh and groaned, "Oh, Graham, I had forgotten—" Then her words were crushed back into her throat as his mouth closed forcefully over hers.

She could not get enough of him. Her need was too great, and every kiss, every stroke of greedy fingers frantically searching out the insistent secrets of his flesh served only to inflame her further. She began to writhe beneath him, trying to shift him into the final embrace. When he resisted, she stared wildly at him with glazed green eyes pleading mutely.

"Be patient, my darling," he whispered with a shiver of sheer masculine triumph; "we have all night." His mouth moved with deliberate slowness down the slender curve of her throat, scorching ever lower as he savored her taste and scent. Her own bewildering hunger had defeated her, and even shaking with desire, he was once more the one in control. When he brushed aside the long strands of ebony hair that veiled her body and his lips closed over her breast, she moaned and arched against him, weaving her fingers into the silvery brightness of his hair. "Sweet, so sweet," he murmured when his tongue tasted the hardness of her nipples. He could smell the scent of milk underlying the musky fragrance of her skin. With indulgent affection he recalled how shy she had been in the carriage during the journey back to Renard Chase, how she had blushed when he watched her feed her baby. . . .

Baby! The word resounded in Raeburn's skull, making him shudder. His hand stroked the flatness of her belly once more, and before him flashed a vision of Jessica's body stretched with child, his child. . . . He tried to put the thought away from him, but the image seemed to brand itself into his brain, engorging him with its heat. He felt himself tremble, and he was suddenly certain that he would be unable to maintain the control necessary to protect her from the consequences of their union.

Then he knew with equal certainty that he had no intention of withdrawing; that no matter what she had been or what circumstance had forced her to do, she was his now, his woman, countess of his heart, and if necessary he would bind her elusive spirit to him in the most primitive and elemental way of all. . . .

By the time his fingers found the inviting secret of her desire, she was burning with a strange new heat, as if the sun that had beamed so relentlessly that long-ago summer day had somehow become centered deep in her loins. Under his questing hands she moaned with a delight that was almost pain, and clutching at Raeburn in her arms, she tried once more to guide him to her, thinking she would die if he did not take her now, now. . . . But at last he was ready, and as she sobbed his name hoarsely, with one swift movement he lifted her beneath him and plunged deep into the welcoming darkness of her body.

Her need was too great for coyness. She stared up wildly at him with eyes made blind by the sun storm of sensation raging through her, and as he watched and felt and heard her instant response he too was dragged gasping into the feverish tempest.

She fell asleep in his arms like one washed ashore after a hurricane: disoriented, exhausted, clinging to him as the only security in a still-heaving world. In the wavering candlelight he smiled down at her tenderly, lovingly, brushing strands of hair away from her flushed cheeks with fingers that still trembled slightly. He knew a moment's chagrin that she had dozed off so quickly: there was much he had to say to her. And yet, he admitted with a wry shrug, conscious of his thudding heart, perhaps it was just as well: he did not know if he was yet capable of coherent thought, much less speech. He slid deeper beneath the bedclothes and shifted her unsubstantial weight more comfortably in the crook of his arm. When her bandaged wrist twitched as if it hurt, he brushed the gauze with his lips and arranged the blankets so that they would not constrict and irritate the wound. Then, sighing heavily, he relaxed against the pillow and closed his eyes.

Chapter Eight

"Your Lordship . . ."

The voice was low, little more than a hiss. Raeburn stirred uneasily and settled back against the pillow, even in his sleep his arms tightening instinctively around the woman beside him.

"Your Lordship!"

The voice came again, still hushed but more strident, piercing his dream, and this time it was accompanied by the light touch of a hand shaking his bare shoulder. Raeburn blinked slumber-fogged gray eyes and shifted his head so that he could squint up at the intruder. With a start he recognized the bland face of Willa Brown.

His gaze flicked back to Jessica, who still slept deeply, one arm thrown across his broad chest as if she clung to him; then he looked up at Willa again. He felt his jaw tighten with hot embarrassment, and he wondered if he blushed.

But the maid's expression remained unreadable, and when she saw that she had his attention at last, she said quietly, neutrally, "Your Lordship, it's almost dawn. Soon the household will be afoot."

Raeburn nodded imperceptibly. By "household" he knew that Willa meant the staff, who rose with the sun winter or summer; his family and guests would lie abed till almost noon. There would be none but servants to spy on his hasty departure from Jessica's room, and surely he could command their silence. . . . He hesitated, glancing at her yet again, savoring the feel of her warm, damp flesh curled so pliantly about him, and he felt a nagging resentment that circumstance forced him to creep furtively from her bed. Just for a second he wondered what would happen if he did not leave her, if he let himself be discovered with her, in this way making clear publicly and defiantly that she was his now, convention be damned. . . .

As if reading his mind, Willa shook her head, and her brown eyes met his gray ones evenly, for one moment communicating not as master and servant, but as two people made equal by their mutual love for a third. She said, "No, Your Lordship. She'll not thank you if she wakes to find you here."

Raeburn considered this; then he agreed with a sigh. "Of course you're right." He turned his head to brush his lips across Jessica's cheek, and very gently he lifted her hand away from his chest and tucked it under the covers, careful not to rouse her. Stretching out a long, bare arm to flip back the blankets, he looked at Willa and said, "I'm going to get up now." She stepped back, and he thought she was going to turn and leave the room, but instead she simply picked up his shirt and breeches from the untidy heap on the floor, shook out the wrinkles, and stood waiting to help him dress, as impassive as his own valet might have been. One of Raeburn's thick fair brows arched in surprise; then with the faintest of shrugs he slipped out of bed.

As he tugged on his tight breeches he thought grimly that Willa's absolute lack of reaction to his nakedness gave him more insight into the life she had once been forced to lead than all the disapproving tales that had been whispered to him by Flora Talmadge and others like her. For a moment he put aside his concern for Jessica and considered with fierce anger the injustice of a society where a girl not yet twenty was left utterly devoid of illusion. He gazed pensively at Willa and with a sinking heart tried to remember how often in the past he himself had blithely taken advantage of . . . not her, but women like her, uncaring of the consequences to them, heedless of anything but his own ephemeral pleasure. Streetwalker, opera singer, titled divorcée, he had always paid fairly, in coin or gowns or jeweled trinkets, and he professed nothing but contempt for men who satisfied their lusts with physical abuse, but . . .

He looked down at Jessica, who had shifted her position slightly when he left her. She now slept like a child with one hand close to her face, the fingers curled and clutching tightly at the ticking of the pillow. Again he winced at the sight of the bloodstained bandage on her wrist. Except by degree, he wondered humbly, was he really any different from the band of ruffians who had degraded the maid and driven her to the brink of suicide. . . .

"Your Lordship, please!" Willa said urgently.

He nodded and fumbled with the buttons of his shirt; then he stared at his boots and debated the necessity of pulling them on. After the warmth of Jessica's bed . . . and body . . . the marble floors seemed forbidding and unbearably cold, but he'd make far less noise in his bare feet. Reluctantly he turned to leave. Willa tagged dutifully behind him. At the door into the corridor he paused and regarded the maid steadily. "Take care of her for me, Willa," he said simply.

"Of course, Your Lordship. With my life."

He reached for the doorknob, then hesitated. "Willa," he asked curiously, his deep voice thick with concern, "why does she sleep with her fists clenched?"

Just for a second Willa's face dropped that calm mask she cultivated so carefully, and Raeburn saw in her brown eyes a depth of melancholy knowledge that no girl, however placed, should ever possess. Her mouth curved up in a mirthless smile. "Maybe . . . maybe she's just trying to hold on to her dreams," she suggested softly—then her expression became shuttered again, and she bobbed a curtsy as Raeburn glanced both ways and stepped quickly into the hallway.

"Am I to gather that Mrs. Foxe is not joining us for dinner?" John Mason remarked to the gathering at large as footmen removed the platters of fish and turkey that made up the first course and set out dishes of glazed sweetbreads and asparagus. His yellow eyes sketched the vacant chair beside Claire.

From his vantage point at the head of the table, the Earl of Raeburn watched four additional pairs of eyes follow the artist's gaze curiously, then dart back to the food laid out before them. Knives and forks scraped chillingly over china plates. The atmosphere in the dining room was tense and charged, conversation desultory. Raeburn was reminded of soldiers on the eve of battle, after the flagons had been drained and the camp followers sent away, when the silence reverberated with the bugle call that would sound soon, too soon. . . . An explosion was imminent; he could feel it in the air.

He knew the source of that tension, of course. He had seen it in the sidelong glances, quickly veiled, that had been cast his way all day as he tried to carry on the routine business of the estate. Since early that morning when, still drowsy, he had met with Tomkins, who had uttered tight-lipped assurances that the Irish groom would be packed off to Belfast as soon as his back was healed, Raeburn had been aware of an undertone of reproach, like the drone of bees on a hot summer day, tainting all his dealings with his household. Even the butler Barston had seemed unusually stiff when he announced dinner. Raeburn was unused to anything but respectful deference from his staff, but he supposed the servants' attitude was to be expected. He had never flogged a servant before—whatever the provocation, he ought to have had his steward do it—but Christ, whenever he thought of that creature's hands touching Jessica, pawing her . . . That tacit air of disapproval made him feel uncomfortable and faintly impatient. He wished Jessica were with him, to lend him support. He was certain she was avoiding him—indeed, she seemed to be avoiding everyone—and he found her uncharacteristic cowardice peculiarly irritating. He wanted matters settled now.

He glanced at Daphne sitting at his right hand, blandly unprepossessing in a flimsy muslin dress that did not become her, and his jaw tightened with a resentment that shamed him. It was not his fiancée's fault that he no longer desired her—although in truth, despite Daphne's uncontestable suitability, he realized that he had never *desired* her—but dammit, he wanted Jessica beside him now! He supposed he always had. At table or in bed, he wanted her within easy reach, he needed her close at hand where he could smile into her shining eyes, talk to her when he was troubled, touch her. . . .

When Raeburn felt his body stirring potently, he sternly put such thoughts behind him and turned his attention once more to his guests. He noticed Lord Crowell's thick fingers toying with the stem of his wineglass, a troubled expression marking his heavy features. The young duke seemed edgy, and Raeburn wondered how much he suspected, not about the incident in the stable but about Raeburn's intentions toward Daphne. He had long ago given up trying to deduce the mysterious way rumor spread throughout the manor, but he did not doubt that by now even the tenants on the farthermost borders of the estate had heard that the earl was having second thoughts about his engagement. Thus his announcement was bound to come as no surprise to any of his family or guests, but considering the way Crowell had haggled over his sister's marriage settlement, Raeburn knew he was not going to take kindly to her being jilted.

Despite the poor light in which Raeburn must inevitably appear, he was anxious to make his declaration. Better to have it all over and done with. . . . Looking past the candles and covered dishes to his sister, who sat at the far end of the table with her head bowed over her plate so that only her crest of bright, riotous curls was visible to him, he asked, "Claire, do you know where Jessica is?"

Slowly Claire lifted her head to meet her brother's gaze. Raeburn saw with surprise that her young face was even whiter than usual, the pallor normal for redheads having bleached to an unhealthy pasty color, and her eyes seemed puffy and swollen. Raeburn frowned with concern, wondering if she was ill. "Clairie, are you all right?" he questioned gently, and the girl smiled blearily.

"It's—it's just a slight cold," Claire said, a noticeable quaver making her light voice rather husky.

Flora jerked up her head and peered narrowly at her charge. "You didn't tell me you were unwell," she accused. "Too many late nights, I expect. You must go to bed at once and—"

"Oh, Aunt, do be quiet," Claire snapped rudely. When Raeburn's thick brows came together sharply at her tone, the girl sighed with a noticeable lack of contrition, "I'm sorry . . . but I'm no longer a toddler to be packed off to the nursery, you know."

Her brother nodded slowly. "No, you're not," he agreed, squelching Flora's instinctive protest. "Of course you may stay up as late as you like, so long as you take care of yourself. Christmas is but three days hence. You don't want to be sick."

Claire nodded, and her dismal expression lightened momentarily at this unprecedented acknowledgment of her maturity. But she frowned again when Raeburn repeated, "Do you know where Jessica is? Did she say anything about not coming down for dinner?"

"I haven't seen her at all today," Claire said. "I—I went to her room this morning—there was . . . something I needed

194

to talk about, to—to explain . . . but her maid said she—she wasn't able to see anyone."

John Mason interjected meaningly, "Are you saying that Mrs. Foxe is ill, my lady? How unexpected . . . She was in most excellent spirits the last time I saw her—almost as if she cherished some happy secret, perhaps an announcement of some sort. I have no doubt that if I were to send up a message reminding her of our last encounter, it might . . . hasten her recovery."

Raeburn stared blankly at the artist, and he felt his color rise at the man's insolence. "What the devil is that supposed to mean, Mason?" he demanded hotly.

"My lord—" Mason began, but from Raeburn's side Daphne interrupted him.

"Graham," she said stiltedly, "you would do well not to question Mrs. Foxe's absence. It seems to me that she is displaying a discretion and sensibility that I would never have expected from one of her sort."

" 'Her sort'?" Raeburn echoed softly, too softly, and from across the table Lord Crowell muttered, "Easy now, Daph. . . ."

But Daphne would not be silenced. Aware that she now had the attention of every person at table, she reiterated, "Yes, Graham, 'her sort.' You cannot pretend ignorance of what every other member of the household already knows: that Mrs. Foxe has conducted herself in a manner so outrageous that it—" Abruptly she broke off her accusation when the door opened a few inches and Willa poked her head inside.

Barston stepped forward, scandalized by the maid's intrusion, but Willa ignored him. "Your Lordship," she addressed Raeburn quietly, "may I have a word with you, please?"

The butler interrupted pompously, "Girl, if you have a message for His Lordship, the correct procedure is to give it to me, and if I think it warrants his attention, I will—"

"No, Barston," Raeburn said, "I'll talk to Willa myself. Come here, girl."

Willa glanced uneasily at the assemblage, then drew her head back like a turtle retreating into its shell. "If—if we could be private, sir . . ." she pleaded.

One brow arched curiously. Conscious of the watchful eyes of the people around the table, Raeburn shoved back his chair and strode to the door; the instant he pulled it shut behind him he heard agitated conversation spring up in his wake. He gazed down at the maid, trying not to flush as he remembered the circumstances under which he had last spoken to her. "Well, Willa?" he asked.

She bobbed a quick curtsy. "Your Lordship, my mistress asked me to beg you to excuse her from dinner."

"She's not feeling well?" Raeburn queried.

"A . . . slight headache, Your Lordship."

Raeburn felt his temper rise. He closed his eyes and took a deep breath to compose himself. Damn her, so she was going to play the craven, cower in her room while she left him to attend to the announcements, the settlements. How could Jess be so poor-spirited? Didn't she know that he needed her here, now? He blinked and opened his mouth to order the maid to fetch Jessica, no matter how many headaches she pretended, but he snapped his mouth shut without issuing the command. He would deal with Jess later, privately—very privately. . . .

"I see," he said harshly, pivoting to stalk back into the dining room. "Thank you for telling me." A footman drew out his chair again, and he flopped heavily into it, causing the wood to creak in protest. The other people stared at him, but his expression forbade questions. Then almost at the same moment, the door slid open once again, and the woman he had sought entered the room.

She paused in the archway, her head held high and proud in the face of the insinuating gazes confronting her. She wore a gown of crimson wool that clung to her willowy figure

196

despite the demureness of its design, and Raeburn had to clamp his jaw tight to keep from gaping. He was not certain he had ever seen her wear red before, and against her ivory skin and the blue-black luster of her hair the color made her look exotic and regal, like a Spanish princess. "Jess," he said huskily, rising to greet her, anger obliterated by the hunger that swept through him.

Before speaking to him, she turned to her maid, who hovered as if on guard in the doorway. "Forgive me for sending you on a fool's errand, Willa," she said; "I changed my mind almost the instant you left my room. I decided nothing would be gained by coddling myself."

" 'Tis of no importance," Willa murmured, searching her mistress's face intently for signs of the distress that had wracked her most of the day. "I'm just glad you're feeling . . . more the thing."

Jessica looked at Raeburn. "Forgive me for being so tardy, Graham," she said stiltedly, with a smile that only he could see did not reach her eyes. "I fear I let . . . personal concerns . . . get the better of my good manners. I hope I haven't inconvenienced anyone."

He said, "Nothing matters as long as you're here." He looked past her to a loitering footman. "Help Mrs. Foxe with her chair and then bring back the turkey for her."

The manservant bowed his powdered wig and stepped over to pull back the chair beside Claire, but as he did, Daphne declared indignantly, "Graham, I will not have *that woman* at my table!"

"Daphne!"

"My lady!"

"For God's sake, you stupid chit, hold your tongue!"

From around the table, the response was instant and varied. Claire was aghast, Flora confused, and John Mason's sallow face seemed thoughtful and cunning, as if he were mentally recording every word. Lord Crowell looked as if he wanted to strike his sister. Only Raeburn's broad features betrayed no emotion. He glanced up at Jessica, who stood stricken, motionless, one hand clenched about a carved finial on the back of the chair in which she had been about to sit, and he noted the way Willa slipped into the room to move protectively closer; then he turned to regard Daphne with narrowed eyes. "Perhaps you'd better explain yourself," he said dangerously.

Daphne's cheeks pinked at his tone, but she lifted her chin stubbornly. "I hardly think explanations are necessary, Graham," she said tensely. "It is true that despite her questionable background, Mrs. Foxe is your kinswoman, and of course for that reason you must make allowances. But consistently you indulge her in behavior unthinkable in a woman of your own class. In fact, were the idea not so utterly absurd, one might almost credit you with a particular . . ."

Daphne shrugged away the asinine notion that suddenly took shape in her mind. "But Graham," she continued hardily, "in four months' time I am to be your *wife*. I will be mistress of your house and"—her blush deepened—"mother of your children. If you will not send Mrs. Foxe away out of respect for my sensibilities, then kindly remember that once we are married I will be responsible for the moral well-being of all who dwell under your roof. And I cannot countenance the presence of a woman so lacking in morals, so—so degraded that she carries on illicitly with—with stableboys!"

"No!" Claire choked, jumping to her feet, spots of hectic color glowing clownishly against her white skin.

"Hush, Claire," Jessica muttered, coming to life at last. "Don't say a word."

Claire shook her head fiercely, bright curls bouncing with disconcerting merriment about her strained features. "No, Jess, I must." She turned to her brother's fiancée. "Daphne, you're wrong," she insisted. "It wasn't like—"

"Claire," Daphne said coldly, "you would do well to stay out of this. I can see that your brother and your chaperon

198

have neglected your education sadly. A lady does not speak of such matters, except when they become so egregious that they cannot be ignored, as in this case. Everyone, even my own maid, knows what happened last night: Graham discovered Mrs. Foxe and a groom in their sordid little liaison, and after she deserted her paramour, Graham rightly took a horsewhip to the man for his insolence. It is bad enough that you have been exposed to a person so—''

"But you're wrong!'' Claire repeated, her voice becoming shrill with guilt and temper. Tears beaded on her red-gold lashes. "You're all wrong: it wasn't Jessica who met Fred O'Shea in the stables last night. *It was I!*''

The girl's declaration reverberated around the dining room in the stunned silence that followed it. Jessica watched Claire sink weakly back into her chair, all defiance spent, and she shook her head sadly. "Oh, Claire''—she sighed—"why didn't you keep quiet? Truly I could have handled it.'' She glanced toward the head of the table, where Raeburn sat motionless, his strong features slack with shock. She said gently, "It's not as bad as you think, Graham; just a—an impetuous prank, that's all. I followed Claire to the stables, where I overheard enough of their conversation to realize that she had gone to O'Shea in all innocence, and I intruded upon the scene before he could harm her.''

Raeburn tore his flinty gaze away from his sister's face and looked up at Jessica, who stood beside the girl, her chin held high. One slim hand rested with maternal protectiveness on Claire's shoulder, and just under the flounced cuff Raeburn could see the edge of the gauze that circled her wrist; he noticed inconsequentially that the bandage had been reapplied more skillfully, probably with Willa's assistance. "And you would not have told me anything?'' he husked. "You would have let me go on believing . . .''

"My shoulders are broader than Claire's,'' Jessica said.

Raeburn caught his breath with a hiss. "Oh, Lord,'' he

groaned, "what a coil." He surveyed the company assembled, their varying expressions of confusion and distress. With dismay his eyes settled briefly on John Mason, whose cadaverous features imperfectly concealed an expression of near-triumphant gloating. It was insupportable that such a man should be made party to Claire's indiscretion. Suddenly he remembered obscure stories he had heard whispered about the artist, and he wondered grimly if he was to be approached with a request for patronage, in exchange for Mason's silence. . . . With a mixture of pity and exasperation Raeburn regarded his sister's tear-stained cheeks. Not for an instant did he doubt her innocence, although he felt like shaking her for being so—so criminally stupid. A *groom*, for God's sake! Yet, perhaps it was partly his own fault. She was so very young, and, he admitted, since Andrew's death he had not given her the attention she needed. In the face of his neglect he supposed it was only natural that she would turn to the nearest man available for affection.

With an effort at lightness he chuckled. "I swear, Clairie, you're fast becoming too much for me to handle; must be your red hair. . . . Perhaps we'd better take you to Town and set about finding you a husband who will know how to deal with all that fire in you."

Claire blinked away the moisture in her eyes and stared at her brother, her face lighting with hope. "You—you mean it, Graham? You'll let me have my come-out this spring after all?"

Raeburn smiled indulgently. "I think it's not a moment before time, don't you agree?"

Beside him Daphne declared pettishly, "You pamper her far too much, Graham. To reward such an indecent escapade! And what about our wedding plans? Won't a formal debut interfere? I thought we had agreed—"

"Daphne," Raeburn began deeply, "there's something that you and I need to—"

On the other side of the table Lord Crowell heard the ominous undertone in his host's voice. He lifted his head from his wineglass and interrupted with heavy joviality, "Daph's right, you know, Raeburn. A wedding *and* a presentation at the same time would make a hubble-bubble so frantic that a man might consider enlisting for the Peninsula just to get a little peace! On the other hand, I know another solution that would make everyone happy. . . . Why don't we make it a *double* wedding?"

Raeburn swiveled his head to regard the young duke blankly. "What on earth are you suggesting?"

Lord Crowell flushed slightly. "I—I should think it would be obvious. A double wedding: you and my sister, me and—and . . ." His voice faded as Raeburn's eyes narrowed quellingly. Gulping down the last dregs of his wine, he sputtered sullenly, "By God, Raeburn, don't—don't scowl at me like that. I know I ought to have applied to you privately first, but, dammit, man, we're practically brothers! Surely you—you realize . . ." His tongue stumbled thickly over the formal words. "It—it cannot have es-escaped your notice that I find Lady Claire a most delightful and ap-appealing young—"

"No!"

Once more a cry of shocked feminine protest echoed through the room, but when the people around the table turned automatically to Claire, they saw that she looked as startled as they. Polite confusion altered to gasping amazement when Willa Brown left Jessica's side and ran to Raeburn, squeezing into the space between his chair and Daphne's. She fell to her knees, shaking and white-faced, and she clutched at his sleeve with work-roughened fingers. "Your Lordship," she pleaded hoarsely, her voice quavering, "I beg of you, listen to me. If—if you love your sister, do not even think about giving her to that—that man. You don't know him, what he is truly like. He is—he is *evil!*"

Lord Crowell jumped to his feet, his thick body trembling

with outrage. "Of all the damned impudence!" he exploded. "By God, I'll—" He made as if to lunge across the table at Willa, but Raeburn waved him back.

"Leave her alone, Crowell," he said with grim force, his narrowed eyes glinting like gunmetal.

"Graham!" Daphne squawked, mortally offended, but her brother silenced her.

"Shut up, Daph," he growled before facing Raeburn again. The sallow skin of his puffy cheeks glistened feverishly above the points of his heavily starched collar. "Raeburn," he demanded, sneering, "are you so spineless that you're going to permit a—a *servant* to insult me, your guest, your future brother-in-law, in your own home?"

For a long moment Raeburn studied the younger man thoughtfully. At last he answered with an enigmatic smile, his voice quiet and controlled. "Yes, I am—if I think she's telling the truth."

Crowell blinked, uncertain he had heard correctly. "T-truth?" he blustered, subsiding jerkily into his chair when he saw that Raeburn was serious. "Wh-what truth? What is she accusing me of? I've never laid eyes on that wench in my life!" He fell silent, and the only sound about the table was the clink of crystal as he groped for the wine decanter.

Raeburn looked down at Willa, who still crouched at his feet, her head bent in petition so that only the top of her mobcap was visible. He tapped her shoulder lightly, and she looked up at him with fearful brown eyes, glancing uncertainly at the large hand that touched her with a gentleness she had never before known from a man. With a pang he realized that she reminded him of a whipped puppy that is afraid to be petted. He urged soothingly, "Stand up, Willa. No one is going to hurt you, I promise. No one is going to call you a liar. I think I know you well enough to be certain that you would not have spoken as you did unless you were sure you had good cause. So, stand up now, girl, and say what you have to say."

Slowly, awkwardly, Willa rose to her feet. She wiped her damp palms on her skirt and tucked an errant tendril of her yellow hair back beneath the ruffle of her cap. She gazed at Jessica, who still stood beside Claire, and in her mistress's green eyes she saw compassion and encouragement and dawning comprehension.

"Yes, tell us, Willa," Jessica said softly, a hint of steel in her silky voice. "It's high time there was a little justice in this world."

Willa nodded and stood a little straighter, lifting her chin. Her face growing rosy with triumph, she shot a glance of fulminating contempt at Lord Crowell. "He's never seen me before, he says," she muttered with ironic disgust. "Ever since he came to Renard Chase I've been hiding from him, afraid he'd recognize me . . . and now I find out he doesn't even remember!" She took a ragged breath and addressed Raeburn again, her voice deeply respectful, ringing out in the charged silence.

"Your Lordship," she said, meeting his gaze evenly, "you know me for what I am—and you know how it was with me before. It's never been any secret that from the time I was a child I walked the streets, not by my own choice but because—well, because that's just the way of the world, I suppose. There's many like me, too many. . . ." She sighed, then shrugged. "Anyway, Your Lordship, as I was saying, you know what I was, so I won't pretend otherwise, just as I won't try to lie about what I was doing in front of St. Paul's that night. The—the woman who employed me expected her girls to stay round Covent Garden—that's where the really flash coves go when they're looking for a bit of . . . But whenever I could get away from her I'd sneak over to the church and hide behind the pillars. I felt safer there, and if some bloke *did* happen my way, I could get a good look at him first, before I approached him. . . ."

Willa paused, and when she spoke again, her voice was thick with recollected pain. Her eyes clouded and she said huskily, "It was getting late, Your Lordship, and I'd been there in the shadows for hours. I knew I had to get out and—and find someone, or else I'd get a cane taken to me if I came home without any money, so when this swank carriage pulled up beside me and this man—him!" she elaborated, pointing at Crowell, "leaned out the window and showed me a guinea, I—I climbed inside. I remember thinking as how I might not get whipped for a week if I brought home real gold. . . . So I asked him how—how he wanted me to do him, and he kind of chuckled and said, 'Not in a carriage, I value my comfort more than that,' and we drove down by the river.

"I thought he was one of those as kept a room rented somewhere so their families won't guess what they're up to. But when we stopped and the door was opened, I saw that we were in an alley, black as pitch. I could hear people moving around, but they were just shadows, and I was afraid, but when I tried to get back into the coach, he—Lord Crowell—pushed me out again. Someone flashed a dark lantern in my face, and someone else laughed, 'It looks like you caught us a juicy young one this time, Billy'. Then the lantern was closed and they—they grabbed me. . . ."

By the time Willa paused in her recitation, Jessica was sobbing quietly. "Oh, Miss Jess"—Willa sighed, gazing at her tenderly—"forgive me. I never meant you to hear." She turned back to Raeburn. "There were seven of them, Your Lordship," she said tersely. "The only one whose face I saw was him there, but I counted their voices, and from the way they talked I knew they were all gentry. I used to think that I had learned to survive anything, but by the time they—they finished with me, all I wanted to do was die. . . ."

She looked again at her mistress, who was now being comforted by Claire; then she stared straight at Lord Crowell, who shrank back in his chair, his piggy blue eyes narrowed as if he were puzzling over something. To Raeburn she concluded with weary dispassion, "If it weren't for that dear lady crying for me there, I would have drowned myself in the river . . . and when I got to hell I know I would have found out that the devil has Lord Crowell's face."

The only sounds in the room were the crackle of the fire in the hearth and Jessica's weeping muffled against Claire's shoulder; then Raeburn turned to Barston and said, "See that Lord Crowell's luggage is packed and loaded onto the carriage within the hour."

"Very good, my lord," the butler replied stolidly, signaling to the footmen with a movement of his powdered head.

The duke jerked upright in his seat. "By God, Raeburn," he sputtered, "you—you can't mean . . . you'd take the word of a little slut like—"

"Oh, do be quiet, Billy," John Mason drawled, reaching past Crowell for the wine decanter. "Have the good grace for once to admit that your sins have found you out."

Crowell turned furiously to the artist. "Dammit, Johnny, you promised no one would ever know!"

Splashing burgundy into his glass, Mason shrugged. "No, Billy. What I said was that I would do all in my power to keep your unsavory little habits a secret. I can hardly be held responsible if you were fool enough to let one of your pigeons recognize you. . . ."

"Sweet Jesus," Raeburn groaned, sickened, "are you telling me that you too were party to this—this . . ."

Mason's yellow eyes regarded his host benignly. "Oh, no, my lord. Membership in that rather, shall we say, exclusive group was—is—open only to certain . . . adventurous . . . peers. I was not aware of its existence until just a few months ago when I came into possession of some letters written by a young viscount who has since fallen in His Majesty's service at Galicia."

Crowell choked, and Raeburn ventured acutely, "And since acquiring those letters you've been using them to extort money and favors, is that it? How did you do it, Mason? Did you blackmail them with the threat of those cartoons of yours?"

Mason pursed his mouth in thought, sucking in his cheeks so that his face looked more skull-like than ever. He said mildly, "My lord, 'blackmail' is such an ugly word. I prefer to think of myself as an older, wiser influence trying to curb . . . youthful exuberance."

Raeburn swore so viciously that the women jumped, especially Daphne, when he turned on her. "Well, Daphne," he demanded harshly, "did you know about this too?"

Daphne grimaced with distaste. "I have always made it a point never to probe into my brother's private life, but I can't say these revelations surprise me. Everyone knows that men are animals."

"Indeed," Raeburn said coldly, staring down at her as if he had never seen her before. "If that is your true opinion of my sex, then I am right amazed that you should wish to marry."

"If there were any alternative—" Daphne began, only just catching herself. She took a deep breath and regarded Raeburn steadily. "I will do my duty, Graham."

Raeburn gazed down at the woman he had chosen to be his bride, the mother of his children, and he wondered bleakly if when he proposed he could have been suffering a temporary derangement brought on by the double shock of Andrew's death and Jessica's disappearance. Nothing else could explain it. The thought of taking Daphne into his arms, embracing that scrawny body while she lay stiffly beneath him and "did her duty" : . . His mind returned irresistibly to the night he had just spent with Jessica, so willing, so giving; the nights they would spend together in future . . . With the faintest twinge of guilt at the way he was treating Daphne, he said to her, "No, my dear, I am not a barbarian to demand such a sacrifice from you. I want no martyrs in my bed. And because it is so patently clear that you and I should not suit, I must withdraw my offer of marriage."

Daphne gaped at him, her mouth working mutely. When she found her voice she stammered, "You—you're *j-jilting* me?"

"I'm afraid so," he admitted with a moue of remorse. "But it is for your own good. I am convinced that to proceed further with our engagement would bring nothing but misery to either of us."

"But—but . . ."

Raeburn sighed. "I will of course accept all the blame, and, fortunately, since the betrothal was not to be announced officially until Christmas night, you will be spared the embarrassment of having to publish a retraction—"

"Damnation, Raeburn," Lord Crowell exploded, banging his fist on the table, "you can't just throw my sister over like that! I won't let you get away with it, there's too much at stake! Renard Chase, the—the settlement . . . I'll—by God, I'll sue for breach of—"

"I think not," Raeburn cut in, his tone changing to one of cool authority. "You would never expose your sister to public scandal. . . ." His voice hardened, and he continued implacably, "Nor, I think, would you care for me to explain under oath that the primary reason I broke the engagement was to prevent my family's name from being soiled by even collateral alliance with someone like you." He paused again; then he said meaningly, "Crowell, perhaps I did not make myself clear earlier when I instructed my servants to pack your belongings: from this moment hence, you are no longer welcome in my home." After glancing dismissively at John Mason, he added, "Your, um, protege may leave as well."

Above the collection of stifled gasps echoing about the

room, Daphne's voice rose with uncharacteristic force, strident and enraged. "Goddamn you, Graham Foxe, you—you lying bastard, leave my brother alone!"

Everyone turned to stare in amazement at her, and even Flora Talmadge was moved to reprove shakily, "My lady, you m-mustn't say things like th-that. Such words are—are . . ."

Daphne ignored her, glaring up at Raeburn with eyes that glinted with pale fire. "How dare you denounce my brother?" she gritted. "What kind of credulous fools do you take us for? Who are you to talk so pompously of 'scandal'? In the past two years there has been enough scandal about your family to make the Foxe name notorious for generations!"

Angrily pushing back her chair, she rose to her feet, her muslin skirts flying, and over the heads of the onlookers she pointed a shaky finger at Jessica. "There she is, there's the real reason you've decided to abandon and humiliate me: Jessica, the drawing teacher, the parson's chit! Everything was fine until she turned up again, her and that squawling red-haired brat of hers who was born so conveniently after her husband's death. Have you given careful thought to the paternity of that so-called niece of yours, Graham?"

Through clenched teeth Raeburn muttered, "Take care what you say, Daphne. I know you're upset, but you're not thinking clearly."

Daphne laughed raucously, her harsh words utterly devoid of humor. "Not thinking clearly? I think my mind must be working properly for the first time in months!" She watched Jessica's pallor increase with each new accusation. "A clergyman's daughter?" she snorted. "Christ, man, everyone knows her own family disowned the little lightskirt after she seduced your brother! God alone knows what you men see in her, what kind of whore's tricks she's used to captivate first Andrew, then you. . . ." Nostrils flaring, she glowered again at Raeburn. "I've seen the way you look at her. Don't bother to deny it."

Raeburn met Daphne's gaze squarely. "I wouldn't dream of denying it," he snapped. "I'm going to marry Jessica."

At the far end of the table Jessica gasped. The rigor that had kept her silent during Daphne's tirade softened enough to allow her to stammer uncertainly, "M-marriage, Graham?" Suddenly her green eyes were blind to everything but the face of the man she loved.

He smiled tenderly at her confusion. "I think it would be advisable, don't you, darling?" He glanced about him wryly, noting his enrapt audience. Mason especially seemed about to explode. Raeburn guessed that they had better become resigned to being caricatured in the gazettes for months. He said, "Of course I hadn't intended to make my declaration in quite this way or quite so . . . public, but—"

Claire squealed with delight and hugged Jessica. "How perfectly wonderful: you'll be my sister twice!"

At Raeburn's side Daphne reeled. She clutched his sleeve and protested breathlessly, "You can't make her your wife! Offer her a carte blanche if you must, but to actually *marry* a woman like that after spurning me, a Templeton . . ."

"And Graham," Flora ventured timidly, "have you seriously thought of the consequences? Jessica is poor Andrew's widow, and for you to wed after living together in the same house. . . . There could be . . . gossip. . . ."

With growing frustration Raeburn eyed the circle of people clamoring about him, coming between him and the woman he loved. Except for his sister, he would willingly consign them all to perdition, for he could see that Jessica remained stunned, unconvinced of his sincerity. Oh, God, he needed to be alone with her so that he could talk to her, touch her, reassure her in the most basic and personal of ways. . . .

"But, Graham, think of the scandal," Flora wailed.

"There will be no scandal when Jessica is my countess," he retorted hotly. "I will see that *no one* dares make light of our family name!" He glowered significantly at Mason and

Crowell, and he was surprised when the artist lurched to his feet, so agitated that he stumbled against the table and made the crockery rattle.

"Don't you think it's a little late for such precautions, my lord?" Mason blurted. Everyone stared. Jessica stood mesmerized as his yellow eyes glinted ferally at her, like those of a jackal closing in on a wounded fawn. "I warned you, madam," he grated, and she could only nod wretchedly, helpless to stop what was coming, knowing that the fleeting and unexpected glimpse of heaven that Raeburn had just shown her would make her purgatory away from him all the more bitter.

Raeburn watched that exchange of glances, his eyes narrowing menacingly at Jessica's instinctive recoil. "What the hell is going on here, Mason?" he demanded.

Mason drew himself up to his full height, expanding his sunken chest importantly. A lock of his sandy, thinning hair fell forward over his eyes, and he brushed it back carefully into place across his bald spot. When he saw that his spectators were all attention, he cleared his throat and began unctuously, "My lord, although it is clear that you have misinterpreted my simple desire to spare your sensibilities any distress by not telling you what I knew about Lord Crowell, I am sure—"

"To the point, man; get to the point!" Raeburn interrupted with raw impatience.

"Very well, my lord," Mason said, deflating slightly as he abandoned his oratorical air, "the point is this: you would be committing a tragic and ironic error of almost monumental proportions if you marry this woman in order to give her the protection of your good name, for she is the one person who has deliberately and insidiously sought to destroy the virtue of that name. Jessica Foxe, your sister-in-law, the woman who lives under your roof and eats at your table, is in truth none other than the scurrilous cartoonist Erinys!"

Time faltered: gray eyes met green across a chasm of

210

disbelief and admission and guilt; then with a guttural squeal Jessica ran.

She darted for the door, but Raeburn intercepted her before she could reach it, before the other people in the dining room could do more than gape in vacant astonishment. When his large hands clamped like manacles over her arms, she cried out in protest and flailed at him, her eyes screwed shut so that she would not have to see the disgust on his beloved face. "Let me *go*!" she wailed, thrashing wildly, but he restrained her movements with no more effort than if she had been Lottie's size. As he caught her close against the hard wall of his broad chest he glanced dismissively over the top of her head at the shaken onlookers. "Out. All of you," he rasped, and no one dared gainsay him.

Magically Barston materialized in the archway again, summoned as if by second sight. He drew back the door to make room for the people trooping out, and Raeburn asked him tersely, "Is the carriage ready?"

"Yes, my lord," the butler replied, impassive as always, giving no notice of the woman squirming in his master's arms. "The coachman did request that I inform you that because of the snow on the roadway, travel is likely to be slow and extremely uncomfortable, although not impossible."

Raeburn shrugged. "I expect Lord Crowell and Mr. Mason to be sent on their way at once—snow or no snow."

"Very good, my lord," Barston replied again, and this time Raeburn was surprised to note the man's stern mouth twitch.

"Barston, my luggage also," Daphne commanded tersely, passing Raeburn with averted eyes as she followed the others from the room. He called her name softly. She glanced over her shoulder, but at the sight of Jessica she quickly looked away again. Raeburn said quietly, "Daphne, I sincerely regret the embarrassment this situation must inevitably cause you. As some slight recompense, if you will permit it, I should like to see that you . . . are provided for in such a way that your future independence might be assured."

He could see his former fiancée's shoulders stiffen with outrage, and he thought she was about to whirl around to confront him. Instead, after a moment she relaxed, murmuring dully, "Thank you, Graham. That is most generous of you." With an air of odd dignity she lifted her chin and walked out of the Earl of Raeburn's dining room—and his life.

At the sound of the door closing behind Daphne, Jessica struggled impotently, expending all her strength in a futile attempt to escape him. "Let me go, Graham," she cried again, moisture squeezing out from under her clenched eyelids and beading on her long lashes. "I can't bear it!"

"Can't bear what, Jess?" he demanded grimly. "Can't bear for me to touch you? I know better than that, my girl!"

She shook her head in furious denial, making tears stream in gleaming but erratic rivulets down her bloodless cheeks. "Yes . . . no . . ." Her thrashing stilled, and she collapsed limply against his chest, the steady thud of his heart under her ear a soothing counterpoint to her own frenetic pulse. "Oh, dammit, Graham," she sniffled, "don't you understand? I can't bear for you to look at me and hate me, knowing what I've done to you, the way I've—I've . . ." Her tongue stumbled over the words.

Raeburn said, "Open your eyes, Jess." She trembled and burrowed her face deeper into the lapels of his coat. He repeated, "Open your eyes. Don't be a coward."

"But I am a coward," she insisted. "I knew what Mason was going to say, and I—I just couldn't stand the thought of your anger. I so wanted to be brave, to stand up to the truth the way poor Willa did. . . ."

"Willa Brown is rather a remarkable young woman," Raeburn observed drily. "I sincerely hope that some day some good man will see beyond the prejudice of society and recognize her many virtues."

Gradually Jessica was becoming aware that his tone was soft, almost gentle, with only an underlying note of confusion roughening it. When his blunt fingertips stroked across her damp cheek and hooked lightly under her chin, tilting her face upward, she blinked rapidly as she peeked through tear-clumped lashes. "Why aren't you angry with me?" she asked in puzzlement.

Raeburn said, "Maybe I will be . . . once I understand what's going on. Tell me, Jess. Explain to me how in the name of God you came to be a satirical cartoonist."

Her awkward position was straining her neck, so she pushed at his chest lightly, and he released her. She stepped away from him and faced him directly, sighing wryly. "It was an impulse, Graham, like—like almost everything I do. I've always drawn funny sketches of people, especially when I was angry or bored—if you could have seen what I did to the margins of my prayerbook during my father's sermons!—but I'd never given any thought to the possibility that they might be worth money until after Willa and I reached Brighton."

"Brighton," Raeburn said thickly. "I thought—"

"Yes, I know what you thought," Jessica said. "You thought some man was keeping me. . . ." With a shrug she elaborated, "We stopped in Brighton because that was as far as we could go on the money from pawning my wedding ring. We were getting desperate. Funds were running short, and I was unwell—because of Lottie, you understand. One morning at Willa's insistence I sent her to the apothecary for a potion that my mother used to take whenever she was increasing. I had written the ingredients on the back of an old scrap of paper, never noticing that on the other side was a drawing of a man we had spotted at an inn, some would-be Corinthian with shirt points so high he almost blinded himself whenever he turned his head. . . . When Willa came home, she told me that the chemist had been so taken with the sketch that he had accepted it as payment for my medicine; he said it was better than some of the cartoons he had seen in the print shops in London. . . . That gave me the idea. I knew it was a gamble, yet there seemed little alternative. I sent out samples of my work, and finally Haxton and Welles in Clerkenwell wrote back that they'd buy all the drawings I could produce."

For a very long moment Raeburn regarded her silently, his wide brow furrowed. At last he asked heavily, "Did they tell you whom they wanted satirized?"

The question she had most dreaded, but the one she was now determined to answer honestly. "No, Graham," she admitted throatily, "the subjects and treatments were all my ideas."

"Even the one that likened me to a centaur?"

"Yes, Graham."

"And that very elaborate one entitled 'Cornelia Weeps' —the picture that depicted Prinny and me as nasty, spoiled children, with our mother, Britannia, shown as a Roman matron wailing that all her jewels had turned to dross? Was that also your idea?"

"I'm afraid so. But you must understand that I—I had been terribly hurt by you . . . or so I thought."

He frowned. "Hurt or not, Jessica, that . . . that was not very kind."

She winced. "I know," she said in a tiny voice.

Silence stretched between them, as cold and taut as her nerves. Then suddenly, startlingly, like the west wind blasting life-giving warmth across the bleak and frozen countryside, Raeburn roared with laughter, "No, it may not have been kind, Jess—but, by God, it was funny!"

She stared in disbelief as his stern expression melted away under the onslaught of his humor; then with a sob she flung herself back into his arms. "Forgive me!" she begged, twining her arms around his neck and planting frantic kisses along the hard line of his jaw. "Please, Graham, tell me you forgive me!"

"Forgive you for what—being brilliant?" he echoed in disbelief. "Talent like yours isn't something to forgive; it's a gift to be cherished and nurtured! You idiot, why didn't you tell me? Why did you let me go on thinking . . .?"

"I—I was afraid you would take Lottie from me and s-send me away," she stammered helplessly. "You—you said . . ."

Raeburn's arms tightened convulsively about Jessica, crushing the breath from her as he groaned into the inky luster of her hair, "Oh, God, Jess, couldn't you tell that the only reason I ever uttered those threats was because I loved you so much and I was desperate for some excuse to make you come back to me, where you belonged? Do you truly think me capable of such despicable cruelty that I would separate a mother and her child?"

She shook her head, caught somewhere between her own laughter and tears, glorying in the bruising stricture of his embrace. "N-no, of course not!" she insisted shakily. "It's just—it's just that I think I've been a little mad ever since Andrew died. . . ."

Raeburn growled fiercely, "I've been mad longer than that, my girl; ever since that very first day by the roadside when I was insane enough to let you slip through my fingers. God, how blind can a man be? All this talk about looking for a 'suitable' bride, when it's patently obvious that you and I are two of a kind . . . It should have been I who swept you up onto my horse and carried you off to Scotland!"

Despite the seduction of his words, Jessica hesitated. She loved this man with all her heart, but there was something she had to make clear, something that had to be faced, no matter how much it might displease him. "Graham," she said, her voice low and serious, "I did love Andrew."

215

She felt the tremor of emotion that passed through him. Jealousy? she wondered. Regret?

The answer was not long in coming. With a wistful sigh that seemed incongruous issuing from someone of his great stature, Raeburn kissed Jessica lightly on the forehead and said, "Yes, sweetheart, I know you loved Andy, and I thank God you did. With my poor brother's life doomed to be as brief as it was, it's comforting to know that he had his taste of happiness, that his memory lives on in the child he left behind. . . ."

His broad hands cupped Jessica's face for a moment; then he reached down and caught her slim fingers in his own. He removed his carved sapphire signet ring and slipped it onto her wedding finger; it was far too large for her, and he had to curl her hand into a fist to keep it from falling off. Pressing his lips against her knuckles, he murmured, "The past is done, Jess, and now you are *my* wife. You know that, don't you? In our hearts and minds we are already married, you and I, even if the snow and the holidays mean we must delay a few days before we find a bishop who can issue a special license to make our union a legal fact."

Jessica stared down at the ring, her pale face glowing. When she made no demur, Raeburn lifted her chin again and grinned wickedly. "Well, wife," he drawled in a voice weighted with sheer masculine satisfaction, "I do hope you aren't planning to make your poor husband sleep alone until we can locate that bishop?"

"I wouldn't dream of it," Jessica said, her green eyes growing drowsy with anticipation.

Delighted that she was being so acquiescent, Raeburn pursued, "And, naturally, you will inform your publisher that the meteoric but short-lived career of Erinys is at an end, will you not? I do think it would be best for everyone if henceforth you devoted your talent for portraiture to paintings for the gallery here. I rather imagine that eventually you'll be able to fill an entire wall with pictures of our children. . . ."

Jessica hesitated, thinking of her still-undisclosed bank account. No matter how much she loved this man, it seemed to her that a woman ought to retain a little independence. . . . "Whatever you say, Graham," she answered with deceptive meekness, and standing on tiptoe she wove her fingers into his bright hair and drew his mouth down to hers.

ABOUT THE AUTHOR

Julia Jeffries was born in Arkansas, but she has been a resident of California since childhood. Very early she developed a taste for the great romances of literature, and she began composing her own stories before she entered high school. Although she studied music and languages in college, her lifelong love of writing triumphed when she chose her career. Miss Jeffries makes her home in Sacramento with her husband Richard Ward, a computer expert, and their three young sons. *The Chadwick Ring,* her first Regency novel, is also available in a Signet edition.